A Bevy of Girls

By

L. T. Meade

A Bevy of Girls

Chapter One

The Departure

The girls stood in a cluster round Miss Aldworth. They surrounded her to right and left, both before and behind. She was a tall, dark-eyed, grave looking girl herself; her age was about twenty. The girls were schoolgirls; they were none of them more than fifteen years of age. They adored Marcia Aldworth; she was the favourite teacher in the school. She was going away to England suddenly, her mother was very ill, and she might not return. The girls all spoke to her in her native tongue. They belonged to several nationalities; some German, some French, some Dutch, some Hungarian; there was a sprinkling of Spanish girls and a good many English. The school was supposed to be conducted on English principles, and the head teacher was an Englishwoman.

There was a distant sound of music in the concert room not far away, but the girls, the principal girls of the school, took no notice of it.

"You will write to us, dear, dear Marcia," said Gunda Lehman. "I'll forget all my English and I'll make all sorts of mistakes. You'll write to me, and if I send you an English letter you'll correct it, won't you, dear, dear Miss?"

Miss Aldworth made the necessary promise, which was echoed from one to another amongst the girls. There was an American girl with a head of tousled hair, very bright china-blue eyes, and a sort of mocking face. She had not spoken at all up to the present, but now she came forward, took Miss Aldworth's hand, and said:

"I'll never forget you, and if ever you come to my country be sure you ask for me, Marie M. Belloc. I won't forget you, and you won't forget me, will you?"

"No, I won't forget you, Marie. I'll ask for you if ever I come to your country."

Miss Aldworth moved off into the hall. Here the head mistress began to speak to her.

"Move aside, girls," she said, "move aside. You have said your good-byes. Oh, here are your flowers—"

A porter appeared with a huge basket of flowers. These were tied up with different coloured ribbons. They were presented by each girl in succession to her favourite English teacher.

"How am I to carry them away with me?" thought poor Miss Aldworth, as she received them; but her eyes filled with tears all the same, and she thanked each loving young personality in the way she knew best.

A few minutes later she found herself alone in the cab which was to bear her to the railway station. Mrs Silchester's school at Frankfort was left behind; the now silenced voices began to echo in her ears. When she found herself virtually alone in the railway carriage, she arranged her flowers in order, then seated herself in a corner of the carriage and burst into uncontrollable crying. She was going home! Her bright life at the school was over. Her stepmother wanted her; her stepmother was ill. She knew exactly what it all meant. She had resisted several letters which she had received from home lately. They had come from her younger sisters, they had come from her brother; they had come from her father. Still she had rebelled and had struggled to keep away. She sent them half her salary, but it was no use. Her mother wanted her; she must come back.

At last there arrived a more alarming message, a more indignant remonstrance. She could not help herself any longer. It was not as though it were her own mother; it was only her stepmother who wanted her, and she had never been specially good to Marcia, who had always been something of a drudge in the family. Her salary was not half as important as her services. She must come back.

She consulted Mrs Silchester; she even gave her a hint of the truth. Mrs Silchester had hesitated, had longed to advise the girl to remain with them.

"You are the making of the school," she said. "You keep all those unruly girls in order. They adore you; you teach them English most beautifully, and you are my right hand. Why should you leave me?"

"I suppose it is my duty," said Marcia. She paused for a minute and looked straight before her. She and Mrs Silchester were in a private sitting room belonging to the latter lady, who glanced firmly at the tall, fine, handsome girl.

"Duty," she said, "it is a sorry bugbear sometimes, isn't it?"

"To me it is," said Marcia. "I have sacrificed all my life to my sense of duty; but perhaps I am mistaken."

"I do not think so; it seems the only thing to do."

"Then in that case I will write and say that I will go back at once."

"I tell you what, my dear, if your mother is better when you return, and you can so arrange matters, I will keep this place open for you. I will get a lady in as a substitute for a short time; I won't have a permanent teacher, but I will have you back. When you return to England, write to me and tell me if there is any use my pursuing this idea."

Marcia said firmly:

"I know I shall never be able to return; once I am back I shall have to stay. There is no use in thinking of anything else."

Now the whole thing was over; the girls had cried and had clung to her, had lavished their love upon her, and the other teachers were sorry, and Mrs Silchester had almost shed tears—she who never cried. But it was over; the wrench had been made, the parting was at an end. Their bright lives would go on; they would still enjoy their fun and their lessons; they could go to the opera, to the theatre; they would still have their little tea parties, and their friends would take them about, and they would have a better time than English girls of their class usually have. They would talk privately to each other just the same as ever, about their future homes, and their probable dots, and of the sort of husbands that had been arranged for them to marry, and how much linen their good mothers were putting away into great linen chests for them to carry away with them. They would talk to each other of all these things, and she, who had been part and parcel of the life, would be out of it. She always would be out of it in the future.

Nevertheless, her sense of duty carried her forward. She felt that under no possibility could she do otherwise. She had a long and rather tiresome journey, and arrived at her destination on the following evening.

Her home was in the North of England, in an outlying suburb of the great bustling town of Newcastle-on-Tyne. Marcia arrived first at the general station; she then took a local train and in about a quarter of an hour she arrived at the suburb where her family resided. There a tall gaunt figure in a long overcoat was pacing up and down the platform. Several other people got out of the train; they were mostly business men, returning from their day's work. The tall figure did not notice them, but when the girl sprang out of the train the man in the overcoat pulled himself together and came forward with a quickened movement and took both her hands.

"Thank God you have come, Marcia," he said. "Molly and Ethel and Nesta were all in terror that you would send a wire at the last moment. Horace said he thought you had spunk enough to do your duty, but the rest of us were afraid. You have come, thank God. That's all right."

"Yes, father," she said in a lifeless sort of voice, "I have come. Am I wanted so very badly!"

"Wanted?" he said. "Now let's see to your luggage; I'll tell you about that afterwards as we are walking home."

Marcia produced her ticket, and after a short delay her two modest trunks were secured from the luggage van. A porter was desired to bring them to Number 7 Alison Road as quickly as possible, and the father and daughter left the railway station and turned their steps homeward.

Marcia opened her eyes and shut them again. Then she opened them wide. Was it a dream after all? Had she really been at delightful Frankfort, at the gay school with its gay life not two days ago? And was she now—what she had been doing the greater part of her life—walking by her father's side, down the well-known road, turning round by the well-known corner, seeing the row of neat, dull, semi-detached houses, the little gardens in front, the little gates that most of them never kept shut, but which clapped and clapped with the wind; the little hall doors, made half of glass, to look artistic, and to let in a little more cold than they would otherwise have done, a picture of the little nail, the dingy linoleum on the floor; the look of the whole place?

By-and-by they reached their own gate; of course it needed mending.

"Oh, father," Marcia could not help saying, "you ought to see to that."

"Yes, but Molly has put it off week after week. She said you'd do it when you came home."

"I'll manage it. But how is mother? Is she very bad?"

"She is worse than usual; she requires more care, constant attention. There was no one else who would suit," he added. "Come along now, I'll tell you all presently."

"You don't want me to see her to-night, do you?"

"Not unless you wish to. She is upstairs."

"Does she know I have come?"

"Yes, she knows; at least she hopes with the rest of us that you have come. You had better run in and see her for a few minutes; you needn't begin your duties until to-morrow."

"Thank God for that reprieve," thought Marcia.

The next instant there was a loud clamour in the hall, and three exceedingly pretty girls, varying in age from fourteen to eighteen, bustled out and surrounded Marcia.

"You have come! What an old dear you are! Now you'll tell us all about Germany. Oh, isn't it fun!"

Nesta's voice was the most ringing. She was the youngest of the girls, and her hair was not yet put up. She was wearing it in a long plait down her back. It curled gracefully round her pretty temples. She had sweet blue eyes and a caressing manner; she was rather untidy in her dress, but there was a little attempt at finery about her. The other two sisters were more commonplace. Molly was very round and fat, with rosy cheeks, small, dark eyes and a good-humoured mouth, a gay laugh and a somewhat tiresome habit of giggling on the smallest provocation.

Ethel was the exact counterpart of Molly, but not quite so good-looking. These three girls were Marcia's step-sisters.

In the distance there appeared the towering form of a young man with very broad shoulders, and a resolute face. He was Marcia's own brother. She gave one really glad cry when she saw him, and flung herself into his arms.

"Good old girl! I said you'd have the spunk to do your duty," he whispered in her ear, and he patted her on the shoulder.

She felt a strange sense of comfort; she had hardly thought of him during the journey; once he had been all in all to her, but circumstances had divided them. He had been angry with her, and she had felt his anger very much. He had preached duty to her until she was sick of the word and hated the subject. She had rejected his advice. Now he was here, and he approved of her, so things would not be quite so bad. His love was worth that of a hundred schoolgirls.

"Oh, yes, yes," she whispered back, and he saw the pent-up emotion in her at once.

"Marcia, come upstairs," said Nesta. "I want to see you. You needn't go to Mummy yet. She said you weren't to be worried. Mummy is too delighted for anything. We have put a new dressing gown on her, and she looks so smart, and we've tidied up the room."

"Of course," said Ethel, "we've, tidied up the room."

"We have," said Molly, "and we've put a white coverlet over the bed, and Mummy looks ever so pleased. She says you'll read to her for hours and hours."

"Of course you will, Marcia," said Nesta. "It does so tire my throat when I read aloud for a long time."

"And mine!" said Molly.

"And mine!" said Ethel.

"You know Ethel and Molly are out now," said Nesta. "They're asked a good deal to tea parties and dances."

"Yes, we are," said Molly; "we're going to a dance to-morrow night."

"Yes, yes!" said Ethel, skipping about. "I want to show you our dresses."

"They made them themselves," said Nesta.

"We did; we did, wasn't it clever of us?" said the other two, speaking almost in a breath.

"They're awfully fashionable looking," went on Nesta—"the dresses I mean."

Molly giggled in her commonplace way. Ethel did not giggle, but she laughed. Nesta squeezed Marcia's arm.

"You dear darling, what a tower of strength you are," she said. "We thought of course you wouldn't come."

"We thought you'd be much too selfish," said Molly.

"Yes, we did truly," said Ethel.

"We were certain you wouldn't do it," said Nesta. "We said: 'She'll have to give up, and why should she give up?' That's what we said; but Horace said you'd do it, if it was put to you strongly."

"Put to me strongly?" said Marcia. "Oh, girls, I have had a long, tiring journey, and my head aches. Is this my room? Would you think me frightfully unkind if I asked you for a jug of hot water, and to let me be alone for ten minutes?"

"Oh dear, dear, but don't you want us three in the room with you? We have such a lot to tell you."

"Darlings, you shall come in afterwards. I just want ten minutes to rest and to be quiet."

"Girls, come downstairs at once," said Horace from below.

The girls hurried off, glancing behind them, nodding to Marcia, kissing their hands to her, giggling, bubbling over with irrepressible mirth. Oh, it did not matter to them; their prison doors were open wide.

"So," thought Marcia, "they are going to put it all on me in the future, even Horace. Oh, how can I bear it?"

Chapter Two

Share and Share Alike

The next morning Marcia commenced her duties. She had said to herself the night before that the prison doors were closing on her. They were firmly closed the next morning. She saw her stepmother for a few minutes on the night of her arrival. She was a tall, very lanky, tired-looking woman, who was the victim of nerves; her irritability was well-known and dreaded. Marcia had lived with it for some years of her life; the younger girls had been brought up with it, and now, when they were pretty and young, and "coming out," as Molly expressed it, they were tired of it. The invalid was not dangerously ill. If she would only exert herself she might even get quite well; but Mrs Aldworth had not the least intention of exerting herself. She liked to make the worst of her ailments. As a matter of fact she lived on them; she pondered them over in the dead of night, and in the morning she told whoever her faithful companion might happen to be, what had occurred. She spoke of fresh symptoms during the day, and often sobbed and bemoaned herself, and she rated her companion and made her life a terrible burden. Marcia knew all about it. She thought of it as she lay in bed that first night, and firmly determined to make a strong line.

"I have given up Frankfort," she thought, "and the pleasures of my school life, and the chance of earning money, and some distinction—for they own that I am the best English mistress they have ever had; I have given up the friendship of those dear girls, and the opera, and the music, and all that I most delight in; but I will not—I vow it—give up all my liberty. It is right, of course, that I, who am not so young as my sisters, should have some of the burden; but they must share it."

She went downstairs, therefore, to breakfast, resolved to speak her mind. The girls were there, looking very pretty and merry. Nesta said eagerly:

"Molly, you will be able to go to the Chattertons to-day."

"I mean to," said Molly. "Ethel, you mustn't be jealous, but I am coming with you."

"And she's got a charming new hat," said Nesta.

"I know," said Ethel. "She trimmed it yesterday with some of the ribbon left over from my new ball dress."

"She'll wear it," said Nesta, "and she'll look as pretty as you, Ethel."

Ethel shook herself somewhat disdainfully.

"And I'm going to play tennis with Matilda Fortescue," continued Nesta. "Oh, hurrah! hurrah! Isn't it nice to have a day of freedom?"

"What do you mean, girls?" said Marcia at that moment.

Her voice had a new quality in it; the girls were arrested in their idle talk.

"What do we mean?" said Nesta, who was far and away the most pert of the sisters. "Why, this is what we mean: Dear old Marcia, the old darling, has come back, and we're free."

"I wish to tell you," said Marcia, "that this is a mistake."

"What do you mean?" said Molly. "Do you mean to insinuate that you are not our sister, our dear old sister?"

"I mean to assure you," said Marcia, "that I am your sister, and I have come back to share your work and to help you, but not to take your duties from you."

"Our duties!" cried Molly, with a laugh. "Why, of course we have heaps of duties—more than we can attend to. We make our own clothes, don't we, Nesta?"

"And beautifully we do it," said Nesta. "And don't we trim our own hats?"

"Yes, I'm not talking about those things. Those are pleasures."

"Pleasures? But we must be clothed?"

"Yes, dears; but you will understand me when I speak quite plainly. Part of your duty is to try to make your poor mother's life as happy as you can."

"But you will do that, darling," said Nesta, coming close up to her sister and putting her arms round her neck.

Nesta had a very pretty and confiding way, and at another time Marcia would have done what the little girl expected, clasped her to her heart and said that she would do all, and leave her dear little young sister to her gay pleasures. But Marcia on this occasion said nothing of the sort.

"I wish to be absolutely candid," she said. "I will look after mother every second morning, and every second afternoon. There are four of us altogether, and I will have every day either my morning or my afternoon to myself. I will take her one day from after breakfast until after early dinner, and afterwards on the day that I do that, I shall be quite at liberty to pursue my own way until the following morning. On alternate days, I will go to her after early dinner, and stay with her until she is settled for the night. More I will not do; for I will go out—I will have time to write letters, and to study, and to pursue some of those things which mean the whole of life to me. If you don't approve of this arrangement, girls, I will go back to Frankfort."

Marcia's determined speech, the firm stand she took, the resolute look on her face, absolutely frightened the girls.

"You will go back to Frankfort?" said Nesta, tears trembling in her eyes.

Just at that instant Mr Aldworth and Horace came into the room.

"My dear girls, how nice to see you all four together," said the father.

"Marcia, I trust you are rested," said Horace.

"Oh, Horace," said Nesta, "she has been saying such cruel things."

"Not at all," said Marcia. "I am very glad you have come in, father, and I am glad you have come in, Horace. You must listen to me, all of you. I am twenty, and I am my own mistress. My stepmother does not stand in quite the same relation to me as my own mother would have done. She is not as near to me as she is to Ethel, and Molly, and Nesta; but I love her, and am willing, abundantly willing, to take more than my share of nursing her."

"That's right, Marcia," said her father.

"Listen, father. I haven't said all I mean to say. I will not give the girls absolute liberty at the expense of deserting their mother. I refuse to do so; I have told them that I will look after my stepmother for half of every day, sometimes in the morning, and sometimes in the afternoon; but I will not do more, so Molly or Ethel or Nesta, who is no baby, must share the looking after her with me. You can take this proposal of mine, girls, or leave it. If you take it, well and good; if you leave it I return to Frankfort to-morrow."

Had a bombshell burst in the midst of that eager, animated group, it could not have caused greater consternation. Marcia, the eldest sister, who had always been somewhat downtrodden, who had always worked very, very hard, who always spared others and toiled herself, had suddenly turned round and dared them to take all her liberty from her.

But even as she spoke her heart sank. It was one thing to resolve and to tell her family so; but quite another thing to get that family to carry out her wishes. Nesta flung herself into her father's arms and sobbed. Molly and Ethel frowned, and tears rolled down Ethel's cheeks. But Horace went up to Marcia, and put his hand on her shoulder.

"I do think you are right," he said. "It is fair enough. The only thing is that you must train them a bit, Marcia, just a bit, for they have not your orderly or sweet and gracious ways."

"Then you take her part, do you?" cried the younger sisters in tones of different degrees of emotion.

"Yes, I do, and, father, you ought to."

"It doesn't matter," said Marcia, who somehow seemed not even to feel Horace's approval of much moment just then. "I do what I said; I stay here for a month if you accede to my proposal. At the end of a month, if you have broken my wishes, and not taken your proper share of the nursing of your mother, I go back to Frankfort. Mrs Silchester has promised to keep my situation open for me for that time. Now I think you understand."

Marcia went out of the room: she had obtained at least a moral victory, but how battered, how tired, how worn out she felt.

Chapter Three

Taking Mother

"Now, my dear," said Mrs Aldworth, when Marcia entered her room, "I really expect to have some comfort. You have such a nice understanding way, Marcia. Oh, my dear, don't let so much light into the room. How stupid. Do you see how that ray of sunlight will creep up my bed in a few moments and fall on my face. I assure you, Marcia, my nerves are so sensitive that if the sun were even to touch my cheek for an instant, I should have a sort of sunstroke. I endured agonies from Nesta's carelessness in that way a few days ago."

"Well, it will be all right now, mother," said Marcia in a cheerful tone.

She was brave enough; she would take up her burden, what burden she thought it right to carry, with all the strength of her sweet, gracious womanhood.

Mrs Aldworth required a great deal of looking after, and Marcia spent a very busy morning. First of all there was the untidy room to put straight; then there was the invalid to wash and comfort and coddle. Presently she induced Mrs Aldworth to rise from her bed and lie on the sofa.

"It is a great exertion, and I shall suffer terribly afterwards," said the good woman. "But you always were masterful, Marcia."

"Well, you see," said Marcia gently, "if I nurse you at all, I must do it according to my own lights. You are not feverish. The day is lovely, and there is no earthly reason why you should stay in bed."

"But the exertion, with my weak heart."

"Oh, mother, let me feel your pulse. Your heart is beating quite steadily."

"Marcia, I do hope you are not learning to be unfeeling."

"No," replied the girl, "I am learning to be sensible."

"You look so nice. Do sit opposite to me where I can watch your face, and tell me about your school, exactly what you did, what the girls were like; what the head mistress was like, and what the town of Frankfort is like."

(Four pages missing here.)

"I am sorry, dear."

"How could we go? Whoever is with mother this afternoon will be too fagged to go. We simply couldn't go. And to think that this is to go on for ever. It's more than we can stand."

"I am waiting to know, not what you can stand, or what you cannot, but which of you will look after mother this afternoon? You won't have a very hard time; her room is in perfect order, and her meals for the entire day are arranged. You have but to sit with her and chat, and amuse her."

"We're none of us fit to go near her, you know that perfectly well," said Molly.

"Very well," replied Marcia in a resolute tone. "You all know my firm resolve. You have got to face this thing, girls, and the more cheerfully you do it the better."

In the end it was Molly who was induced to undertake the unwelcome task. She shrugged her shoulders and prepared to leave the room, her head drooping.

"Come, Molly," said Marcia, following her. "You mustn't go to mother in that spirit."

She took Molly's hand when they got into the hall.

"Can you not remember, dear, that she is your mother?"

"Oh, don't I remember it. Isn't it dinned into me morning, noon, and night? I often wish—"

"Don't say the dreadful words, Molly, even if you have the thought. Don't utter the words, for she is your mother. She tended you when you could not help yourself. She brought you into the world in pain and sorrow. She is your mother. No one else could ever take her place."

"If you would only take her to-day, Marcia, we would try to behave to-morrow. If you would only take her this one day; it is such a blow to us all, you know," said Molly.

Marcia almost longed to yield; but no, it would not do. If the girls saw any trace of weakness about her now, she would never be able to uphold her position in the future.

"I tell you what I will do," she said, "I will go with you into mother's room, and see you comfortably settled, and perhaps—I am not promising—but perhaps I'll have tea with you in mother's room presently; but you must do the work, Molly; until mother is in bed to-night she is in your charge. Now, come along."

Marcia took her sister to her own room.

"Let me brush your hair," she said.

"But you'll disarrange it."

"Now, Molly, did not I always improve your style of hair dressing? Your hair looks a show now, and I could make it look quite pretty."

In another moment Molly found herself under Marcia's controlling fingers. Her soft, abundant hair was arranged in a new style which suited her, so that she was quite delighted, and began to laugh and show her pretty white teeth.

"Here is some blue ribbon which I have brought you as a little present," said Marcia.—"You might tie it in a knot round the neck of your white blouse. There, you look quite sweet; now put some smiles on your face and come along, dear, for mother must be tired of waiting."

Mrs Aldworth was amazed when she saw the two girls enter the room hand in hand.

"Oh, Molly," she said. "Good-morning, dear, you haven't been to see your old mother yet to-day, but I'll excuse you, my love. How very nice you look, quite pretty. I must say, Marcia dear, that my children are the beauties of the family."

Marcia smiled. She went straight up to the open window. Molly fidgeted about near her mother.

"Sit down, Molly, won't you?" said Marcia.

"But why should she?" said Mrs Aldworth. "The poor child is longing to go out for a bit of fun, and I'm sure I don't wonder. Run along, Molly, my love. Marcia and I are going to have such a busy afternoon."

"No," said Marcia suddenly. She turned round and faced Mrs Aldworth. "I must tell you," she continued, "I am really sorry for you and the girls, but they must take their share in looking after you. I will come to you at this time to-morrow, and spend the rest of the day with you. Molly, you can explain the rest of the situation. Do your duty, love, and, dear mother, believe that I love you. But there are four of us in the house and it must be our pleasure, and our duty, and it ought to be our high privilege, to devote part of our time to nursing you."

Chapter Four

A Refreshing Tea

The door closed behind Marcia. Mrs Aldworth was so astonished that she had not time to find her breath before the daring culprit had disappeared. She looked now at Molly. Molly, who had quite forgotten her rôle, turned to her mother for sympathy.

"Oh, mother, could you have believed it of her? She is just the meanest old cat in existence."

"But what is it, Molly? Do you mean to say that Marcia—Marcia—won't be with me, her mother, this afternoon?"

"Catch her, indeed," said the angry Molly. "Didn't you say, mother, and didn't you hear father say that when Marcia came home, we three girls would have a fine time of freedom? It was always, always like that—'Wait till Marcia comes back.' Now she is back, and she—oh, mother, I couldn't believe it of her, I couldn't! I couldn't!"

Molly sobbed and sobbed. At another moment Mrs Aldworth would have sent Molly from her room, but now she was so thoroughly angry with Marcia that she was inclined to sympathise with her.

"I will tell you everything, mother. It really is too marvellous. It is almost past belief."

"Sit down, Molly, and try to stop crying. It is so disfiguring to your face. You are wonderfully like what I used to be when I was a girl. That is, before my poor health gave way, and my poor dear nerves failed me. If you cry like that you will suffer in the end, as I am suffering. You will be a helpless, neglected, disliked invalid."

"Oh, mother," said Molly, "I should not be at all surprised, and I only eighteen. You know Marcia is two years older, quite old, you know, out of her teens. When a girl gets out of her teens you expect her to be a little bit steady, don't you, mother?"

"Of course, dear, of course. But stop crying. I can't hear you when you sob between each word."

"It's enough to make anybody sob. We were so happy yesterday, we three. Ethel and I had everything planned—we were going to the Carters' dance to-night. You know Edward was to be there, and—and—Rob, who is so taken with Ethel, and our dresses were ready and everything."

"But why cannot you go, my dear child? You must go."

"It is impossible, mother, and it is all Marcia's doing. Our only fear was that perhaps Marcia would not come; but when she did enter the house we did feel ourselves safe. Nesta, poor pet, was going to play tennis with the Fortescues, but everything is knocked on the head now."

"There's an unpleasant draught over my feet," said Mrs Aldworth. "Please, Molly, get me a light shawl to throw over them. No, not that one, the light one, the light one with the grey border. Just put it over my feet and tuck it in a little round the edge—not too much. You are not very skilful. Now, Marcia—"

"Oh, mother, you'll have to do without much of your precious Marcia. It was an awful mistake to let her go to Frankfort; it has ruined her. She has come back most terribly conceited and most, most selfish."

"I never did greatly admire her," said Mrs Aldworth. "As a child she was exceedingly obstinate."

"Like a mule, I've no doubt," said Molly. "Oh, dear, dear! I know I've got a quick temper, but as to being mulish—I wouldn't make others unhappy, and she has made three girls so wretched."

"Well, out with it, Molly."

Mrs Aldworth was so much interested and so much amazed, that now that her feet had just the right degree of heat provided for them by the shawl with the grey border, she was inclined to listen with curiosity.

"It was at breakfast, mother; we had planned our day, and then all of a sudden Marcia turned round and faced us. She said that she was going to look after you one day in the morning and the next day in the afternoon, and that we three girls were to look after you during the alternate times, and she said—"

"She surely didn't say anything so monstrous and inhuman in the presence of your father?"

"That's the worst of it, mother, you wouldn't believe for a single moment that she could, but she did."

"I don't believe you, Molly."

"Well, mother, I'll call her back, she will tell you, she has practically said so already before you, now, hasn't she? She said she didn't want to leave Frankfort, but that she had come, and she would stay and do her duty; but that we were to do our duty too, and if we refused, she'd go back to Frankfort. She will be of age almost immediately, and father says she cannot be coerced, and the fact is she will go unless we do it. And oh, Mothery, Horace too is on her side. There's no hope at all, and we are three miserable girls! What is to be done? What is to be done?"

Molly flung herself on her knees by her mother's side and sobbed against her mother's thin white hand, and Mrs Aldworth never recognised the selfish nature or perceived the shallow heart of her eldest child. After a time, however, Number One rose paramount in the good lady's heart.

"Now get up, my dear. Of course this little matter will be put right. You had better stay with me this afternoon, but Marcia must come in and we can talk things, over."

"She half promised to come in to tea. I don't believe she will; she'll be too much afraid."

"Oh, my dear, she won't defy me long. She'll do what I wish; you leave it in my hands. I don't say for a single moment that you may not have to give up this one dance, but that is all. Marcia has returned to look after me, to be with me morning, noon, and night, to read to me, and amuse me, and alter my dresses and do everything that I require, and you, my three little girls, are to have your pleasure. But you must come to visit your poor old mother daily, won't you, Molly?"

"Oh, darling, of course we will. We just love to come."

"And you must tell me all about your parties and your fun generally, won't you, Molly?"

"Oh, yes, yes, mother."

"And whisper, Molly. Marcia has very good taste; she is an exceedingly clever girl."

"Hardly a girl, mother; she will be twenty-one, soon."

"Anyhow, dear, she is young, I must admit that, and she has very good taste, and perhaps she'll help me to make some little extra finery for you. Now, dear child, get up and go on with that novel. I am so anxious to hear if Miss Melville really did accept Lord Dorchester or not."

Mrs Aldworth's taste in reading had degenerated very much since the days when she had won a first prize for literature at the second-rate school which had had the honour of educating her. She now preferred stories which appeared in penny papers to any others, and was deeply interested in the fate of Miss Melville at that moment.

Molly read badly, in a most slovenly style. Mrs Aldworth snapped her up every minute or two.

"Don't drop your voice so, Molly; I didn't hear what you said. Sit nearer, and don't fidget. Oh, don't you know how you torture my poor nerves?"

This sort of thing went on for a couple of hours. Molly grew sleepier and sleepier, and her face crosser and crosser. The room was no longer comfortable; the sun was pouring hotly in, the blinds were up, and neither Mrs Aldworth nor her daughter had the least idea how to mend matters.

But by-and-by—oh, welcome sound—there came a step in the corridor, and Marcia entered, bearing a beautifully arranged tea tray. She carried it herself, and there was a smile on her sweet face. She was all in white, and she looked most charming.

"I thought I'd give you both a surprise," she said, "Shall I make tea for you this afternoon?"

Molly glanced at her mother. Was the culprit to be received with the coldness she deserved, or on the other hand, was this most welcome interruption to be hailed with delight. Molly flung down her paper and Mrs Aldworth roused herself.

"This room is too hot," said Marcia. "Molly, allow me. Another day, dear, when you are taking charge of mother, draw this Venetian blind down at this hour, and move mother's sofa a little into the shade. See how hot her cheeks are. Please run for a little warm water, Molly, I want to bathe your mother's face and hands. You will feel so refreshed, dear, before you take your tea." Molly skipped out of the room.

"Oh, if only I might run away and not go back," she thought; but she did not dare.

When she brought the water Mrs Aldworth was lying with cool, freshly arranged pillows under her head, her hair combed smoothly back from her discontented fare, and Marcia now having mixed a little aromatic vinegar with the warm water, proceeded to bathe her hot cheeks and to cool her white hands.

The tea itself was a surprise and a delight. There were hot cakes which Marcia had made in the kitchen; fragrant tea, real cream, thin bread and butter. Mrs Aldworth admitted that it was a treat.

"You're a wonderful girl, Marcia," she said, "and notwithstanding the fact that you have behaved in a very cruel and unnatural way, I forgive you. Yes, I forgive you, and I shall thoroughly forgive you and let bygones be bygones if you will give Molly her freedom for the rest of this afternoon, and sit with me yourself. I can explain a few little things to you then, which will cause the hearts of my three dear girls to leap for joy."

"Oh, mother, can you?"

Molly's blue eyes danced. She looked with a sense of triumph, half amusement and half daring, from her mother to Marcia. But, alas, Marcia's face showed not the slightest sign of yielding.

"I think, mother," she said, "that you and I must wait for our conversation until to-morrow afternoon. I am exceedingly busy just now, and Molly knows our compact. Have you finished your tea, Molly? If so, I will take away the tray. Good-bye, mother, for the present. Good-bye, Molly."

As quickly as she had come so did the angel of order and comfort retire. Mrs Aldworth was now in a fury.

"Really, Molly," she said, "this is insufferable. I would much rather she went altogether. To think of her daring to go against my wishes in my own house." But bad as things were at present, Molly knew that if Marcia went they would be worse. A certain amount of freedom could now be safely claimed, but if Marcia went things would go on in their slovenly, slipshod, good-for-nothing style; the invalid's bell always ringing, the girls never at liberty, the house always in disorder.

"Oh, mother," said Molly, "don't rouse her; she is capable of anything, I assure you. She has given us just a month to be on our trial, and she says that if we don't do our part in that time she will return to Frankfort. That horrid Miss Silchester has turned her head, and that's a fact. She has praised her and petted her and made much of her, and would you believe it, mother, she has absolutely offered to keep the post open for Marcia for a whole month. Mother, dear, do be careful what you say to her, for, I assure you, she has no heart. She would actually allow us three girls—" Molly stopped to gulp down a sob— "to wear ourselves to death, rather than to do one little thing to help us. It's awfully cruel, I call it. Oh, mother, it is cruel."

Now all this was from Molly's point of view, and so it happened that Mrs Aldworth, for the time being, took her child's part; she did not think of herself. Besides, Marcia had dared to defy her authority, and a sensation of fury visited her.

"You had better call the others," she said. "We must have a conclave over this. We really must. I will not submit to insurrection in my house. We must arrange with the girls what we shall do, and then call your father in. His must be the casting vote."

Molly flew out of the room. She found Nesta presently, enjoying herself in the swing. She jumped lightly from it when she saw Molly.

"Well," she said, "what has happened! Whatever did mother say?"

"Mother is in the most awful rage. Marcia has openly defied her. I wouldn't be in Marcia's shoes for a good deal. Mother thoroughly sympathises with us; she feels that we are most badly used, and she wants you, Nesta, you and Ethel. Wherever is Ethel?"

"Ethel has gone over to the Carters' to explain about to-night. Poor Ethel, her head was banging; I expect the heat of the sun will give her sunstroke. But Marcia wouldn't care. Not she."

"Well, you had better come along, Nesta," said Molly. "Mother will be awfully annoyed at Ethel being out. What a pity she went. It's very important for our future."

The two sisters went up together to their mother's room, arm in arm. As a rule they often quarrelled, but on this occasion they were unanimous against their common fate. Mrs Aldworth, however, had changed her mood during Molly's absence. She had begun to think what all this was about, and what all the agony of Molly's tears really represented. The great trial in the minds of her daughters, was having to nurse her. She was their mother.

"Am I such a nuisance, so terribly in every one's way?" she thought, and she began to sob feebly. She wished herself, as she was fond of saying, out of the way. "If only I might die!" she moaned. "They would be very sorry then. They would think a great deal of what their poor mother was to them in life. But they're all selfish, every one of them."

It was in this changed mood that the two girls, Molly and Nesta, entered Mrs Aldworth's room. She greeted them when they appeared in the doorway.

"Don't walk arm in arm in that ridiculous fashion. You know you are always quarrelling, you two. You are just in league against poor Marcia."

"Poor Marcia!" cried Molly.

"Yes, poor Marcia. But where's Ethel; why doesn't she come when her mother sends for her? Am I indeed openly defied in my own house?"

"Oh, mother," said Molly, in some trepidation, "it isn't us, it is Marcia."

"It's much more you, you are my children—Marcia isn't. I am your mother. Live as long as you may you will never be able to get a second mother."

Here Mrs Aldworth burst into sobs herself. But Nesta was an adept at knowing how to manage the invalid when such scenes came on.

"As though we wanted to," she said. "Darling little mother; sweet, pretty little mother."

She knelt by the sofa, she put her soft arms round her mother's poor tired neck, she laid her soft, cool cheek against the hot one, she looked with her blue eyes into the eyes from which tears were streaming.

"You know, mother, that we just worship you."

"But, of course, mother, it's only natural," said Molly, "that we should sometimes want to have a little fresh air."

"It is just as true," continued Nesta, "that one cannot be young twice, as that one cannot have a real ownest mother over again."

"Of course it is," said Mrs Aldworth, whose emotions were like the weathercock, and changed instant by instant. "I quite sympathise with you, my darlings. You adore me, don't you?"

"We live for you," said Molly. "You are our first thought morning, noon, and night."

"Then where is Ethel? Why doesn't she come?"

"She has gone to the Carters to explain that we cannot possibly be present at the dance this evening."

"Poor darling," said Nesta, "she'll have sunstroke on the way, her head was so bad."

"Sunstroke?" said Mrs Aldworth, who was now seriously alarmed, "and the afternoon is so very hot. Why did you let her go out with a bad headache?"

"She had to go, mother," said Nesta. "The Carters would be so offended."

"Of course they would," said Molly. "She simply had to go. But for Marcia it would have been all right."

"Certainly that girl does bring discord and misery into the house," said Mrs Aldworth.

"But she won't long, mother; not when you manage her."

"You can manage anybody, you know, mother," said Nesta.

Mrs Aldworth allowed herself to smile. She mopped the tears from her eyes and sat up a little higher on her sofa.

"Now, darling," she said, "draw up that blind. Marcia has made the room too dark."

"Catch her doing anything right!" said Nesta.

She pulled up the Venetian blind with a bang. Alas, one of the cords snapped. Immediately the rods of wood became crooked, and the light darted on to Mrs Aldworth's face.

"You tiresome, clumsy child," said the mother. "Now what is to be done?"

"I don't know, I'm sure. I'm very sorry," said Nesta. "I'm all thumbs—I have always said so. I suppose it's because I'm so ridiculously young."

Mrs Aldworth scolded in the fretful way in which she could scold; the girls between them managed to move the sofa, and after a time peace was restored; but the room was disorderly, and the crooked blind wobbling in a most disreputable manner against the partly opened window, did not improve its appearance.

"What will you do, mother?" said Nesta. "Do tell us what you will do?"

"Well," said Mrs Aldworth, "I shall insist firmly on obedience."

"There's no use coercing her too roughly, mother; there really isn't," said Molly. "She will simply do what she said."

"You leave her to me, dears. When does her so-called duty recommence?"

"To-morrow afternoon, mother, Ethel will look after you to-morrow morning," said Nesta, in some terror for fear the unwelcome task should devolve on herself.

"Yes, of course, Ethel will take her turn," said Molly, then she added, glancing at Nesta, "and it will be your turn on the following afternoon."

"Oh, but I cannot possibly come then, for I have promised to go for a walk with Flossie Griffiths. It has been such a looked-forward-to treat. Mother, you couldn't deprive me of the pleasure."

"I tell you it will be all right by then," said Mrs Aldworth. "Now, go away, Nesta, your voice is much too loud, and remember, that after all it is a great privilege for you to have a mother to attend to when she is so devoted to you."

"Yes, yes, darling; yes, yes," said Nesta.

She kissed the hot cheek again and went slowly out of the room. In the passage, however, she uttered a low whoop of rejoicing at her recovered liberty, and a minute later she flew down the garden path to enjoy herself in the swing.

Chapter Five

Seeking Sympathy

The Carters were a numerous family. They lived about a mile away from the Aldworths. The Aldworths lived in a small house in the town and the Carters in a large country place with spacious grounds and every imaginable luxury. Mr Carter had suddenly made a great pile of money in iron, had retired to private life, and had given his six children everything that money could buy. The Carters conducted themselves always according to their special will; they had no mother to look after them, their mother having died when Penelope, the youngest girl, was a baby. There were two sons in the family and four daughters. The sons were called Jim and Harry, the girls were Clara, Mabel, Annie, and Penelope. They were ordinary, good-natured, good-humoured sort of girls; they took life easily. Clara, the eldest, believed herself to be the mistress of the house, and a very sorry mistress she would have made but for the fact that there was an invaluable old nurse, a servant, who had lived with Mrs Carter before she died, and who really held the household reins. This kind-hearted, motherly body kept the young people in check, although she never appeared to cross them. They consulted her without knowing that they did so. She superintended the servants; she saw to the linen press; she arranged the food; she kept all the supplies with a liberal hand, and gave Clara and the other girls carte blanche with regard to what they might do with their time, and when they might entertain their friends.

The old house, Court Prospect by name, on account of its extensive view, was very suitable for entertainments. Once it had been the property of a gracious and noble family; but hard times had come upon them and Sir John St. Just had been glad to receive the money which the rich Mr Carter was prepared to offer. In consequence, the St. Justs had disappeared from the neighbourhood. Beautiful Angela St. Just no longer delighted the people when she walked down the aisle of the little village church. She no longer sang with a voice which seemed to the parishioners like that of an angel, in the choir. She went away with her father, and the Carters, it must be owned, had a bad time of it during the first year of their residence at Court Prospect.

But money can effect wonders. The place was according to the Carters' ideas completely renovated. The hideous, ugly out-of-date furniture was replaced by maple with plush and gilt and modern taste. The gardens were laid out according to the ideas of a landscape gardener who had certainly never consulted the true ideas of Nature. Some of the old timber had been cut down to enlarge the view, as Clara expressed it.

This young lady was now exactly eighteen years of age. She was out, and so was her twin sister, Mabel. Annie, who was only seventeen, was still supposed to be in the school-room, but she was very much en évidence at all the parties and entertainments; but Penelope, who was only fourteen, was obliged to be to a certain extent under tutelage.

The Carters' ball, or rather, as they expressed it themselves, their little impromptu dance, had been the talk of all the girls and young men who were lucky enough to be invited to it. It was a great honour to be intimate with the Carters; they were jolly, good-natured girls, and certainly without a trace of snobbishness in their compositions. They were so rich that they did not want to be bothered, as they expressed it, with monied people; they liked to choose their own friends. Molly and Ethel and Nesta had attracted Clara and Mabel some time ago, and their brothers, too, had considered the girls very pretty; for the young Aldworths were of the laughing, joking, gay sort of girls, who could talk in a pert, frank fashion; who were not troubled with an overplus of brains, and, in consequence, were exceedingly popular with certain individuals.

It was to visit the Carters, therefore, and to unburden her mind of its load, that Ethel, with her aching head, proceeded to go on this hot summer afternoon. She found the girls and two boy friends from the neighbourhood having tea under the wide-spreading cedar tree on the lawn. This cedar tree had been the pride of Sir John St. Just, but Mr Carter seriously thought of cutting it down in order to still further enlarge the view; therefore the poor old cedar was at present on sufferance, and the young people were enjoying its shade when Ethel appeared with crimson cheeks, and eyes which still bore traces of the heavy tears which she had shed. They jumped up, and Mabel ran to meet her.

"This is good; and so you have followed your horrid, detestable note. Why, of course, you are coming to-night. Clara and I won't hear of a refusal."

"We cannot, really," said Ethel. "We can't either of us come."

"Let me introduce you to Mr John and Mr Henry Grace," said Mabel, bringing Ethel up to the rest of the party.

"Have some tea, Ethel, do," said Clara, holding out her hand a little languidly. "How awfully hot you look."

Ethel sank down on a chair which one of the others had vacated and allowed herself to be cooled and petted. Clara suddenly began on the subject of the ball.

"What a queer note you sent; what does it all mean?" she asked.

"I will tell you afterwards; I have come over to explain," said Ethel, "if I can see you—you and dear Mabel for a few minutes alone before I leave."

"Dear me, what is the mystery?" said Jim, who had flung himself on the grass. "Why can't you tell us all? It would be no end of a lark. Another rumpus with the mother. Is she more cantankerous than ever?"

"No, mother is quite nice, particularly nice," said Ethel, who had often explained to the young Carters what a trial her mother was.

"Well, then, come and have a game," said Jim. "Come along, do, and forget all the worries. If it isn't the mother it can't be anything very serious."

"Yes, but it is, and I cannot tell you," said Ethel.

She looked so forlorn that everyone present pitied her. Her soft brown eyes filled with sudden tears and overflowed.

"Oh, how my head is aching. I've been lying down all the afternoon. I just managed to come out to tell you, for I felt you must know."

"Is it as bad as that? Then we had best make ourselves scarce," said Jim. "Come along, let us go away, we who are the unfavoured; we'll leave the select few to listen to confidences."

A game of tennis was presently in active progress, Clara and Mabel, who both longed to join, did not feel too sympathetic.

"Well," said Clara, "whatever is it? Do tell all. If you won't come to-night and you won't play, why—"

"Oh, you mean me to go," said Ethel. "It's always like that—I might have expected it."

"Oh, no; don't go," said Mabel, who was more good-natured than her sister, "that is," she corrected herself, "if we can do anything to help you."

"I must tell you—I won't keep you more than a few minutes. You know Marcia—you have heard of her?"

"Of your elder sister? Oh, how funny! There came a letter yesterday from Colonel St. Just to father, and he said that his sister, Mrs Silchester, is coming to spend the holidays with them, and that she had mentioned your sister, Miss Marcia Aldworth. She said what a splendid girl she was. Colonel St. Just told us to tell you—he thought you would be pleased."

"Oh, she is deceived in her," said Ethel, her face getting redder than ever. "She is deceived in her. I wish she knew. Well, I'll tell you all about it. You know Marcia isn't our real sister—"

"Oh, my dear, of course, that is no news," said Clara more crossly than ever.

"But she is older—she is older than I am, and older than Molly. She is twenty."

This was said with effect, and a long pause followed. "She will be twenty-one before long. You can't call that young, can you?"

"Well, not as young as eighteen, of course."

"But it isn't young at all," said Ethel, in a fretful tone. "Now I am only seventeen, and dear Molly is only eighteen; we are quite young."

"And so are we, we are both eighteen, aren't we, darling old Clay?" said Mabel, patting her sister on the face.

"Yes, but don't call me Clay—it does sound so earthy," said Clara. "But do go on, Ethel. Out with this trouble."

"Well, it is this—father sent for Marcia."

"What, from that delightful school where Mrs Silchester adores her so much?"

"Yes, why not? She is his child, and he sent for her, and she came, and Horace approved of the plan."

"I am always so frightened of that Horace of yours," said Mabel. "But do hurry up."

"Well, she came. We feared she wouldn't, for she is awfully selfish; but she did; she came, and we were so happy. It was, you know, liberation for us, for dear mother, poor darling, does take up such a lot of time. One of us has always to be with her, and sometimes two have to be with her, for father insists on her never being alone, and we are not rich like you, and cannot afford a hired nurse."

"And who would give a hired nurse to one's mother?" said Mabel.

"Well, anyhow, that is how it is; we wouldn't, of course, and Marcia came. She came last night. She is very staid, you know, not a bit like us."

One of the boys shouted across to ask Clara when she would be finished and ready to make up a set.

"I really cannot stay," said Clara. "Oh, you aren't a bit sympathising. I thought you would be; but I don't suppose any one will be. Well, she came, and she absolutely refused to give more than a little bit of her time to mother. We're to be tied as much as usual, and we cannot come to-night. You know Molly and I never do anything apart, and Molly won't be free, for mother is never settled till between nine and ten o'clock, and it would be much, much too late. We'll never be able to go anywhere. Marcia will manage that we're to be tied and bound as much as ever we were, and Marcia will have all the honour and glory. Oh dear, we can only be young once. I think Marcia might have remembered that— Marcia, whose youth is quite over. I do think she might—I do!"

"Poor Ethel," said Clara, with more sympathy. "It does seem hard. Well, we'll try and get some fun for you on your free days. After all she is your mother. Coming, Jim, coming. Sorry you can't be here to-night, Ethel; but we'll get up some fun again in a hurry. Now, cheer up, old girl, cheer up."

Chapter Six

The Joy of her Life

The next morning passed somehow. The girls had decided that they would send Marcia to Coventry. They had made up their minds in a solemn conclave late the night before.

"We daren't oppose her for the present," said Ethel, who had thought of this daring plan, "but we'll make her life so miserable that she just won't be able to bear it."

"She used to be so affectionate; I remember that," said Molly. "She was very good to me when I had the measles. She used to sit in the room and never think of herself at all."

"She caught them afterwards, don't you remember, horrid things?" said Nesta.

"And I don't think I went to sit with her at all," said Molly.

"It was rather piggish of you, wasn't it?" said Ethel.

"Well, well; don't rake up my old faults now. Am I not sad enough? Do you really think, Nesta and Ethel, that we had best send her to Coventry? Do you mean really to Coventry?"

"Yes; don't let's speak to her. We'll try the effect for a week. We'll do our duty, of course. We'll go into mother's room in turn, and we'll give up everything for our mother's sake, and we'll deny ourselves, and we'll never speak to Marcia at all. When we are at meals, if she forces us to speak, we'll say yes and no, but that's all, unless Horace or father is present. We'll leave her quite to herself; she shall have her free hours, and her time for writing, and we wish her joy of it."

This plan of action being determined on, the girls went to bed with a certain sense of consolation.

It was Ethel's turn to spend the morning with the invalid on the following day, and she determinedly went there without a word. The effect of the Coventry system seemed at first to be but small. During breakfast that morning Marcia was absorbed in some letters she had received. She asked her father the best way to get to Hurst Castle.

"Why do you want to go there?" asked her parent.

"I have had a letter from Angela St. Just. She is most anxious to see me."

Ethel very nearly dropped the cup of tea which she was raising to her lips.

"Angela St. Just?" she murmured under her breath. Even Mr Aldworth looked interested.

"Do you know her?" he asked.

"Of course I do; she was one of Mrs Silchester's pupils. She wants me to go and see her, and, if I can be spared, to spend a little time there in the summer. I have had a long letter from her."

"She was a remarkably handsome girl; I remember that," said Mr Aldworth. "Well, to be sure, and so she was at that school."

"You forget, father," said Marcia, "that Mrs Silchester is Sir Edward St. Just's sister-in-law."

"Indeed? That is news."

Horace made one or two remarks.

"I am glad you know her so well, Marcia, and I hope you will have a pleasant time when you go to Hurst Castle. You say Sir Edward is staying there at present?"

"Yes, with some relatives."

"And Angela?"

"Yes, they're going to spend some months there this summer."

Marcia then calmly read her remaining letters and then, just nodding towards Ethel, she said:

"I think it is your turn to look after mother, dear," and she left the room.

But just as she reached the door she came back.

"Be very careful, dear Ethel, not to allow her to sit in the sun. It is such a beautiful day that I think you might wheel her on to the balcony, where she can get some fresh air. Just do your best to make her happy. I shall be so pleased if I see her looking bright and comfortable this afternoon."

To these remarks Ethel proudly withheld any comment Marcia, not in the least disturbed, hurried away.

"Well," said Nesta, when her father and brother and elder sister had made themselves scarce, "she doesn't seem to be much put out by the beginning of Coventry; does she, Molly?"

"She's so eaten up with pride," said Molly, "talking about her Angela St. Just and her Hurst Castle—snobbish, I call it, don't you, Ethel?"

"I don't know that I shouldn't like a little bit of it myself," replied Ethel. "You should hear how the people talk of her in the town. They don't think anything at all of the Carters, I can tell you."

"You have never explained what happened during your visit yesterday," said Molly.

Marcia was passing the window. She looked in.

"It's time you went to mother, Ethel," she said.

Ethel rose with a crimson face.

"Hateful old prig!" she said.

"There, girls, I can't tell you now. I'm in for a jolly time, and you'll be amusing yourselves in the garden, and she'll amuse herself."

"Well, you can think of me to-morrow," said Nesta, "giving up my walk with Florrie Griffiths. That's what I call hard, and you and Ethel will have a jolly afternoon all to yourselves, and a jolly morning to-morrow. It's I who am to be pitied. I don't think I can stand it. I think I'll run away."

"Don't be a goose, Netty. You know you'll have to bear the burden as well as Miss Mule Selfish."

"Oh, what a funny name," said Nesta, laughing.

"Do let us call her Mule Selfish. It does sound so funny."

Ethel, having propounded this remarkable specimen of wit, went upstairs, considerably satisfied with herself. Her post that morning was no sinecure. Mrs Aldworth was in a terrible temper, and she was really weak and ill, too. It was one of her worst days. Ethel, always clumsy, was more so than usual. The sun poured in through the open window, and when the doctor arrived he was not pleased with the appearance of the room, and told Ethel so sharply.

"You are a very bad nurse," he said, "for all the training you've had. Now don't allow that blind to be in such a condition a moment longer. Get one of the servants to come and mend it. I am exceedingly annoyed to see your mother in such an uncomfortable condition."

Ethel was forced to go off in search of a servant. The blind was mended after a fashion; the invalid was pitied by the doctor, who ordered a fresh tonic for her. So the weary hours flew by, and at last Ethel's task was over. She rushed downstairs. The load was lifted from her mind; she was free for a bit. She immediately asked Molly how they might spend the afternoon.

Lunch was on the table and Marcia appeared. Marcia spoke to the young lady.

"How is mother?"

"I don't know," said Ethel.

"You don't know? But you have been with her all the morning."

"The doctor called; you had better ask him."

"She will turn at that. I would like to catch her in a rage," thought Ethel.

Marcia did not turn. She guessed what was passing through her young sister's mind. It would pass presently. They would take the discipline she was bringing them through presently. She was sorry for them; she loved them very dearly; but give them an indulgent life to the detriment of their characters, and to her own misery, she would not.

By-and-by lunch came to an end, and then Marcia rose.

"Now, you go to your imprisonment," thought Molly.

Marcia went into the garden. She gathered some flowers, then went into the fruit garden and picked some very fine gooseberries. She laid them in a little basket with some leaves over them, and with the fruit and flowers in her hand, and a pretty basket containing all kinds of fancy work, she went up to the sick-room.

Mrs Aldworth could not but smile when she saw the calm face, the pretty white dress, the elegant young figure. Of course, she must scold this recalcitrant step-daughter, but it was nice to see her, and the flowers smelt so sweet, and she had just been pining for some gooseberries. Why hadn't one of her own girls thought of it?

Marcia spent nearly an hour putting the room in order. The Venetian blind did not work; the servant had mended it badly. She soon put that straight. She then sat down opposite to Mrs Aldworth.

"Our afternoons will be our pleasantest times," she said. "There is so much to be done in the mornings, but in the afternoons we can have long talks, and I can amuse you with some of the school-life stories. I have something quite interesting to tell you to-day, and I have brought up a book which I should like to read to you, that is, if you are inclined to listen. And, oh, mother, I think you would like this new sort of fancy work. I have got all the materials for it. It would make some charming ornamental work for the drawing room. We ought to make the drawing room pretty by the time you come back to it."

"Oh, but I shall never come back to it," said Mrs Aldworth.

"Indeed you will, and very soon too. I'm not going to allow you to be long in this bedroom. You will be downstairs again in a few days."

"Never," said Mrs Aldworth.

"Indeed you will. And anyhow we ought to have the drawing room pretty now that Molly and Ethel are out—or consider themselves so. And, mother, dear,"—Marcia's voice assumed a new and serious tone—"I have so much to talk to you about the dear girls."

Mrs Aldworth trembled. Now, indeed, was the moment when she ought to begin, but somehow, try as she would, she found it impossible to be cross with Marcia. Still, the memory of Molly and her wrongs, of Nesta, and the burden she was unexpectedly forced to carry, of Ethel, and her tendency to sunstroke, came over her.

"Before you say anything, I must be frank," she said.

"Oh, yes, mother; that's what I should like, and expect," said Marcia, not losing any of her cheerfulness, but laying down her work and preparing herself to listen.

She did not stare as her young sisters would have done, for she knew that Mrs Aldworth hated being stared at. She only glanced now and then, and her look was full of sympathy, and there was not a trace of anger on her face.

"You really are very nice, Marcia; there's no denying it. I do wish that in some ways—not perhaps in looks, but in some ways, that my girls were more like you. But, dear, this is it—are you not a little hard on them? They're so young."

"So young?" said Marcia. "Molly is eighteen. She is only two years younger than I am."

"But you will be twenty-one in three months' time."

"I think, mother, if you compare birthdays, you will find that Molly will be nineteen in four months' time. There is little more than two years between us."

Mrs Aldworth was always irritated when opposed.

"That's true," she said. "But don't quibble, Marcia; that is a very disagreeable trait in any girl, particularly when she is addressing a woman so much older than herself. The girls are younger than you, not only in years but in character."

"That I quite corroborate," said Marcia firmly.

"Why do you speak in that tone, as though you were finding fault with them, poor darlings, for being young and sweet and childish, and innocent?"

"Mother," said Marcia, and now she rose from her seat and dropped on her knees by the invalid's couch, "do you think that I really blame them for being young and innocent? But I do blame them for something else."

"And what is that?"

"For being selfish: for thinking of themselves more than for others."

"I don't understand you."

"If you will consider for a moment I think you will quite understand what I mean."

"Marcia, my head aches; I cannot stand a long argument."

"Nor will I give it to you. I have come back here to help you—"

"Why, of course, you were sent for for that purpose."

Marcia felt a very fierce wave of passion rising for a moment in her heart. After all, she had her passions, her strong feelings, her idiosyncrasies. She was not tame; she was not submissive; hers was a firm, steadfast, reliable nature. Hers also was a proud and rebellious one. Nevertheless, she soon conquered the rising irritation. She knew that this bad hour would have to be lived through.

"I am glad you are talking to me quite plainly," she said, "and I on my part will answer you in the same spirit. I have come back here not because I must, for as a matter of fact, I am my own mistress. You see, by my own dear mother's will I have sufficient money of my own—not a great deal, but enough to support me. I can, therefore, be quite independent; and the fact that by my mother's will I was made of age at twenty, puts all possibility of misconstruction of my meaning out of the question."

"Marcia, you are so terribly learned; you use such long words; you talk as though you were forty. Now, my poor children—"

"Mother, you are quite a clever woman yourself, and of course you know what I mean. I have come back to help you, because I wished to—not because I was forced to do so."

"Molly says you are terribly conceited; I am afraid she is right."

Marcia took no notice of this.

"Although I have come back to help you, I have not come back to ruin my young sisters."

"Now, Marcia, you really are talking the wildest nonsense."

"Not at all. Don't you want them to love you?"

Mrs Aldworth burst into tears.

"What a dreadful creature you are," she said. "As though my own sweet children did not love me. Why, they're madly devoted to me. If my little finger aches they're in such a state—you never knew anything like it. I have seen my poor Molly obliged to rush from the room when I have been having a bad attack of my neuralgia, just because her own precious nerves could not stand the agony. Not love me? How dare you insinuate such a thing?"

"Mother, we evidently have different ideas with regard to love. My idea is this—that you ought to sacrifice yourself for the one you love. Now, if I came here and took the complete charge of you away from your own daughters; if I gave them nothing whatever to do for you, and if they were to spend their entire time amusing themselves, and not once considering you, I should do them a cruel wrong; I should injure their characters, and I should make them, what they are already inclined to be—most terribly selfish. That, God helping me, I will not do. I will share the charge of you with them, or I will return to Frankfort to Mrs Silchester, whom I love; to the life that I delight in; to the friends I have made. I will not budge an inch; I will nurse you with the girls, or not at all."

Mrs Aldworth looked up. After all, with a captious, fretful, irritable invalid, a woman with so vacillating a nature as Mrs Aldworth's, there was nothing so effective as firmness. She succumbed. In a minute she had flung her arms round Marcia's neck.

"My darling," she said, "I do see what you mean. And you are right; you will train them, you will be, in my absence, a mother to them."

"Not a mother, for I, like them, am young; but I will be to them an elder sister, and I will teach them—not in words, but by precept and by sympathy and by love, what I should like them to learn. They want a great deal of looking after; and, first of all, they want a complete change in their method of living."

"I am afraid even for them, and for you, I cannot quite ignore my pain, my constant suffering, my weary nights, my long, long, fatiguing days."

"Of course you cannot, and I have said enough for the present. Now, let us have a jolly time. See, I am going to have a particularly nice tea for you this afternoon. I have told Susan to bring it up when it is ready. We'll have it on that balcony."

"Oh, but I shall catch cold."

"Indeed you won't. Do you see that shady corner, and how the scent-laden air is pervading the whole place, and the sun will be shining across the other half, and you can see a long way down the garden? I'll sit near you and read to you when you like, out of such a funny book."

"My taste and yours don't agree with regard to reading," said Mrs Aldworth, always glad to hail any interruption. "I suppose I have degenerated; I am certainly not an intellectual woman; I don't pretend that I am. I like the stories that are in the penny papers. We get two or three of them, and we always enjoy them. Will you read me one of those?"

"No, mother."

"Oh, how cross you are!"

"I am very sorry, mother, but I will read you something just as amusing. Did you ever hear of 'The Reminiscences of an Irish R.M.'?"

"No, it sounds very dull."

"Wait till you hear it. It will make you laugh a great deal more than the stories in the penny papers."

"They make me cry a great deal. Molly reads rather badly, but yesterday I found myself weeping in the middle of the night over the woes of the poor little heroine. I am sure the next number of the paper has come in, and I am so anxious to know if she is really married to the Earl of Dorchester."

"It will be Nesta's turn to-morrow, and she can read to you. Now for the balcony and a pleasant time." They had a pleasant time, and the hours flew by on wings. Marcia told stories; she laughed, she chatted, and she read a little from "The Reminiscences of an Irish R.M." Mrs Aldworth laughed till the tears ran down her cheeks.

"Oh, rich! rich!" she exclaimed. "That scene with the dog is inimitable. How funny, how truly funny! But, Marcia, isn't it bad for my nerves to laugh so much?"

"It's the best thing for them in all the world."

"Marcia, you are wonderful!"

"Now for the new fancy work," said Marcia.

She taught the invalid a different sort of stitch from any which she had before learned. She gave her bright-coloured silks, and a piece of art cloth to embroider upon, and soon her stepmother was so fascinated that she allowed her young companion to work in silence, often raising her eyes to look across the distant garden.

The girls were spending the afternoon in the garden; but presently they went out, all three of them gaudily and badly dressed. They walked through the garden, gathered some roses, and then disappeared through a little wicket gate at the further end.

Marcia felt quite sure that they did this for the purpose of showing her how they were enjoying themselves, while she was in prison. She smiled to herself.

"Poor little things," she thought. "I wonder how soon I shall win their hearts."

She had marked out a plan of action for herself. She had practically secured Mrs Aldworth—not for long, of course, for Nesta would turn her round the next day, and Molly the day after. It would be a constant repetition of the battle; but in the end she would win her. The girls, of course, were different. Unselfishness must be born within them before they really did what Marcia wanted them to do. Unselfishness, brave hearts, pure spirits, noble ways.

"Two, three months should do it," thought the girl; "then I can go back with Angela St. Just in the autumn; for she is returning to Frankfort, I know, just to be with Mrs Silchester, and I can take her back. Oh, little Angela!"

Marcia recalled the soft touch of Angela's blooming cheek; the look in her lovely eyes; the refinement in all her bearing.

Mrs Aldworth indulged in a nap; but now tea appeared and there was again bustle and movement, and when Mr Aldworth entered the room presently, he was so surprised at the improvement in his wife that he scarcely knew her.

"Marcia, you are a magician," he said.

"You must uphold me with regard to the girls," said Marcia.

"Of course, dear, you must uphold her. She has been explaining things to me," said the wife. "She says that my children are exceedingly selfish."

"I have always known that," replied Mr Aldworth, looking at his daughter.

Mrs Aldworth began to frown. "I must say I think it is very unkind of you to say so; but of course you stick up for Marcia, and you abuse my poor children. That is always the way. I suppose just because Marcia's mother thought herself a fine county lady and I—my people only in common trade, that—"

"Oh, hush, Amelia," said her husband.

"Mother—dear mother!" said Marcia.

Mr Aldworth backed out of the room as quickly as he could. He met his son on the stairs.

"Don't go in," he said. "She's as jealous as ever she can be. Like a bear with a sore head. The girls are all out enjoying themselves and Marcia is keeping guard. I must say that she makes an excellent nurse. I believe your mother will be ever so much better in a short time. She has her out on the balcony, prettily dressed, surrounded by coloured silks and all that sort of thing, and Marcia herself is looking like a picture."

"She is very handsome," interrupted Horace. "I'll go in and have a peep. I don't often visit mother."

If there was a person in the whole world whom Mrs Aldworth respected, it was her stepson. She was, of course, a little bit afraid of him; she was not in the least afraid of her husband. She had led him a sorry sort of life, poor man, since he had brought her home, an exceedingly pretty, self-willed, rather vulgar little bride. Horace and Marcia had a bad time during those early days, but Marcia had a worse time than Horace, for Horace never submitted, never brooked injustice, and managed before she was a year his stepmother to turn that same little stepmother round his fingers. Marcia, luckily for herself, was sent to school when she was old enough, but Horace lived on in the house. He took up his father's business and did well in it, and was his father's prop and right hand.

"Horace, dear," exclaimed Marcia, when she saw her brother.

Horace came out through the open window, bending his tall head to do so.

"Upon my word," he said, "this is very pleasant. How nice you look, mother, and how well. Marcia, I congratulate you."

"Horace, she has been reading me such a lecture—your poor old mother. She says that my children are so selfish."

"A most self-evident fact," replied Horace.

"Horace! You too?"

"Come, mother, you must acknowledge it."

"Marcia is going to take them in hand."

"Good girl, capital!" said Horace, giving his sister a glance of approval.

"Don't you think we needn't talk of it just now?" said Marcia. "We don't see so much of you, Horace. Have you nothing funny to tell mother?"

"I have, I have all kinds of stories. But you look tired, old girl. Run away and rest in the garden for an hour. I'll stay with mother for just that time."

Marcia gave him a glance of real gratitude. Oh, she was tired. The invalid was difficult; the afternoon hours seemed as though they would never end.

When she went back again Horace had soothed his mother into a most beatific state of bliss. She told Marcia that she was the best girl in all the world; that she would confide the entire future of her three girls to dear Marcia, that Marcia should train them, should make them noble like herself.

"And I'll tell them so: I'll tell that naughty little Nesta to-morrow afternoon. I'll tell her she must look after me: I'll be firm; I'll put down my foot," said Mrs Aldworth.

Marcia made no response. Another long hour and a half had to be got through and then the invalid was safe in bed, with all her small requirements at hand. She opened her eyes sleepily.

"God bless you, Marcia dear. You are a very good girl, and the joy of my life."

Chapter Seven

Shirking Duty

Now Nesta was perhaps the naughtiest of the three Aldworth girls. She had been more spoiled than the others, and was naturally of a somewhat braver and more determined nature. She was fully resolved that nothing would really induce her to give up her walk with Flossie Griffiths. Flossie was her dearest friend. Between Flossie and Nesta had sprung up that sort of adoring friendship that often exists between two young girls in that period of their lives. Flossie and Nesta declared that they thought alike, that when a thought darted through the brain of one, it immediately visited the other. Every idea was in common; all their plans were made to suit the convenience of each other. Nesta used to say that Flossie was like her true sister, for her own sisters were of course absorbed in each other.

"There are Molly and Ethel, they are always hugger-muggering," she used to say. "What should I do but for my Flossie? I am quite happy because I have got my Flossie."

Therefore, to have to tell her that she could not walk with her, could not confide secrets to her, could not be so much in her company just because there was a tiresome old mother at home, who ought to be nursed by an equally tiresome elder sister, a confirmed old maid, was more than Nesta could brook. She had made up her mind, therefore, what she would do. She would not confide her scheme to her sisters, but after dinner, instead of going to her mother's room, she would slip out of the house, rush down a side path in the garden, get into the wood, and go off to Flossie's house. The idea had come into her venturesome brain that morning; but she was quite cautious enough to keep it to herself. She knew well that with regard to such an escapade she would have no sympathy from her elder sisters. They were highly pleased with the complete day of liberty which lay before them. They had planned it delightfully. They were resolved to ask the Carters to have tea with them in the summerhouse at the far end of the garden. They had so often been at the Carters' house, now it would be their turn to entertain them, and they should have a right good time. They had coaxed Susan, the parlour maid, into their conspiracy, and Susan had proved herself agreeable. She said that hot cakes and several dainty sweets should be forthcoming, and that the two Miss Carters should have as good a tea as she and cook could devise between them.

"But not a word to Marcia," said Molly, "and for goodness' sake, not a word to Nesta. She is so greedy that she would be capable of coming down and helping herself to the things in the pantry if she knew."

Nesta did know, however; for nothing ever went on in that house that she did not contrive to learn all about, but as she herself had a scheme quite ripe for action, she was determined to leave her sisters alone.

"One of them will have to go to mother," she thought, "and goodness me what a fuss there'll be. Of course, mother can't be left alone, and I cannot be got back in a hurry, particularly when Flossie and I'll be out and away the very minute I get to her house. Marcia is going by train to visit that tiresome Angela St. Just. I heard her telling father so this morning. I wouldn't be in Molly's shoes, or in Ethel's shoes. Yes, it will be Molly's turn—I wouldn't be in Molly's shoes. Dear, dear! What fun it is! It is quite exciting, we live in a continual sort of battle, each of us dodging the others."

Nesta had to be very careful, and to keep the watchful eyes of her companions from fixing themselves too much on her face.

Marcia came down to lunch that day neatly dressed, with her hat on.

"Did you leave mother to put your hat on?" asked Ethel, in a vindictive tone.

"No, mother helped me to dress. She was most particular. She has very good taste when she likes."

"She is everything that is good; don't run her down to us," said Molly.

They had, it may be perceived, almost dropped the Coventry system. It was tiresome and uninteresting when nobody took any notice of it.

"Nesta, dear," said Marcia during lunch, "you will be very careful about mother. I think you are going to have a nice afternoon. I have left her so well and comfortable, and so inclined to enjoy herself."

"Oh, yes," said Nesta.

"That's a good girl," said Marcia. "I see by your face that you are going to make us all happy."

"I hope so," replied Nesta.

These remarks would have aroused the suspicions of Molly and Ethel on another occasion, for they would have considered them wonderfully unlike the pert Nesta; but they were absorbed by the thought of their own tea party, and took no notice.

Marcia had to hurry through her lunch in order to catch her train. She told her sisters she would be back about nine o'clock that evening and went away.

"Now, Nesta, it is your turn," said Molly. "You ought to be going to mother. Do go along and make yourself scarce. Do your duty; it's no use grumbling. She's off now for her fill of pleasure, and we cannot get her back. Horrid, mean, spiteful old cat!"

"You can't be called Miss Mule Selfish for nothing, can you?" said Nesta.

Molly laughed at this.

"Doesn't it sound funny?" she said. "I'll tell—"

She stopped herself. She was about to say that she would tell the Carters, who would keenly relish the joke.

Nesta slipped out of the room. She had already secreted her hat under the stairs. It was soon on her head, and a minute or two later she had dashed down the sidewalk, passed through the wicket gate, and was away through the woods.

The Griffiths lived about three-quarters of a mile away. They were not rich like the Carters, but they had a little house in the opposite suburb of the town, a little house with a fairly big garden, and with woods quite near. Flossie was an only child; she was a great pet with her father and mother, whom she contrived completely to turn round her little finger.

She was standing now at the gate, waiting anxiously for the moment when her darling Nesta would arrive. She and Nesta were to go for a picnic all by themselves to a distant ruin. Flossie was to bring the eatables; Nesta knew nothing of this delectable plan, for Flossie had resolved to keep it a secret all to herself. But now, with her basket packed—that basket which contained tea, milk, sugar, various cakes, a small pot of jam, some bread, and a little pat of butter, as well as a second basket filled with ripe gooseberries—she anxiously waited for her visitor.

By-and-by Nesta was seen. She was running, and looked very untidy, and not like her usually spruce self.

"Dear, dear!" called out Flossie. "How do you do, Nesta? What in the world is the matter? You haven't put on your best frock or anything."

"I'm very lucky to be here at all," said Nesta. "For goodness' sake don't speak to me for a minute, until I have got back my breath. I have run all the way, and I am choking—oh, my heart will burst."

"Lean against me," said Flossie.

Nesta flung herself against her friend. Flossie was slender and dark, with very curly hair. Nesta was a large girl, built on a generous scale. When she flung herself now against poor Flossie, the latter almost staggered.

"Oh, come," said Flossie, "not quite so violent as that. Here, let us flop down under this tree. You can take your breath and tell me what it is all about."

"Oh, I can't," said Nesta, who was beginning to recover herself already. "We must be off as fast as possible. Oh, I have had a time of it coming to you. Goodness gracious me, whatever is that?"

She pointed to the tea basket.

"We're going to Norland's Cliff, you and I, to have tea all by ourselves. Isn't it prime? Isn't it golloptious?" said Flossie.

"Flossie! Has your mother said you might?"

"Yes, yes, of course, she has. I asked her this morning, and she said: 'Certainly, dear.'"

"But I thought there were donkey races there to-day."

"There are; but I didn't say a word about that to mother. She never guessed. Luckily, father was out of the room. It will be much more fun going there to-day, for we'll see the races; that is if we are quick. But I'm sure, Nesta, I did think you'd come looking a little bit smart, and you've got your very oldest hat on too, and that dress."

"Oh, if you're ashamed of me," began Nesta, tears springing to her blue eyes— they could always rise there at a moment's warning.

"I didn't mean to hurt you, dear," said Flossie, who was really deeply attached to her friend; "but whatever is it?"

"You must take me as I am, or I'll go home again if you like," said Nesta. "It would be much better for me to go home. I wouldn't get into quite such an awful row as I shall get into all for love of you, if I went home now. I'll go if you wish. I'll just be in time to escape the very worst of the fuss. What am I to do, dear?"

"Never mind about your dress. I'd lend you something of mine, only you are twice as big."

"Well, I'll carry this basket," said Nesta, picking up the tea basket. "Now, do let us go; I shan't have an easy moment until we are well out of sight of the house."

The girls walked on briskly. They had, for some time, to walk along the dusty road, but soon they came to a stile which led across some fields, delightfully green and inviting looking at this time of the year. The fields led again into a wood, and this wood, by an upland path, came at last to Norland's Cliff. Norland's Cliff was the highest point in that part of the country, and on this eminence had once been built by an eccentric Sir Guy Norland, a tower. He had built it as a sort of a vantage tower, in order to see as far round him as possible; but in the end, in a fit of madness, he had thrown himself from the tower, and his mangled body was found there on a certain winter's night. Afterwards no one had gone near the tower except as a sort of show place; and it was, of course, supposed to be haunted, particularly at night, when Sir Guy Norland was said to ride round and round on horseback.

But it was a beautiful summer day on the present occasion, and the girls thought of no ghosts, and when they were in the shelter of the woods Nesta began to recount her wrongs.

"She has come back, the old spitfire," she said, and she explained the whole situation.

Flossie was full of commiseration.

"She wanted you to give up your delightful time with me—this Saturday to which we have been looking forward for such a long time—just to sit with your mother?"

"That's it, Floss; that's the truth, Floss. Oh, Floss, how am I to bear it?"

"And you ran away then?"

"Yes, I ran away, I just could do nothing else; I couldn't give up my afternoon with you. It is all very well to talk of filial affection, but the deepest affection of my heart is given to you, Floss."

"That's very kind of you," said Flossie, but she did not speak with the intense rapture that Nesta expected.

"Aren't you awfully, awfully shocked about it all?" said Nesta, noticing the tone, and becoming annoyed by it.

"I am dreadfully sorry that anything should have occurred to prevent your coming to me; but it does seem fair that you should sometimes be with your mother. When my darling old mothery has a headache I like to sit with her and bathe her forehead with eau de Cologne."

"Oh, that's all very well," said Nesta, "and so would I like to sit with my dear mothery, if she only had a headache once a month or so; but when it is every day, and all day long, and all night too, you get about tired of it."

"I expect you do," said Flossie, who was not at all strong-minded, and was easily brought round to Nesta's point of view. "Well, at any rate, here you are, and we'll try and have all the fun we can. Oh, do look at those donkeys down there, and the crowd of men, and girls and boys. Isn't it gay?"

"I wonder if we can get into the tower," said Nesta.

"We must get into the tower," remarked Flossie. "I have determined all along that we will have tea just on the very spot where Sir Guy threw himself over the wall. I know the very niche. It will seem so exciting to-night when we are dropping off to sleep. I do like to have a sort of eerie feeling when I'm in a very snug bedroom, close to my father and mother, with the door just a teeny bit open between us. I love it. I wouldn't like it if there was anything to be frightened about, but to know that you have been close to something queer and uncanny, it makes you seem to sort of hug yourself up, don't you know the feeling, Nesta?"

"I do, and I don't," said Nesta. "I sleep in the room with Molly and Ethel, and we always jabber and jabber until we drop asleep. That's what we do, but we have great fun all the same."

Flossie gave a faint sigh. They approached the tower; but to their surprise a custodian stood at the entrance and informed the two little girls that this was a very special show day, and that no one could be admitted into the tower under the large sum of twopence. Neither Nesta nor Flossie had brought a farthing with them, and they stood back, feeling dismayed.

"Never mind," said Nesta, "let us go and have tea in the wood, it will be just as good fun."

"I suppose it will; only I did want to see the donkey races. Where are the races, please?" continued Flossie, turning to the man.

But here again disappointment awaited them. They would not be allowed within sight of the donkey races without paying a penny each.

"I have heaps of money at home," said Flossie, "a whole little savings bank of pennies."

"And I have half a crown which I have not broken into yet," said Nesta. "It's too bad."

"Well, we have an excellent tea, and it is very shady and pleasant in the woods, much better than sitting in your mother's room, getting scolded," said Flossie, "so do come along and let us enjoy ourselves."

Chapter Eight

A Feast to Delight the Eyes

Meanwhile matters were not going on quite so comfortably at the Aldworths' house. They began smoothly enough. Mrs Aldworth had spent a morning full of perfect happiness, order, and comfort with her eldest daughter. Marcia had done everything that was possible for the well-being of the invalid. She had given instructions also with regard to the food which she was to be supplied with that afternoon, and last, but not least, had not left her, until she saw her enjoying a delicious little dinner of roast chicken, fresh green peas, and a basket of strawberries.

Mrs Aldworth was already beginning to feel the benefit of the change. Until Marcia arrived on the scene she had been, not nursed, but fussed over, often left alone for long hours together to fret and bemoan herself, to make the worst of her trials, and the least of her blessings. Her girls did not mean to be unkind, but they were very often all out together, and the one who was in, was always in a state of grumbling. Now the house seemed suddenly to have the calm and sweet genius of order and love presiding over it. Mrs Aldworth was conscious of the agreeable change, without analysing it too closely. She was glad, yes, quite glad, that dear Marcia should have a happy time with the St. Justs. She knew all about her husband's first marriage. He had married a penniless girl of very good family, who had been a governess in a nobleman's house. He had come across her when he was a poor lawyer, before he rose to his present very comfortable position. He had married her and she had loved him, and as long as she lived he had been a very happy man. But Marcia's mother had died, and Mrs Aldworth was his second wife. She had been jealous of the first wife in a way a nature like hers would be jealous, jealous of a certain grace and charm about her, which the neighbours had told her of, and which she herself had perceived in the beautiful oil portrait which hung in Marcia's room. She had always hated that portrait, and had longed to turn it with its face to the wall. But these sort of petty doings had gone out of fashion, and the neighbours would be angry with her if they knew. Then her own children had come, and ill health had fallen upon her, and she had sunk beneath the burden.

Yes, she knew all these things. Her past life seemed to go before her on this pleasant summer's afternoon like a phantasmagoria. She was not agitated by any reminiscences that came before her eyes, but she was conscious of a sense of soothing. Marcia was nice—Marcia was so clever, and Marcia was wise. She was glad Marcia was out. She too would vie with her in being unselfish; she too would become wise; she too would be clever.

She thought of Marcia's promise, that whatever happened she would visit her for a few moments that evening just to tell her about Angela. Mrs Aldworth, with all the rest of the inhabitants of the little suburb, had worshipped the St. Justs. She had seen Angela occasionally, and had craned her neck when the girl passed by in their open carriage with her aristocratic-looking father by her side. She had felt herself flushing when she mentioned the name. She had been conscious, very conscious on a certain day when Angela had spoken to her. On that occasion it was to inquire for Marcia, and Mrs Aldworth had been wildly proud of the fact that she was Marcia's stepmother. But Marcia could talk about Angela in the calmest way in the world, evidently being fond of her, but not specially elated at the thought of her friendship.

"I suppose that is called breeding," thought the good woman. "Well, well, I mustn't grumble. My own dear children are far prettier, that is one thing. Of course, whatever advances Marcia's welfare she will share with them, for she is really quite unselfish. Now, I wonder why my little Nesta doesn't come. I am quite longing to kiss my darling girl."

Mrs Aldworth was not angry with Nesta for being a bit late.

"It is her little way," she thought. "The child is so forgetful; she is certain to have to run out to the garden twenty times, or to stroke pussie, or to remember that she has not given old Rover his bone, or to do one hundred and one things which she knows I would be annoyed at if she forgot."

So for the first half-hour after dinner, Mrs Aldworth was quite happy. But for the next quarter of an hour she was not quite so calm. The sun had come round, and it was time to have the blind rearranged. It was also time for Nesta, who had been given explicit instructions by Marcia, to wheel her mother on to the balcony. Mrs Aldworth felt hot; she felt thirsty; she longed to have a drink of that cold water which was sparkling just beyond her reach. Even the penny paper was nowhere in sight; her fancy work had dropped to the floor, and she had lost her thimble. How annoying of naughty little Nesta—why, the child was already an hour late!

Mrs Aldworth managed in her very peevish way to ring her bell, which was, of course, within reach. The first ring was not attended to; she rang twice, with no better result. Then with her finger pressed on the electric button, with her face very red and her poor hand trembling, she kept up a continued peal until Susan opened the door.

Susan had been busy rushing backwards and forwards to the garden, putting everything in order for the advent of the Carters.

"I beg your pardon, ma'am," she said. "I am sorry I kept you waiting; but isn't Miss Nesta here?"

"No, she is not; why didn't you answer my ring at once?"

"The young ladies, ma'am, are expecting one or two friends in the garden, and I was helping them. I thought, of course, Miss Nesta was with you."

"She is not; I have been shamefully neglected. Tell Miss Nesta to come to me at once."

"Yes, ma'am."

"Before you go, Susan, please pull down that blind."

"Yes, ma'am, of course. I am sorry—the room is much too 'ot. Whatever would Miss Marcia say?"

Susan, who was exceedingly good-natured, did all in her power for her mistress; picked up her fancy work, found the thimble, moved the sofa a little out of the sun's rays, and then saying she would find Nesta in a jiffy and bring her to her mother in double haste, she left the room.

But the jiffy, if that should be a measurement of time, proved to be a long one. When Susan did come back it was with a face full of concern.

"I'm ever so sorry, ma'am, but Miss Nesta ain't anywhere in the house. I've been all over the house and all over the garden, and there ain't a sign of her anywhere. Shall I call Miss Marcia, ma'am?"

"Nonsense, Susan, you know quite well that Miss Marcia has gone to Hurst Castle. She has gone to see the St. Justs."

Susan was not impressed by this fact.

"Whatever is to be done?" she said.

"Send one of the other young ladies to me. Send Miss Molly, it is her turn, I think, but send one of them."

Now this was exactly what naughty Nesta had prophesied would happen, Molly, dressed in a pale blue muslin, which she had made herself, a pale blue muslin with little bows of forget-me-not ribbon all down the front of the bodice, her hair becomingly dressed, her hands clean and white, with a little old-fashioned ring of her mother's on one finger, was waiting to greet the Carters. The Carters were to come in by the lower gate; they were to come right through the garden and straight along the path to the summerhouse. Ethel was in the summerhouse. She was in white; she was giving the final touches to the feast. It was a feast to delight the eyes of any tired guest, such strawberries, so large, so ripe, so luscious; a great jug of cream, white, soft sugar, a pile of hot cakes, jam sandwiches, fragrant tea, the best Sèvres china having been purloined from the cupboard in the drawing room for the occasion.

"They haven't china like that at the Carters', rich as they are," said Molly.

Oh, it was a time to think over afterwards with delight; a time to enjoy to the full measure of bliss in the present. And they were coming—already just above the garden wall Molly could see Clara's hat with its pink bow and white bird-of-paradise feather, and Mabel's hat with its blue bow and seagull's wings. And beside them was somebody else, some one in a straw hat with a band of black ribbon round it. Why, it was Jim! This was just too much; the cup of bliss began to overflow!

Molly rushed on tiptoe into the summerhouse.

"They're coming!" she whispered, "and Jim is with them! Have we got enough cups and saucers? Oh, yes, good Susan! Now I am going to stand at the gate."

The gate was opened and the three visitors appeared. Molly shook hands most gracefully; Jim gave her an admiring glance.

It was just then that Susan, distracted, her face crimson, hurried out.

"Miss Molly," she said, "Miss Molly!"

"Bring the tea, please," said Molly, in a manner which seemed to say—"Keep yourself at a distance, if you please."

"Miss Molly, you must go to the missus at once."

"Why?" said Molly.

"She's that flustered she's a'most in hysterics. That naughty Miss Nesta has gone and run away. She ain't been with her at all. Missus has been alone the whole blessed afternoon."

"I can't go now," said Molly, "and I won't."

"Miss Molly, you must."

"Go away, Susan. Clara, dear, I'm sorry that the day should be such a hot one, but you will it so refreshing in the summerhouse."

"You have quite a nice garden," said Clara, in a patronising voice, but Mabel turned and looked full at Molly.

"Did your servant say your mother wanted you?"

"Oh, there's no hurry," said Molly, who felt all her calm forsaking her, and crimson spots rising to her cheeks.

"Oh, do go, please," said Clara. "Here's Ethel; she will look after us. Oh, what good strawberries; I'm ever so thirsty! Run along, Molly, you must go if your mother wants you."

"Of course you must," said Jim.

"You must go at once, please," said Clara. "Do go. I heard what the servant said, she was in quite a state, poor thing."

Thus adjured Molly went away. It is true she kept her temper until she got out of sight of her guests; but once in the house her fury broke bounds. She was really scarcely accountable for her actions for a minute or two. Then she went upstairs and entered her mother's room with anything but a soothing manner to the poor invalid.

"Is that you, Nesta?" said Mrs Aldworth, who from her position, on the sofa could not see who had entered the room.

"No," said Molly, "it's not Nesta, it is I, Molly, and it is not my day to be with you, mother. We have friends in the garden. Please, what is the matter? I can't stay now, really; I can't possibly stay."

"Oh, Molly, oh, I am ill, I am ill," said Mrs Aldworth. "Oh, this is too much. Oh, my head, my head! The salts, Molly, the salts! I am going to faint; my heart is stopping! Oh, let some one go for the doctor—my heart is stopping!"

Molly knelt by her parent; for a minute or two she was really alarmed, for the flush had died from Mrs Aldworth's face, and she lay panting and breathless on her sofa. But when Molly bent over her and kissed her, and said: "Poor little mother, here are the salts; now you are better, are you not? Poor mother!" Mrs Aldworth revived; tears rose to her eyes, she looked full at her child.

"You do look pretty," she said, "very, very pretty. I never saw you in that dress before."

"Oh, mothery, it is too bad," said Molly, her own grievances returning the moment she perceived that her mother was better. "It's that wicked little Nesta. Oh, mother, what punishment shall we give her?"

"But tell me," said Mrs Aldworth earnestly, "what is the matter? What are you doing?"

"Mother, you won't be angry—you know you are so fond of us, and we are so devoted to you. Oh, if you would excuse me, and let me go down and pour out tea for them. They are, my dear darling, Clay and Mabel Carter, and we have tea in the summerhouse, and it's so nice."

"Dear me," said Mrs Aldworth, "tea in the summerhouse, and you never told me?"

"It was our own little private tea, mother. We thought it was our day off, and that you wouldn't want us."

"And you didn't want me," said Mrs Aldworth.

"Oh, mother, it isn't that we don't want you, but we do want to have our fun. We can't be young twice, you know."

"Nesta said that—Nesta is tired of me, too."

"We are none of us tired of you."

"Yes, you are," said Mrs Aldworth. "You know you are, you are all tired of me; Marcia is right. You may go, Molly."

At that strange new tone, that look on the invalid's white face, a girl with a better heart, with any sort of real comprehension of character, with any sort of unselfishness, would immediately have yielded; but Molly was shallow, frothy, selfish, unreliable.

"If you really mean it," she said—"we could quite well spare Susan."

"It doesn't matter; you can go."

"I'll send Ethel up presently, mother. It seems so rude just when they have come from such a long way off, in the burning sun and by special invitation. And there is Jim—you know, you always like us to chat with Jim."

"You can go," said Mrs Aldworth. "I would not stand in your way for anything. It's all right."

The sun was pouring in at the window. Mrs Aldworth's head was hot, her feet were cold; her fancy work had fallen to the ground; all her working materials were scattered here, there and everywhere, but she rather hugged her own sense of discomfort.

"Go, dear, go," she said, speaking as gently as she could, and closing her eyes.

"You'd like to have a nap, wouldn't you?" said Molly, her face brightening. "I'll put this shawl over your feet."

"No, thank you, I'm too hot."

The shawl was wrenched with some force from Molly's hand.

"Oh, mothery, don't get into a temper. You are not really vexed with your Molly, are you? I'll be up again soon. I will, really."

"Go," said the weak, querulous voice, and Molly went.

"Is she all right?" asked Ethel when Molly rushed down to the summerhouse.

"Oh, yes," said Molly in a cheerful tone. "She is going to sleep."

"To sleep?" said Ethel in astonishment.

"Yes, she didn't wish me to stay. Dear old mother, she is so unselfish. I made her very comfy and I'll go back again presently. Now, I can look after you; I'm going to help you. Sit down there, Ethel, and let me pour out the tea. Fie, Ethel, you have not given Jim anything."

But for some reason Jim had darted a glance into Molly's eyes, and Molly thought she read disapproval in it. It seemed to her that he did not quite approve of her. But she could not long entertain that feeling, for she was always satisfied with herself. In a few minutes the whole five were laughing and talking, playing games, passing jests backwards and forwards as though there were no invalid mother in the world, no duties in the world to be performed, no naughty Nesta not very far off.

"Now," said Clara, "we must be trotting home, and you may as well walk back with us."

"Are you certain you can be spared?" said Jim.

"Yes, I'm positive," said Molly; "but to make sure I'll go in and see Susan."

Molly went into the house; but she did not go to Susan. She would be too much afraid to inquire of Susan, who, with all her good nature, could be cross enough at times, that is, when she thoroughly disapproved of the young ladies' racketings, as she called them.

What Molly really did was to slip up to her own bedroom, put on her most becoming hat, catch up her white parasol, take up a similar parasol and hat for Ethel, with a pair of gloves for each, and rush swiftly downstairs. No one heard her enter the house, and no one heard her go downstairs again.

"Thanks," said Ethel, when she saw her hat with its accompanying pins, observed the parasol, and welcomed the gloves. "Is mother all right?" she said.

"Yes, she is having a lovely sleep. Now do let us come along."

"You may as well stay and have a game of tennis," said Jim, who after Molly's return to the house concluded that things must be all right.

"Yes, that would be splendid," said Clara, "and you could stay to supper if you liked."

How very nearly had that delightful afternoon been spoiled. This was Molly's thought; but it was the mother herself who had saved it. The dear little mother who wouldn't like her children to be put out. And of course she was in such a lovely sleep. That queer attack she had had when Molly was in the room! But Molly would not let herself think of that. Mother was queer now and then, and sometimes the doctor had to be sent for in a hurry; but it was nothing serious. All mother's attacks were just nervous storms, so the doctor called them. Signs of weakness, was Molly's explanation. Oh, yes, the attack was nothing, nothing at all, and what a splendid time she and Ethel were having.

Chapter Nine

The Truth about Mrs Aldworth

When Marcia left the train at Hurst Castle station she was greeted by, a tall, very slender girl who was waiting on the platform to receive her. The girl had a sufficiently remarkable face to attract the attention of each person who saw her. It was never known in her short life that any one passed Angela St. Just without turning to look at her. Most people looked again after that first glance, but every one, man, woman, and child, bestowed at least one glance at that most radiant, most lovely face. It was difficult to describe Angela, for hers was not the beauty of mere feature; it was the beauty of a very loving, loyal, and noble soul which seemed, in some sort of way, to have got very close to her body, so close that its rays were always shining out. It shone in her eyes, causing them to have a peculiar limpid light, the sort of light which has been described as "Never seen on land or shore," and the same spirit caused those smiles round the girl's beautiful lips, and the kindly words which dropped from her mouth when she spoke, and the sympathy in her manner. For the rest, she was graceful with an abundance of chestnut hair, neatly formed and yet unremarkable features and a creamy white complexion. Her eyebrows were delicately formed, being long and sweeping, and slightly arched. Her eyes were also long, almost almond-shaped, of a soft and yet bright hazel. Her eyelashes were very thick and very dark, making the hazel eyes look almost black at a distance. The girl had all the advantages which a long train of noble ancestors could bestow upon her. Her education had been attended to in the most thorough manner, and now at the age of sixteen and a half, there could scarcely be seen a more perfect young creature than Angela St. Just.

"Oh, Angela," said Marcia, as she found her hand clasped in that of Angela, "this is good. I have just been longing to see you."

"And I to see you, Marcia. The carriage is waiting—I don't mean the ordinary stiff carriage, but the pony trap. Uncle Herbert has lent it to me for the whole afternoon, and there are some delightful woods just a little way out of the town, where we can drive and have a picnic tea. I have brought all the materials for it in a basket in the little pony trap."

Marcia naturally acceded to this delightful proposition, and the girls were soon driving rapidly over the country roads.

Marcia almost wondered as she leant back in the luxurious little carriage and watched her young companion, whether she were in a dream or not. This morning she had been a member of the Aldworths' untidy, disorderly house. She herself was the one spirit of order within it. Now she was by Angela's side, she was close to the most beautiful creature she had ever met, or ever hoped to meet.

Angela was not one to talk very much, but once or twice she glanced at her companion. The sweetest smile just broke the lines of her mouth and then vanished, leaving it grave once more.

They entered the shade of the woods, and presently drew up under a wide-spreading oak tree. The woods near Hurst Castle were celebrated, having once been part of the ancient forest which at one time covered the greater part of England. Here were oaks of matchless size, and of enormous circumference; here were beech trees which looked as though they formed the pillars and the roof of a great cathedral; here were graceful ladies of the forest, with their silvery stems and their slender leaves. Here, also, were the denizens of the woods—birds, rabbits, hares, butterflies innumerable. Marcia gave a sigh.

"What is the matter?" said Angela at once.

"Oh, it is so good, so beautiful, but I can spend such a short time with you."

"I was determined to come all alone, and I wouldn't even let Bob drive me. He was quite disappointed; but I managed the ponies splendidly. Here, we will just fasten them to this tree. Now, darlings, you will be as good as gold, won't you? Jeanette, don't eat your head off. Oh, yes, you must have a little bit of this tender young furze to nibble. Coquette, behave yourself, dear." She lightly pressed a kiss on the forehead of both of her pets, and then taking out the tea basket placed it under the tree.

Two other girls were having tea at that moment in another wood not very far away; but Marcia, luckily for her peace of mind, knew nothing of that. When the meal was half over, Angela turned to her companion.

"Now, I want to hear all about it."

"About what, Angela?"

"Oh, you know—why you suddenly left Aunt Emily; why you gave up the school where you were doing such wonderful things, and influencing the girls so magnificently. What does it all mean? You often told me that you were not wanted at home."

"And I thought so; God forgive me; I was wrong."

"Well, tell me."

"Angela, you know quite well how often you have advocated our direct and instant obedience to the call of duty."

"I certainly have—I often wish duty would call me. I have such an easy life. I long to do something great."

"Well, I will tell you all about myself."

Marcia did give it résumé of what had just happened.

"The girls are dreadful at present," she said. "They are—it's the true word for them, Angela, I cannot help telling you—they are under-bred."

"It must be dreadful, dear; but is it their fault?"

"I fear in a certain measure that this state of things belongs to their natures."

"But natures can be altered," said Angela. "At least I believe so."

She gave a queer little twitch to her brows, looking up as she did so for a moment at Marcia.

"I know," said Marcia, "up to a certain point they can; and people can be made to see their duty and all that; but I think there are certain natures which cannot rise beyond certain heights, at least in this world; don't you agree with me, Angela?"

"I have not thought about it. I have always thought that 'The best for the highest' ought to be our motto—it ought to be the motto of every one—the best for the highest, don't you understand?"

"It is yours," said Marcia.

"Well, anyhow," continued Angela, "I am so interested. I'll come and see you all some day."

"They'd be ever so proud, and so would my stepmother. They think a great deal about you."

Angela did not reply.

"I am going to stay here for a little," she said, after a pause. "Father is quite happy to be with Uncle Herbert, and it is good for him not to have too much of his roaming life. I will ask him if I may not come and see you some day. He wouldn't come—he can't bear to go near Newcastle since dear old Court Prospect was sold."

"I can quite understand that."

"And will you come to see us—are you quite sure you will come during the summer?"

"I hope so."

"Do you think those girls will keep their compact?"

"I don't know."

"Do you mean to keep yours if they break it? that the point," said Angela, and now she leant back against the great clump of fern, and looked at her companion from under the shade of her black hat. Marcia glanced at her.

"I shall do it," she said.

"It would be somewhat painful for you. Your—your mother has got accustomed to you."

"She is not my real mother."

"Ought you to think of that, Marcia? Your real mother doesn't want you; this mother does."

"Yes, I know what you mean, but I will not change; I am determined; I will help the girls to do their duty; I will not take their burden from them."

"But ought they to consider the care of a mother a burden?" said Angela. "I think if I could find my own mother anywhere—"

"Angela, you and they are not made out of the same materials."

"Oh, yes, we are. I should like to talk to them."

"You would have no effect. They would only look at you, and wonder why your hat looked different on you from their hats on them, and why you spoke with such a good accent, and why you are so graceful, and they would be, without knowing it, a little bit jealous."

"You are not talking very kindly of them, are you, Marcia?"

"I don't believe I am; shall we change the subject?"

"Yes, certainly, if you like. What is your plan for the future, Marcia?"

"I will tell you. I have some hopes; I think I have won my stepmother round very much to my views. She is the sort of woman who can be very easily managed, if you only know how to take her. If I had my stepmother altogether to myself and there was no one to interfere, I should not be at all afraid. But you see the thing is this—that while I influence her one day, the others undo all that I have said and done the next, and this, I fear, will go on for some time. Still, I think I have some influence, and I have no doubt when I get back to-night that I shall find Nesta has not transgressed any very open rules."

"Poor Nesta," said Angela, "I understand her point of view a little bit—at least, I think I do."

"I don't," said Marcia. "A life without discipline is worth nothing, but we have been very differently trained. Anyhow, I believe that in three months' time my stepmother will be so much better that she will be able to go downstairs and take her part in the household. Beyond doubt her illness is largely fanciful, and when that is the case, and when the girls have come to recognise the fact that they must devote a portion of their time to her, things will go well, and I shall be able to return to Frankfort for another year."

"Oh, delightful," said Angela. "Think of the opera, and the music. Perhaps we might go to Dresden, or to Leipsic. I do want to see those places and the pictures, and to hear the music, and to do all that is to be done."

Marcia smiled; she allowed Angela to talk on. By-and-by it was time for them to return to the railway station. The train was a little late, and Marcia and Angela paced up and down the little platform, and talked as girls will talk, until at last the local train drew up, and Marcia took her seat.

She found herself alone with one man. At first she did not recognise him, then she gave a start. It was Dr Anstruther, the medical man who attended her mother. He came at once towards her, holding out his hand.

"How do you do, Miss Marcia? I am very glad to see you, and to have the pleasure of travelling with you as far as Newcastle."

Marcia replied that the pleasure was also hers, and then she began to ask him one or two questions with regard to her stepmother.

"I cannot tell you how thankful I am," he said, "that you have returned; her case perplexes me a good deal."

"Her case perplexes you, doctor?"

"Well, yes. Things are going from bad to worse."

"But surely," said Marcia, with a little gasp and a tightening at her heart, "you are not seriously alarmed about my stepmother."

"Not seriously alarmed at present, but I soon should be if the present state of things went on."

"I always thought," said Marcia, "and I gathered that opinion partly from your words, that her case was not at all serious, and that you believed most of her symptoms to be purely imaginary."

"On purpose I always encouraged her to think so, and a good many of her symptoms are imaginary, or rather they are only the consequence of weakened nerves; her nerves are very weak."

"But that kind of thing is never dangerous, is it?" said Marcia, who with her twenty years on her shoulders, and her buoyant strength and youth, had a rooted contempt for what people called nerves.

"Nervous diseases in themselves are scarcely dangerous, but in your mother's case there is a serious heart affection, which requires and must always require, an immensity of care. She has not the slightest idea of that herself, and I should be very sorry to enlighten her on the point. I could not tell your sisters, who would not comprehend me if I did, but I have often been on the point of mentioning the fact to your father, or to your brother."

"How long," said Marcia, in a low, strained voice, "how long have you known this?"

"I have suspected it for a year, but I have been positively certain only within the last three months. I was then called in to attend on your mother when she had had a very serious collapse. She was quite unconscious when I got to the house and for a short time I despaired of her life. She came to, however, and I made as lightly as I could of the attack; but it was then that I told your father I thought he ought to have somebody more capable of looking after his wife than his young daughters. The next day I examined my patient's heart very carefully, and I found that the mischief which would cause such an attack did exist to a larger extent than I had the least idea of before."

"When you asked my father to get a more competent nurse for her, what did he say?"

"He said he would not have a hired nurse in the house on any terms, and immediately mentioned you."

"Dr Anstruther, I will also speak plainly to you. There is time enough, may I?"

"Certainly, Miss Aldworth."

"I am not her real daughter."

"Does that count? She came to you when you were a very little child."

"That is true, and had she no daughter of her own, I should never mention the fact. I would attend to her as I would my real mother, and be glad to do so; but she has three daughters of her own; two grown-up and the other quite old enough to be useful."

"That is true."

"They should have taken care of her."

"They do not know how to, Miss Aldworth. I cannot express to you the neglect that poor woman suffered. She is not very strong-minded herself, and she never knew how to command, how to order, how to force those girls to do their duty. They need some one with a head on her shoulders to guide them. The poor thing drifted and let them drift, and the state of things was disgraceful. It could not have gone on. Had you failed to come, you would soon have had no stepmother to trouble you."

"I am glad I came," said Marcia, and the tears started to her eyes.

"I knew you would be."

"And yet," continued the girl, "it means a great deal of self-sacrifice on my part."

"I thought you were a teacher in a school."

"In one sense you are right, in another wrong. I am a teacher, or I was a teacher, in Mrs Silchester's school at Frankfort. Mrs Silchester is Miss St. Just's aunt, and Angela St. Just has been my dearest friend for some years."

"Indeed?"

"Yes."

"I saw you together just now."

"I was happy at the school. I was paid nothing, for I have sufficient money of my own. I did what teaching I could, and received instruction in return. No girl could have been happier. I had many friends about me; my life was full. To be with Mrs Silchester alone was a happiness unspeakable, and Angela was, and is to be again, a member of the school. Think what I have lost."

"I am sorry for you, but the path of duty."

"I will walk on it, Dr Anstruther; but the girls must help me."

"Ah, that is quite right, if only you will superintend them and make them do their duty. Oh, here we are slowing into Newcastle. You go on, of course, to the West Station. I get out here. You won't mention a word of what I have said."

"Not even to my father?"

"To no one at present. The fewer who know, the better for her. She is so weak, poor soul; so nervous, that even if she guessed at her true condition, she would have a very serious attack. Good-night, for the present. Be assured of my sympathy. I am glad we have had this talk."

Chapter Ten

An Alarming Attack

Marcia did not know why her heart felt like lead as she walked back the short distance between the railway station and her father's house; why all the joy seemed to have gone out of her, when there was no apparent reason. It was a glorious summer evening, the sky was studded with innumerable stars, which would shine more brightly in an hour or so, as soon as the rays of the sun had quite departed from the western horizon. There was not a cloud anywhere. Nevertheless, a very dense cloud rested over the girl's heart.

She went into the house, and the first thing she noticed was the fact that there were no lights burning anywhere. She glanced up at the invalid's room; there was no light in the window, no brightness. What could be wrong? Oh, nothing, of course. Nesta might not be a good nurse, but she could not be so careless as that.

She let herself in with her latch key, and was met by Susan in the hall. Susan had her hat on.

"What is it, Susan?"

"I beg your pardon, Miss? I have only just come in. It was my evening out. I came back a whole hour before my time because I was anxious about Missis. I suppose cook has seen to her."

"Cook? But where are the young ladies? Where is Miss Nesta?"

"I don't know."

"You don't know? And where are the other young ladies?"

"I don't know either. Oh, yes, though, they had tea in the garden with the Misses Carter and young Mr Carter, and then they went a bit of the way home with them. I ran down the garden and brought in the best china, they would have it from the drawing room, and then I slipped out, for I didn't want to lose any of my time. It was such a good opportunity, you see, Miss, for master and Mr Horace were both dining out at the Club this evening, and I thought the young ladies could manage to light up for themselves."

"They don't seem to have done so. How is my mother? How long has she been alone?"

"I don't know, Miss. Shall I run up and see?"

"No, light up as quickly as you can, please. Get cook to help you if necessary. Don't be out of the way. I will go to my mother."

Marcia had called Mrs Aldworth mother on many occasions; but there was a new tone in the way in which she said "my mother," which fell upon the servant's ears with a feeling of reproach.

"I wonder now—" she thought. "I wouldn't have gone out, but she was in such a beautiful sleep; I just crept in on tiptoe and there she was smiling in her sleep and looking as happy as happy could be. So I said to myself—'Miss Nesta'll be in in no time, and if not there are the other young ladies.' So I went to cook and said—'Cook, be sure you run up to Missis when she rings her bell.'"

Susan had now returned to the kitchen.

"You didn't hear Missis ring by any chance, did you, Fanny?" she said to her fellow servant.

"No, I said I'd go up to her if she did ring."

"Then it's all right," said Susan.

"Why, what's the matter? How white you are."

"I—I don't quite know. But Miss Marcia came back and seemed in no end of a taking, at the house not being lit up."

"Let Miss Marcia mind her own business," said Fanny, in a temper.

"Don't you say anything against her, Fanny. Oh, my word, there's the bell, now. I hope to goodness there's nothing wrong."

Susan rushed upstairs; her knees, as she expressed it, trembling under her. She burst open the door.

"Send Fanny for the doctor at once. Get me some hot water and some brandy. Be quick; don't wait a moment. Above all things, send Fanny for the doctor. Tell her to take a cab and drive to Dr Anstruther's house. Be as quick as ever you can."

Marcia had turned on the gas in her mother's room and lit it, and now she was bending over that mother and holding her hand. The poor woman was alive, but icy cold and apparently quite unconscious. The girl felt herself trembling violently.

"They have neglected her; I can see that by the look of the room," she thought. "The window still open, the blinds still up, the position of this sofa—all show that she was neglected. And I, too, left her. Why did I go? Oh, poor mother; poor mother."

Tears streamed from Marcia's eyes; they fell upon the cold hand. Marcia put her fingers on the pulse; it was still beating, but very feebly.

Susan hurried up with a great jug of hot water, and the brandy bottle.

"Mix some brandy quickly for me, Susan; make it strong. Now, then, give it to me."

With some difficulty Marcia managed to put a few drops between the blue lips, and the next minute the invalid opened her eyes. She fixed them on Marcia, smiled, shuddered, and closed them again, collapsing once more into unconsciousness.

It was in this condition that Dr Anstruther found her when he entered the house a quarter of an hour later.

"I feared it," he paid, just glancing at Marcia.

"No, it is not death," he added, seeing the look of appeal and self-reproach in the girl's eyes; "but it might have been. Had you been a few minutes later we could have done nothing. Now, then, we will get her into bed."

He managed very skilfully, with Marcia's help and with that of the repentant and miserable Susan, to convey the poor invalid to a bed, which had already been warmed for her. She then sat by her, administering brandy and water at short intervals, and holding her wrist between his fingers and thumb.

"That's better," he said, after a time. "Now, then, Miss Marcia, will you go downstairs and prepare a nice cup of bread and milk and bring it up to me? she must manage to eat it. She has been absolutely starved; she has had nothing at all since her early dinner."

Marcia flew out of the room.

"Susan," she said, "Susan, what is the meaning of this?"

"Don't ask me, Miss; 'tain't my fault. When young ladies themselves are born without natural affection, what can a poor servant gel do? Do you think I'd leave my mother? No, that I wouldn't. Poor lady, and she that devoted to them. To be sure she have her little fads and fancies, and her little crotchets, as what invalid but wouldn't have? But, oh, Miss, to think of their unkindness."

"Don't think of it now; they will be sorry enough by-and-by," said Marcia. "Help me to get some bread and milk ready."

She brought it up a few minutes later, steaming hot and tempting looking. The invalid was conscious again now, and her cheeks were flushed with the amount of brandy she had taken. She began to talk in a weak, excited manner.

"I had such a long sleep and got so dreadfully cold," she said. "I thought I was climbing up and up a hill, and I could never get to the top. It was a horrid dream. Marcia, dear, is that you? How nice you look in your grey dress, so quiet looking."

"Hush, Mrs Aldworth," said the doctor, in a cheerful voice, "you must not talk too much just now. You must lie quiet."

"Oh, doctor, I've been lying quiet so long, so many hours. Oh, yes, I remember—it was Molly. She had on a blue dress, a blue muslin and forget-me-not bows, and she looked so sweet, and she said the Carters were here—the Carters and—and—she was very anxious to go down to them. It was natural, wasn't it, doctor?"

"Yes, yes. Aren't you going to eat your bread and milk?"

"I'll feed you, mother," said Marcia.

She knelt by her and put the nourishment between the blue lips.

"You are such a good girl, Marcia; so kind to me."

"Everybody ought to be kind to you," said Marcia, "and everybody will be," she murmured under her breath.

"Marcia is an excellent girl; you have never said a truer word, Mrs Aldworth," remarked the doctor.

"It was very disagreeable—that dream," continued the invalid, her thoughts drifting into another quarter. "I thought—I thought I was climbing up and up, and it was very cold as I climbed, and I thought I was amongst the ice, and the great snows, and Molly was there, but a long way down, and I was falling, and Molly would not come to help me. Then it was Nesta, and she would not help me either, Nesta only laughed, and said something about Flossie—Flossie Griffiths. Marcia, have you seen Flossie Griffiths? You know I don't like her much, do you?"

"I have not seen her, dear. Don't talk too much. It weakens you."

"But I'm not really ill, am I?"

"Oh, no, Mrs Aldworth," said the doctor. "You have just had an attack of weakness, but you are better; it is passing off now, and you have a grand pulse. I wish I had as good a one."

He smiled at her in his cheery way, and by-and-by he went out of the room. Marcia followed him.

"Some one must sit up with her all night," said the doctor, "and I will stay in the house."

"Oh, doctor," said Marcia, "is it as bad as all that?"

"It is so bad that if she has another attack we cannot possibly pull her through. If she survives until the morning, I will call in Dr Benson, the first authority in Newcastle. The thing is to prevent a recurrence of the attack. The longer it is stared off the greater probability there is that there will be no repetition."

"I will sit up with her, of course," said Marcia. "She would rather have me than any hired nurse."

"I know that. I am glad. But some one must see your sisters when they come in."

It was just at that moment that a girl, somewhat fagged, somewhat shabby looking, with a face a good deal torn, for she had got amongst briars and thorns and underwood on her way home, crept up the narrow path towards the house. This girl was her mother's darling, Nesta, the youngest of the family, the baby, as she was called. Her time with Flossie had, after all, been the reverse of agreeable. They had begun their tea with every prospect of having a good time; but soon the mob of rough people who had come to witness the donkey races discovered them, and so terrified both little girls that they ran away and hid, leaving all Flossie's property behind them.

This was thought excellent fun by the roughs of Newcastle; they scoured the woods, looking for the children, and as a matter of fact, poor Nesta had never got a greater fright than when she crouched down in the brambles, devoutly hoping that some of the rough boys would not pull her out of her lair.

Eventually she and Flossie had escaped with only a few scratches and some torn clothes, but she was miserably tired and longing for comfort when she approached the house. So absorbed was she with her own adventures that she absolutely forgot the fact that she had run away and left her mother to the care of the others. As she entered the house, however, it flashed upon her what might be thought of her conduct.

"Dear, dear!" she thought, "I shall have a time of it with Molly to-night; but I don't care. I'm not going to be bullied or browbeaten. I'll just let Miss Molly see that I'm going to have my fun as well as another. I wish though, I didn't sleep in the room with them; they'll be as cross and cantankerous as two tabby cats."

Nesta entered the house. Somehow the house did not seem to be quite as usual; the drawing room was not lit up; it had not been used that evening. She poked her head round the dining-room door. There was no appetising and hearty meal ready for tired people when they returned home. What was the matter? Why, her father must be back by this time. She went into the kitchen.

"Cook!" she said.

"Keep out of my way, Miss Nesta," said the cook.

"What do you mean? Where is my supper? I want my supper. Where are all the others? Where's Molly? Where's Ethel? I suppose that stupid old Marcia is back now? Where are they all?"

"That's more than I can tell you," said cook, and now he turned round and faced the girl. "I only know that it's ten o'clock, and that you have been out when you ought to be in, and as to Miss Molly and Miss Ethel, I don't want to have anything to do with them in the future. Here's Susan—she'll tell you why there ain't no supper for you—she'll speak a bit of her mind. Susan, here's Miss Nesta, come in as gay as you please, and asks for her supper. And where are the others, says she, and where's Marcia, says she. And is she back, says she. Miss Marcia is back, thank the Lord; that's about the only thing we have to be thankful for in this house to-night."

"Dear me, cook, I think you are remarkably impertinent. I shall ask mother not to keep you. Mother never would allow servants to speak to us in that tone. You forget yourself, Susan."

"It's you that forgets yourself, Miss Nesta," said Susan. "There; where's the use of stirring up ill will? Ain't there sorrow enough in this house this blessed night?"

"Sorrow," said Nesta, now really alarmed. "What is it?"

"It's your mother, poor soul," said Susan. She looked into Nesta's face and there and then determined not to spare her.

"Mother? Mother?"

For the first time the girl forgot herself. There fell away from her that terrible cloak of selfishness in which she had wrapped herself.

"Mother? Is anything wrong with her?"

"Dr Anstruther is upstairs, and he is going to spend the night here, and Miss Marcia is with her, and not a living soul of you is to go near her; you wouldn't when you might, and now you long to, you won't be let; so that's about the truth, and if the poor darling holds out till the morning it'll be something to be thankful for. Why, she nearly died, and for all that I can tell you, she may be dying now."

"Nonsense!" said Nesta. "What lies you tell!"

She stalked out of the kitchen. For the life of her she could not have gone out in any other fashion. Had she attempted any other than the utmost bravado, she must have fallen. In the hall she met Molly and Ethel coming in; their faces were bright, their eyes were shining. What a good time they had had. That supper! That little impromptu dance afterwards! The tennis before supper! The walk home with Jim and Harry. Jim escorted Molly home; he had quite forgiven her, and Harry was untiring in his attentions to Ethel. Oh, what a glorious, glorified world they had been living in. But, now, what was the matter! They saw Nesta and looked into her face. Full of wrath they pounced upon her.

"Don't," said Nesta. "Don't speak. Come in here."

She took both their hands, dragged them into her father's study, and shut the door.

"Look here, both of you," she said, "I've been beast; I've been the lowest down sort of a girl that ever lived, but you have been a degree worse, and we have killed mother. Yes, we have killed her."

Ethel dropped into a chair and clasped her side with one hand.

"You needn't believe me, but it's true. She was alone all the afternoon, and Marcia came home, and she saw mother, who was nearly gone, and the doctor is here and he is going to stay all night, and perhaps she'll be dead in the morning, and we have done it—we are her own children and we have done it.

You and Molly and I; we have all done it; we are monsters; we are worse than beasts. We are horrors. I hate us! I hate us! I hate us!"

Each hate as it was hurled from her young lips was uttered with more emphasis than the last, and now she flung herself full length on the carpet— the dirty, faded carpet, and sobbed as though her heart would break.

"We're not to go to her—she won't have any of us near her. She won't have us now—we gave her up—she was alone all the afternoon, and now we are not to go to her, we are to stay away; that's what we are to do."

Molly was the first to recover her voice.

"It can't be as bad as that," she said.

Ethel looked up with a scared face. Molly's face was just as scared as her sisters'. As she uttered the words she sank, too, in a limp fashion, on the nearest chair. Then she unpinned her hat and flung it from her to the farthest end of the room.

"You may stay there, you horrid thing," she said. Her gloves were treated in the same manner. She looked down at the bows on her dress and began unfastening them.

"I hate them," she said. "Mother called them pretty. I hate them!"

"What's the good of undressing yourself in that fashion?" said Ethel.

"She had the beginning of the attack when I was with her," said Molly. "I am worse than you, Nesta, worse than you, Ethel, for you did not see her. I gave her some sal volatile, and she got sleepy, and I put a shawl over her and left her. I am worse than either of you."

"Well," said Ethel, rousing herself, "I don't believe it is as bad as this. I don't think it can be. I'll go up and find out."

She went out of the room, but she tottered very badly as she went up the stairs, glancing behind her as though fearful of her own shadow. There was a light in the spare room; the door was partly open. She peeped in. Dr Anstruther was there. He was pacing up and down.

"Ah!" he said, when he saw Ethel's face. "Come in."

He looked at her again, and then said quietly—"Sit down."

He went to the table, poured something into a glass, mixed it with water, and brought it to the girl.

"Drink this," he said.

"I don't want to," replied Ethel.

"Drink it at once," said the doctor.

She obeyed; it was strong sal volatile and water.

"Now," he said, "you clearly understand that the duty you have to perform to-night in this house, is absolutely to forget yourself—obliterate yourself if necessary. Don't do one single thing that you are told not to do, and if you can, keep your sisters in the background. You may all be wanted at any moment, or you may not. You are not, any of you, to go to your mother's room without my permission. Don't think of yourselves at all. If there is any way in which you can help the servants, do it, but do it quietly, and don't become hysterical; don't add to the trouble in the house to-night."

"But we have all neglected her—"

"You can tell your clergyman that in the morning—you can tell your God to-night—it is not my affair. I have to do with the present. Act now with obedience, with utter quiet, with calm, with self-restraint. Go down now and tell your sisters what I have said."

"I will," said Ethel. She went out of the room.

"Poor child!" thought Dr Anstruther. "I had to be hard on her to keep her up; she'd have broken down otherwise. God grant that those girls have not a rude awakening—they very nearly did have it—God help them, poor things."

When Mr Aldworth and Horace returned late that evening, it was the doctor who drew the poor husband into his own study and told him the truth. He concealed as much as possible of the girls' conduct; he admitted that Mrs Aldworth had been neglected during the day, but he made the best of it.

"In any case," he said, "this attack was quite likely to come. Had there been any one near her it might not have been so prolonged, and the consequences would not have been so serious; but it was bound to come."

"And Marcia?" said the father then.

"Oh, she is all right, she is a brick—she is one in a thousand."

Chapter Eleven

Repentance and Afterwards

The three girls found themselves in their own bedroom.

"Don't turn up the light," said Ethel. "Let's sit in the dark."

"It doesn't matter," said Molly, "we'd best have the light, we may be wanted."

"Yes, I forgot that," replied Ethel.

She turned on the gas, which roared a little and then subsided into a sullen yellow flame. The shade belonging to the gas jet had been broken that morning by Nesta in a game of romps with her two sisters.

"How hot it is," said Nesta presently.

No one took any notice of her remark, and after a time Ethel spoke.

"I ought to tell you," she said.

Molly turned her haggard face.

"What?" she asked. "If it is anything awful, I shall scream."

"You won't—so there!"

"What do you mean? How can you prevent me?"

"I saw," said Ethel, and she gulped down a sob in her throat—"I saw Dr Anstruther, and he said we were to forget ourselves—to obliterate ourselves—that was the word he used—to keep ourselves out of sight. We might be wanted, or we might not. We're of no account—no account at all—that was the kind of thing he said, and I'm not a bit surprised."

"Nor am I," said Nesta; "we're beasts. I wish we could be killed. I wish we could be buried alive. I wish—I wish—anything but what has happened."

Molly went and stood by the window.

"I'm the worst of you," she said after a pause.

"No, you're not," said Nesta—"I'm the worst. Nothing would have happened at all if I hadn't run away in that mean, horrid, detestable fashion. I thought it was such a joke. You both really did think you had a day off, and it was my turn to be with her—with her. Why, I'd give my two hands to be with her now." Nesta held out her two plump little hands as she spoke. "The doctor may cut them off; he may chop me in bits—he may do anything if only I might be with her."

"Well, you cannot," said Ethel; "you're no more to her now than the rest of us. What you say is quite right; you did do worse."

"No, don't say that," interrupted Molly, "I was the worst. I saw the attack begin, and I knew it, for I have seen it before. But I shut it out of my mind; there was a door in my mind, and I shut it firm and locked it, and forced myself to forget, and when she was lying there so white and panting for breath, I just put a shawl over her, and said, you will have such a nice sleep, and I went away back to my fun—my fun! Fancy my eating strawberries and cream, and mother— mother so ill. Fancy it! Think of it?"

"I don't want to think of it," said Ethel. "I wish we could have something to make us go into a dead sleep. I want this night to go by. I don't think that Marcia should have all her own way."

Then she remembered the doctor's words.

"I wish I might dare to open the door very softly," said Nesta, "and just creep, creep upstairs and watch outside. I wish I might. Do you think I might?"

"I don't see why you shouldn't," said Ethel, with a momentary gleam of hope. "You can walk just like a cat when you please. No one ever was as good going down creaking stairs as you when you want to steal things from the pantry. You may as well make yourself useful as not. Go along and report; tell us if all is quiet."

Nesta, with a momentary sense of relief at having something to do, slipped off her shoes and left the room. She came back at the end of five minutes.

"There isn't a sound—I don't think things can be so bad," she said, and she closed the door behind her.

She had scarcely uttered the words before there came a tap, sharp and decisive, and Horace came in. The girls had never loved Horace; it must be owned that he had never done anything to make his young sisters care for him. He had kept them at a distance, and they had been somewhat afraid of him. They saw him now standing on the threshold with a tray in his hand, a tray which contained three cups of hot cocoa and three thick slices of bread and butter, and when they read, not disapproval, but sorrow in his face, it seemed to the three that their hearts threw wide their doors and let him in. Nesta gave a gasp; Molly choked down something. Ethel jumped up and sat down again and clasped her hands.

"I knew you'd be all feeling pretty bad," said Horace, "so I came to sit with you for a minute or two, and here's some cocoa. I made it myself. I'm not much of a cook, but drink it up, you three, and then let us talk."

"Horace—oh, Horace—may we?"

"Drink it up first. Nesta, you begin. Why, whatever have you done to your face?"

"It got torn with some briars, but it doesn't matter," said Nesta. She rubbed her face roughly; she would have liked to make it smart. Any outward torture would be better than the fierce pain that was tugging at her heart. But the cocoa was hot and good, and warm as the summer night was, the three girls were chilly from shock and grief. Horace insisted on their eating and drinking, and then he sat down on a little sofa which was placed at the foot of the two small beds. He coaxed Nesta to sit next to him.

"Ethel, you come and sit on the other side," he said, "and, Molly, here's a chair for you just in front."

He managed to take the three pairs of hands and to warm them all between his own. Then he said cheerily:

"Well, now, the very best thing we can do, is to make ourselves as useful as possible. We won't think of the past."

"But we must—we must, Horace," said Molly. "And I'm the worst. I'd like to confess to you—I wish I might."

"My dear, I'm not a bit of a father confessor, and we have quite trouble enough in the house at present without raking up what you have done. There, if you like, I'll tell you. You have, all three of you, been abominably careless and selfish. We won't add any more to that; it is quite bad enough. There is such a thing as turning over a new leaf, and whether you have the strength to turn over that leaf God only knows—I don't. The thing at present is to face what is before us."

"You will tell us, Horry, won't you?" said Nesta, in a coaxing tone. She could not for the life of her help coaxing any one she came across.

"I will tell you. I haven't come into this room to be mealy-mouthed or to hide anything from you. Our mother is very ill; the doctor thinks it quite possible that she may not live until the morning."

"Then I'll die, too," said Nesta.

"Nonsense, Nesta. Don't give way to selfishness just now. You are in no possible danger."

"I'll die; I know I'll die."

"Hush!" said her brother sternly; "let me go on with what I've got to say. Our mother is in danger; you cannot be with her, for, alas, when you were given the chance you would not take it. You never really nursed her; you never—not for a single moment—saw to her real comforts. Therefore, now in her hour of peril, you three—her own children—are useless. Nevertheless, the doctor thinks it best that you should not undress. You must stay in your room, ready to be called if it is necessary."

"If?" said Molly. "Why, what is going to happen? Why must we be called?"

"Poor children! she may want to speak to you."

"I won't go," said Molly.

She covered her face with her hands and began to shake from head to foot.

"It may not be necessary, child; but do learn to have more self-control. How will you bear all the sorrows of a lifetime if you break down now?"

"I have never been taught to bear anything—I have never been taught," said Molly.

Horace looked at her in absolute perplexity. Molly rose tremblingly; she flung herself across the bed. She was shivering so violently that her whole body shook.

It was at that instant that Marcia softly opened the door and came in.

"Why, what is it? What is it, Horace? How good of you."

"Now, you have come, Marcia, I'll go," said Horace, and he slipped out of the room.

"Marcia, can you speak to us? Can you? Aren't you too angry?"

"Poor children—no, not now. Molly, sit up."

Marcia laid her hand on the girl's shoulder. She raised her up forcibly.

"My darling," she said, "kiss me."

"Will you kiss me after what has happened?"

"I pity you so much. I have come to—to kneel with you—to pray. It would be a very terrible thing for you if our mother were to die to-night. We will ask God to keep her alive."

"Oh, do, Marcia," said Nesta, in a tone of the greatest anguish and the greatest belief. "You are so good. He will be certain to hear you. Kneel down at once, Marcia—say the words, oh, say them, say them!" Marcia did pray, while the three girls clustered round her and joined their sobs to her earnest petitions.

In the morning Mrs Aldworth was still alive. There had been no repetition of the dangerous attack. The great specialist from Newcastle was summoned, and he gave certain directions. A trained nurse was brought into the house, and Nesta, Molly, and Ethel were sent to stay with the Carters.

It was the Carters themselves who had suggested this, and the girls went away, feeling thoroughly brokenhearted. They were really so shocked, so distressed, that they did not know themselves; but as day after day went by, and as Mrs Aldworth by slow degrees got better, and yet better, so much better that the doctor only came to see her once a day, then every second day, then twice a week, and then finally said to Marcia, "You can summon me when you want me—" so did the remorse and the agony of that terrible night pass from the minds of the young Aldworths. They could not help having a good time at the Carters'. The Carters were the essence of good nature. They had been dreadfully sorry for them during their time of anguish; they had done their utmost for the girls, and now they were willing to keep them as their guests.

On a certain day, a month after Mrs Aldworth's serious illness, when she had come back again to that standpoint from which she had so nearly slipped away into the ocean of Eternity, Marcia made up her mind that it was time to put the repentance of her three young sisters to the test. They must return home and renew their duties to their mother. Marcia had given up all idea now of returning to Frankfort. She had written once or twice to Angela, and Angela had replied. She had also written to Mrs Silchester.

"There is little hope of my being able to return this summer. My stepmother has been most alarmingly ill," she wrote.

Angela had come to see her, but Marcia could not give her much of her time. Angela had kissed her, and had looked into her eyes, and Marcia had said:

"I think I understand a little better your remarks about the path of duty, and the grandeur of duty, and I am quite content, and I do not repent at all."

Angela thought a good deal of her friend, and wondered what she could do for her. But she scarcely approved of Marcia's still firmly adhered-to resolution, that the young Aldworths were to resume the care of their mother.

"It will be so trying to you, and do you dare for a single moment to risk leaving her with them?"

"Yes; the doctor has great hopes of her. He says that the new treatment has produced an almost radical change in the condition of her heart, and that with care she will do well, and may even become fairly strong once more. But all this is a question of time, and the girls have been quite long enough away from home, and I am going to fetch them to-morrow."

On a certain day, therefore, when Nurse Davenant had done everything to make the invalid thoroughly comfortable, Marcia put on her hat and walked along the shady road towards the St. Justs' old house.

She had known it fairly well when she was quite a child, but had never cared to go there since the Carters had purchased it. The Carters were absolute strangers to Marcia. She had never once met them. She walked now under the avenue of splendid old beech trees, and thought of her past and future. Things were not going quite so well with herself as she could have hoped. Her life seemed to have narrowed itself into the care of one querulous invalid. It is true that the doctor had declared that but for Marcia Mrs Aldworth would not now be in the world; but there were Mrs Aldworth's own daughters; Marcia's own step-sisters. She must do something for them. What could she do?

She had just turned a certain bend in the avenue, when she heard a mocking voice say in laughing tones:

"I tell you what it is, I don't ever want to go back to stupid old Marcia, nor—nor to the old house. I'm as happy here as the day is long, and now that Mothery is getting well, and you let me have as much of Flossie's society as I want, I don't ever want to go home."

"Hush!" said another voice.

Nesta raised her head and saw Marcia.

"Oh, did you hear me?" she said. "I know I was saying something very naughty; but I almost forget what it was."

"I did hear you, Nesta," said Marcia. "How are you, dear? Of course, I'm not angry with you. You wouldn't have said it to my face, would you?"

"Well, I suppose not," said Nesta.

"Are you Miss Aldworth, really?" said Penelope, the youngest of the Carter girls.

She was a black-eyed girl, with a great lot of fussy curly hair. She had rosy cheeks and white teeth. She looked up merrily at Marcia with a quizzical expression in her dancing eyes.

"Yes, I am Miss Aldworth, and I have come to see my sisters, and to thank you for being so good to them."

"How is mother to-day, Marcia?" said Nesta.

"Much, much better."

Nesta slipped her hand inside Marcia's arm. She wanted, as she expressed it afterwards to Penelope, to make up to Marcia. She wanted to coax her to do something, which she did not think Marcia was likely to do.

"I generally have my own way," she said, "except with that stupid old Marcia. She never yields to any one, although she has such a kind look. Oh, I know she was good to mother that dreadful, dreadful, dreadful night; but I want to shut that tight from my memory."

"Yes, do, for Heaven's sake," said Penelope. "You always give me the jumps when you speak of it."

Now, Nesta was intensely anxious that Marcia should not go up to the house; there was great fun going on on the front lawn. A number of guests had been invited, and Molly and Ethel were having a right good time. Penelope and Nesta were to join them presently, but that was when Flossie arrived. They did not want Marcia—old Mule Selfish, as Nesta still loved to call her, to intrude her stupid presence into the midst of the mirth.

"I am so glad mother is better; I can tell the others all about her. What message have you got for them?"

"I have no message for them," said Marcia somewhat coldly. "I am going up to the house—that is, if I may, Miss Carter?"

Marcia spoke with that sort of air which had such an effect on people slightly beneath herself. The Carters were beneath Marcia in every sense of the word, and they felt it down to their shoes, and rather disliked her in consequence.

"Of course, you must come up to the house," said Penelope, although Nesta gave her such a fierce dig in the ribs for making the remark that she nearly cried out.

"I have come, Nesta," said Marcia, in her kind voice, "to say that you and Molly and Ethel are expected home to-morrow. We have trespassed quite long enough on your kindness, Miss Carter," she continued.

"Oh, indeed, you haven't," cried Penelope. "We like having them—they're a right good sort, all of them. Not that I care so much for your precious Flossie Griffiths," she added, giving Nesta a dig in the ribs in her turn.

"Oh, don't you? That's because you are madly jealous," said Nesta.

The girls wrangled, and fell a little behind. Marcia continued her walk.

Molly had sworn to herself on that dreadful night, when her mother lay apparently dying, that she would never wear the pale blue muslin dress with its forget-me-not bows again. But circumstances alter one's feelings, and she was in that identical dress, freshly washed, and with new forget-me-not bows, on this occasion. And she had a forget-me-not muslin hat to match on her pretty head. Ethel was all in white and looked charming. The girls were standing in a circle of other young people when Marcia appeared. Marcia went gravely up to them; spoke to the Carters, thanked them for their kindness, and then said quietly:

"I have come here to say that father and mother expect you all to return home to-morrow. If you can make it convenient to be back after early dinner, it will suit us best. No, I will not stay now; thank you very much, Miss Carter. It is necessary that the girls should return then, for their duties await them. Mother is so much better, and she will be delighted to see them. I am afraid I must go now. At what hour shall we expect you to-morrow?"

"You needn't expect us all," was on Molly's lips. Ethel frowned and bit hers. Molly raised her eyes and saw Jim looking at her.

"I suppose," she stammered, turning crimson—"I suppose about—about three o'clock."

"Yes, three o'clock will do nicely. I will send a cab up to fetch your luggage."

"You needn't do that," said Jim; "I'll drive the girls down on the dogcart and all their belongings with them," he added.

He walked a little way back with Marcia.

"I am so very glad Mrs Aldworth is better. You know, somehow or other, Miss Aldworth, we felt that we were to blame for that attack. We ought not to have coaxed your sisters to come back with us that night."

"We needn't talk of it now," said Marcia. "Something very dreadful might have happened. God in his goodness prevented it, and I greatly trust, Mr Carter, that Mrs Aldworth will get much better in health now than she has ever been before."

"Well, that is excellent news," he said.

He opened the gate for Marcia.

"I am sorry you won't stay to tea," he said.

"Thank you, very much, but I must hurry back to my invalid."

"What a right good sort she is," thought the lad. "And what a splendid face she has got."

Then he returned to the merry party on the lawn. He went straight up to Molly.

"You must be happy now," he said. "You'll see her to-morrow. You have been telling me all this time how you have been pining for her."

"Oh, yes, I know," said Molly. "I know."

Her voice was subdued.

"You are not vexed—not put out about anything, are you?" said the boy.

"No; oh, no."

"And with such a splendid sister."

"Oh, for Heaven's sake don't begin to praise her," said Ethel, who came up at that moment. "When we think of all that she has made us endure—and now the last thing she has done is this—she has stolen our mother's love. It's a whole month since we saw our dear mother, and she thinks of no one but Marcia; but when Marcia gives the word, forsooth, then we are brought back—not by your leave, or anything else, but just when Marcia wishes it."

"That's nonsense," said Jim. "You are in a bit of a temper, I think. But, come; let's have some fun while we may."

The news that they were all to go back was broken to the different members of the Carter family, who expressed their regret in different ways and different degrees. Not one of them, however, suggested, as both Molly and Ethel hoped, that it was absolutely and completely impossible for them to spare their beloved Aldworths. On the contrary, Clara said that sorry as they were to part, it was in some ways a little convenient, as their friends the Tollemaches were coming to spend a fortnight or three weeks with them, and the Mortimers were also to be guests at Court Prospect.

"We shouldn't have room for you all with so many other people, so it is just as well that you are going, for it is never agreeable to have to ask one's friends to leave," said Clara in her blunt fashion.

"But all the same, we'll miss you very much," said Mabel.

"For my part," cried Annie, "I'm sorry enough to lose you two girls, but I'm rather glad as far as Penelope is concerned. She has run perfectly wild since that Nesta of yours is here. They're always squabbling and fighting over that wretched, commonplace girl, Flossie Griffiths. I asked father about her, and he said that her people were quite common and not worth cultivating."

"Then you only care for people worth cultivating. I wonder you like us," said Ethel, with much sarcasm in her tone.

"Oh, you're the daughters of a professional man," said Mabel.

"And if we were not?"

Mabel laughed.

"I don't expect we'd see much of your society. Our object now is to better ourselves. You see, father is enormously rich, and he wants us to do great things. He wants us to be raised in the social scale. He told me only this morning that he was most anxious to cultivate your step-sister, Miss Aldworth, and I'll tell you why, Miss Aldworth is such a very great friend of Miss Angela St. Just."

"Now," said Ethel, "I'd like to ask you a question. What do you see in that girl?"

"What do we see in her?" exclaimed Clara, who thought it time to take her turn in the conversation, "why, just everything."

"Well, I'd like you to explain."

"Hasn't she got the most beautiful face, the most wonderful manners? She is so graceful, so gracious, and then she has such good style. There is nothing in all the world that we wouldn't any of us do for Miss St. Just."

"And yet you have never spoken to her?"

"Father means that we shall, and he wants you to help us."

Molly was silent. She felt intensely cross and discontented.

"I don't know her myself," said Molly.

"But your precious Marcia does, and we are greatly hoping to get an introduction through her."

That night as the three girls retired to bed, in the large and luxurious room set aside for their use at Court Prospect, they could not help expressing some very bitter remarks.

"We'll never have a chance against Marcia," said Molly. "She just gets everything. She has got our mother's love—Horace thinks the world of her;

father is devoted to her, and now even our own darling friend, our dear Carters, say plainly that they want to know her because she can get them an introduction to that tiresome Angela St. Just. I haven't patience with them."

"It strikes me," said Ethel, "that they're not specially sorry to see the last of us. How do you feel about it, Molly?"

"I'm not going to say," said Molly.

She went to the window and flung it open. The prospect was delightful. Overhead the stars were shining with unwonted brilliancy; there was no touch or smell of town in this rural retreat. Oh, how sweet it was—how delightful to have such a home! But to-morrow they must give it up; the picnics, the laughter, the fun, the gay friends always coming in and going out. They must go back to the little grubby house, to the tiresome monotony of everyday life— to Susan, impertinent Susan; to Fanny, who had dared to speak to Nesta as she had done on that awful night; to the room where they had lived through such tortures and—to their mother.

To tell the truth, they were afraid to see their mother. They had shut away the idea of clasping her hand, of looking into her face. On that night when she lay close to death they would have given themselves gladly to save her, but that night and this were as the poles asunder. All the old selfish ideas, all the old devotion to Number One, that utter disregard for Number Two, were as strong as ever within them. They disliked Marcia more than they had ever disliked her. Their month at the Carters' had effectually spoiled them.

But time and circumstances are relentless. The Aldworths were to return to their home the next day, and although Molly dreamed that something came to prevent it, and although Ethel vowed that she would implore Clara to keep her on as a sort of all-round useful sort of lady companion, and although Nesta threatened—her favourite threat—by the way—to run away, nothing did happen. Nesta did not run away; Ethel was not adopted as Mabel's slave; Molly was forced to go with just a nod and a good-natured regret from Jim.

"I'll miss you a bit at first, but I'll come round and see you, and you'll come to see us; but you are going back to your mother, and you will be pleased."

And then he was off to attend to his school, for he was still a big schoolboy.

Clay and Mabel were heartily tired of the Aldworth girls. Penelope was slightly annoyed at parting from Nesta, but only—and she vowed this quite openly—because she was able to shirk her lessons when Nesta was present. And so they went away, not even in the dogcart, for Jim could not spare the time, but humbly and sadly on foot, and their trunks were to follow later on.

Chapter Twelve

The New Leaf

As soon as ever the three Aldworth girls entered the house, they were met by their father. This in itself was quite unlooked-for. As a rule, he never returned home until time for late dinner in the evening. He was a very busy professional man, and was looked up to by his fellow townspeople. He now stood gravely in the hall, not going forward when he saw the girls, but waiting for them to come up to him.

"Well, Molly," he said, "how do you do? How do you do, Ethel?"

He just touched Nesta's forehead with his lips.

"I want you three in my study," he said.

"Good gracious," said Molly in a whisper, "it's even more awful than we expected."

But Ethel and Nesta felt subdued, they scarcely knew why. They all went into the study, and Mr Aldworth shut the door.

"Now, girls," he said, "you have come back. You are, let me tell you, exceedingly lucky. That which happened a month ago might have brought sorrow into your young lives which you could never have got over. That kind of silent sorrow which lasts through the years, and visits one when one is dying. That sorrow might have come to you, but for your sister Marcia."

"Father," began Molly.

"Hush, Molly, I don't wish for excuses. You were, Horace tells me and so does Marcia, intensely sorry and remorseful that night, and I trust God in his heaven heard your prayers for forgiveness, and that you have come back now, intending to turn over a new leaf."

"Yes, father, of course. We won't any of us neglect dear, dear mother again," said Ethel. "We are most anxious to see her."

"I have taken steps," continued Mr Aldworth, "to see that you do not neglect her. For the present she will have Nurse Davenant—"

"Who is she?" asked Ethel.

"The nurse I was obliged to call in to help Marcia. For the present Nurse Davenant will be with her day and night, and your province will be to sit with her and amuse her under Nurse Davenant's directions. But the doctor wants a complete and radical change, which your sister Marcia will explain to you. Any possible fluctuation on your parts, any shirking of the duties which you are expected to perform, will be immediately followed by your absence from home."

Ethel looked up almost brightly.

"There is your Aunt Elizabeth in the country. I have written to her and she will take one, two, or all three of you. She told me that you could go to her for three or four months. I do not think you will have much fun, or much liberty there. If you don't choose to behave yourselves at home, you go to your Aunt Elizabeth. I have come back specially to say so. And now, welcome home, my dears, and let us have no more nonsense."

The father who had never in the least won his children's affection, left the room, leaving the three girls gazing at each other.

"A pretty state of things," began Nesta, pouting.

"Oh, don't," said Ethel.

"Don't!" said Molly, who was nearer crying than either of them. "To think of Aunt Elizabeth—to have to go to her. Of course, it's all Marcia."

"Of course it's all Marcia," said a voice at the door, and the three girls had the grace to blush hotly as they turned and looked at their sister. She wore that immaculate white which was her invariable custom; her dark hair was becomingly arranged; her face was placid.

"My dear children, welcome home," she said affectionately, "and try not to blame your poor old Marcia too much. It is nice to see you. I have tea ready for you in the little summer parlour. You must be thirsty after your long walk; I thought Jim Carter was going to bring you back in the dogcart."

"He couldn't," began Nesta.

"He couldn't," interrupted Ethel; "he had to go to school for a special field day."

"He would if he could," burst in Molly.

"Well, anyhow, you are here, and I suppose the luggage is to follow."

"Oh, yes; not that it matters," said Molly.

"But it does matter, dear. Now come and have your tea."

Marcia took Molly's damp, hot little hand in her own cool one, and led the way into the summer parlour. It had been a very ugly and neglected room, but it was so no longer. Marcia, by a very simple arrangement of art muslin had contrived to transform it into a pale green bower of beauty. The tea equipage was on the table, and very pretty did the cups and saucers look. There was fruit, the fruit that happened to be in season; there were flowers; there were hot cakes; there was fragrant tea; there were even new-laid eggs.

"Oh, I declare," said Nesta, cheering up, for she was fond of her meals; "this does look good."

"Shall I pour out tea?" said Molly.

"You may in future, Molly. I hope you will, but wouldn't you like me to do so to-day?"

"Yes, please, Marcia."

Marcia sat down and helped her sisters, and while she did so she chatted. She was quite bright and cheerful.

"I have had your rooms altered a little too," she said.

Molly looked up with a frown.

"Yes, I hope you will forgive me, but I think they look rather nice. And instead of that sort of lumber room where you always fling everything you don't want to use at the moment, I have made a second little bedroom for Nesta."

"For me?" said Nesta. "Golloptious! I did want a bedroom to myself."

"I thought you were fearfully crowded, and I wanted besides—"

"What is the matter?" said Molly suddenly.

"To make things as different as possible from what they were during that night."

"I do believe you are kind," said Molly, and something hot came at the back of her eyes, which made them suspiciously bright for a moment.

"If you will only believe that, my darlings, I don't care how hard I work," said the elder sister.

The meal came to an end, the girls had eaten even as much as Nesta's healthy appetite demanded, and accompanied by Marcia they went upstairs. Did they not know those stairs well—that darn in the carpet, that shabby blind at the lobby window, that narrow landing just above? And mother's room at the far end of the passage—mother's room with the green baize door, which was supposed to shut away sound, but did not. Oh, did they not remember it all, and how it looked on that awful night? And this was the way to their room. What had they not endured during that night in their own room? Molly almost staggered.

"Aren't you well, dear?" said Marcia very tenderly.

"I—I don't know. Oh, yes, I suppose so. I'm all right—I mean it's just a little overcoming," she said, after a minute's pause. "Past memories, you know."

"I quite understand. But see your room, it is quite altered."

It was truly, and this was Marcia's surprise to her sisters. With Horace's help, who had come forward rather liberally with his purse, the room had been repapered; it had practically been refurnished. The commonplace beds were exchanged for brass ones, the commonplace furniture for new, artistic washhandstands and chests of drawers and wardrobes. The shabby carpet was replaced by one of neat pale blue felt; there were a few good pictures on the walls; there were pale blue hangings to the windows, and Nesta's room just beyond was a replica of her sisters'.

The girls turned; it was Ethel who made the first step forward.

"I wouldn't have known it—why, you are a darling!"

"And to think we ever called you Miss Mule Selfish!" said Nesta.

"Miss—what!" said Marcia.

"I won't repeat it—forget it."

"But tell me—it did sound so funny. Miss what Selfish?"

"Miss Mule Selfish. Oh, I never will again—I declare I am a greater beast than ever."

"Well, girls, what I want you to do for me is this— In return for the trouble—for I have taken trouble, and Horace has spent money on your rooms as well—I want you to learn self-repression. I want you to put on neat and pretty dresses, and shoes that won't make any sound, and then you may, one by one, come in and see mother. She is longing for you, longing for her own children; for much as she cares for me, I cannot take your place, so you needn't imagine it for one moment."

As Marcia said the last words she left the room. The girls stood and stared at each other.

"She's a brick!" said Molly. "I shouldn't be one scrap ashamed of showing this room to Clay, and I never could bear the thought of her coming up to it in the old days."

"I say, what a jolly bed," said Ethel. "Shouldn't I just like to tumble into it and sleep and sleep."

"And my darling little room all alone, too. Don't you envy me, you two? Won't you be always afraid that I'm eavesdropping and listening to your precious secrets?" cried the irrepressible Nesta.

"Oh, it is good," said Molly, "but I feel quite a big ache at my heart. It's Marcia, and we've been so horrid to her, and she has been so good to us."

"Well, let's try hard to show her that we're really pleased," said Ethel.

The girls washed their hands and combed out their luxurious hair and made themselves as smart as possible, and then, an anxious trio, they went out and stood on the landing. Here it was Nesta who began to tremble.

"It's that old patch in the carpet," she said. "It upsets me more than anything. I remember how I tried to skip over it that night when I went to listen at mother's door. Oh dear, and the carpet is split here too. Marcia might have got new carpets for the stairs instead of titivating our rooms."

"Marcia only thinks of what will please others," said Ethel.

"For goodness' sake, don't praise her too much," said Molly, "or I shall turn round. I always do when people are overpraised."

A door was opened. It led into their mother's room. Marcia stood outside.

"Molly, darling," she said, "you come first."

She took Molly's hand; she led her round the screen and brought her up to her mother. Just for a moment the girl shut her eyes. There flashed before her mental vision the remembrance of that mother as she had lain pale and panting and struggling for life when she had left her, pretending that she was only sleeping. But now Mrs Aldworth was sitting bolt upright on her sofa, and the room was sweet and fresh and in perfect order, and a nice-looking young woman in nurse's uniform stood up when the girls entered the room.

"I will leave you, Mrs Aldworth, and go and get my tea," she said. "You will be glad to welcome your young ladies. But remember not too much talking, please."

Mrs Aldworth raised her faded eyes; she looked full at Molly.

"My little girl!"

"Mothery; oh, mothery!"

The girl dropped on her knees.

"Gently, Molly. Sit down there. Tell mother what a right good time you have had while you have been away," said Marcia.

"I am ever so much better," said Mrs Aldworth, in a cheerful tone. "I am very glad you were with the Carters. You like them so much."

"Yes, mother," said Molly, and then she added, and there was real truth and real sincerity in her tone—"I like best of all to be at home; I like best of all to be with you."

The words were spoken with an effort, but they were true. Molly did feel just like that at the moment.

Mrs Aldworth smiled, and a very pretty colour came into her cheeks.

"I have been quite ill," she said. "I have been ill and weak for an extraordinarily long time. At least so Marcia says; and Nurse Davenant is quite a tyrant in her way, and Dr Anstruther too; but to tell the truth, darling, I have never had an ache or pain, and I can't imagine why people make such a fuss. But there, darling, I am glad to see you and to have you back again. You'll come and sit with your old mother sometimes, won't you, and you won't think it a dreadful trial?"

"Never again," said Molly.

"Go, Molly dear, for the present," said Marcia, "and send Ethel in."

Molly went almost on tiptoe across the room. She got behind the screen and opened the door.

"Go in," she said in a whisper; "she's looking wonderful."

"Don't whisper, girls," said Marcia. "Come right in, Ethel."

Ethel came in and also kissed her mother, and told her that she looked wonderfully well, and that she too was glad to be back, but she was more self-restrained than her sister, and more self-assured, putting a curb upon herself.

It was Nesta, after all, the youngest, the darling, who made her mother perfectly comfortable, for whatever her faults Nesta could not for a single moment be anything but natural. She came in soberly enough; but when she saw her parent she forgot everything, but just that this was Mothery, and once she had been a terrible beast to that same mother, and she made a little run across the room and dropped on her knees and took her mother's hand and kissed it, and kissed it, and kissed it.

"Oh, you darling, you darling! You sweet! You sweet! There never was any one like you, mothery, never, never, never! Do let me press my cheek against yours. Oh, you sweet! You pet!"

Mrs Aldworth gave one glance of loving triumph at Marcia. Was she not right? Did not her children adore her? Marcia must see it now for herself.

Marcia sat down on a chair and breathed a sigh of relief. Little Nesta was right enough. Little Nesta was better in her conduct than either of her sisters.

"You will come in, of course, and say good-night to me, darling," said Mrs Aldworth when Nurse Davenant made her appearance with the invalid's tea most temptingly prepared.

"Oh yes, if we may."

"You may all come in and out as much as you please, and as often as mother wants you," said Marcia.

"There is no restraint; no limit of time. You do just as you like."

"Then I expect my own dear sweet pet mothery will be getting a little tired of me," was Nesta's response, "for I'll be wanting to be always and always with her, see if I don't!" and Nesta kissed her mother's hand again rapturously.

"Oh, what tempting toast," she said, "and how nice that tea looks."

Mrs Aldworth smiled.

"They are dear girls," she said to Marcia when the door closed on Nesta. "I am glad they're home, and how terribly the sweet pets have missed me."

Chapter Thirteen

A Surprise Visit

The girls soon settled down into the old routine of home life. They got accustomed to their pretty room, which truth to tell they kept in anything but perfect order. They were accustomed to the fact that Mrs Aldworth was a greater invalid than before, but was also well looked after, and was so guarded by Marcia and Nurse Davenant that nobody dared to neglect her. The shadow of that awful night receded farther end farther into the back recesses of their brains; they still had the Carters to love and worship; and Nesta still adored her friend Flossie Griffiths.

A week went by—a fortnight. The weather was intensely hot. Had it been possible, the doctor would have ordered Mrs Aldworth to the seaside; but although her strength returned up to a certain point, she did not seem to go beyond it.

It was one day during the first week in August, one of those extremely hot days when it is an effort even to move, that Mrs Aldworth lay panting on her balcony. The trees in the garden were already assuming a brown tint; the flowers were drooping under the sultry heat of the sun; there was a hot quiver in the air when one looked right in front of one. The bees flew in and out of the window; butterflies chased each other over the garden. There was a stillness and yet a heaviness in the air which seemed to betoken a storm not far off.

It was just then that there came a ring at the front door, and Nesta in a great state of excitement entered her mother's room.

"Marcia," she said, "may I speak to you for a minute?"

Marcia, who was doing some light needlework in the neighbourhood of the invalid's sofa, said:

"Come in, Nesta, and tell me what it is all about."

"But I want to see you by yourself," said Nesta.

"My darling," said Mrs Aldworth, "why these constant secrets? Why shouldn't your mothery know?"

"Oh, it's Clara Carter—she's downstairs. She wants to talk to you. Oh, and here's a telegram for you." Nesta thrust a little yellow envelope into her sister's hand. Marcia opened it.

"It's from Angela," she said. "She's coming to see me in a few minutes. What does Clara want?"

"Just to speak to you. Won't you come down?"

"Can you spare me, dear?" said Marcia, turning to the invalid.

"Yes, of course, Marcia. Go, my dear, and don't hurry back. I feel inclined to ask Miss Angela St. Just to come and see me this morning. You have told me so much about her that I should like to see her; she must be a very nice girl."

"She is, very nice and very beautiful. She is one of God's angels. Her name is one of the most appropriate things about her," said Marcia.

"Do you think she would care to come up to see me?"

"She would be delighted, if you are strong enough."

"Yes," said Nurse Davenant, "Mrs Aldworth is doing finely to-day. Now, Miss Nesta, if you don't wish to sit down, please leave the room, for your mother cannot be fatigued by your moving about in that restless fashion."

Nesta decided that she would leave the room.

"I'll go and get some flowers for mothery," she said, glancing at the different flower glasses, and the next minute, making her escape, she overtook Marcia, who was halfway downstairs.

"What is it, Nesta, what are you so excited about?"

"It's because Clay is coming to ask you something most important I do hope you won't say no. They're all most keenly anxious. Molly and Ethel don't want it, but I do. I promised Penelope when I was there, that I'd do my utmost, but the others are against it."

"Whatever can it be?" said Marcia.

"Well, you see, the Carters are most anxious to know the St. Justs, Angela in particular, and Clara is coming here. Oh, don't go so fast, Marcia, I must tell you. Clara is coming here on purpose, for she guessed that Angela would be coming to see you to-day."

"You mean Miss St. Just," said Marcia steadily.

"Why mayn't I call her Angela as well as you?"

"Simply because, Nesta, you don't know her."

"Well, Miss St. Just, whatever you like to call her."

"And how could Miss Carter possibly know that my friend was coming to see me to-day?"

"Because she knew from her father that Sir Edward had to come to Newcastle for an important meeting, and she guessed somehow, that Miss Angela—I must call her that—would come also, and she is just coming on purpose that you may introduce her. She doesn't want to say so, but she wants to talk to you until Miss St. Just arrives, and you mustn't gainsay her. You won't—will you? It's the greatest fun in the world—it means a great deal to me."

"Now, Nesta, what can it mean?"

"I won't tell you. You can't turn her away—you can't be so rude. There she is, sitting by the window. She's a dear old thing."

Nesta did not accompany Marcia into the drawing room. Marcia went forward and shook hands with Clara, who was looking as such a girl must look when she is particularly anxious to make an impression. Clara, in her cotton frock, with her wild, somewhat untidy mop of hair, was at least natural at Court Prospect; but Clara, with that same hair confined in every direction by invisible nets, with her showy hat, and her dress altogether out of taste, her hands forced into gloves a size too small for her, was by no means a very pleasing object to contemplate. She could not boast of good looks, and she had no style to recommend her. She was natural with the younger Aldworths, but Marcia rather frightened her. She came forward, however, and spoke enthusiastically.

"It is good of you, Miss Aldworth, to give me some of your valuable time. I assure you I'm as proud as possible. I said to Mabel this morning, and to Annie, that I would come to see you. Father was driving into Newcastle to attend that meeting of the Agriculturists. Of course father, as you may know, is on the Board." Marcia made no reply.

"He is on the Board, and will be made Chairman at the next election of officers. It is a most important matter, isn't it, Miss Aldworth? You are interested in the welfare of the farmers, are you not?"

"I regret to say that I don't know anything about them," said Marcia. "I have lived a great deal out of England," she continued, "and since I came home I have been much occupied."

"Oh, yes," said Clara with enthusiasm, "we all know how noble you have been—you saved the life of the poor dear girls' mamma, didn't you?"

"No, it was God who did that."

"Oh, thank you so much for reproving me. I didn't mean in that way. But for you, for your finding her just when you did, she might have died. It was very awful, wasn't it? I did so pity Molly and Ethel. You see, they had invited us to tea, and they gave us, poor girls, a very nice meal; we all quite enjoyed it, and Molly looked so pretty in her blue dress. I think Molly is quite pretty, don't you?"

No reply from Marcia.

"You know she went up to her mother because Nesta—naughty Nesta, had run away. Nesta is very naughty, isn't she?"

Marcia very faintly smiled.

"May I draw down this blind?" she said. "The sun is getting into your eyes."

"Thank you, how kind of you—how considerate. Well, as I was saying, a servant came out and spoke to Molly, and said that her mother wanted her. Molly went in, and she came back in a few minutes and seemed quite jolly and happy. She thought that her mother was going to sleep. But it wasn't a real sleep, was it?

Do tell me the truth. I have always been so anxious to know. You see, when the girls came to us, they were in such a dreadful state of grief, that we did not dare to question them, and we have never dared to question them from that day to this. But I should like to know the truth. Was it a natural sleep?"

"I am sorry, very sorry," replied Marcia, "that I cannot enlighten you. That dreadful time is over, and thank God, Mrs Aldworth's life has been spared."

Clara coloured; she felt the reproof in Marcia's tone. "I know you think me a very silly, curious girl," she said; "but I really do want to be nice and good and to improve myself. Now you, Miss Aldworth—"

Marcia fidgeted. She rose, and opened the window.

"The day is very hot," she said.

"Indeed it is. We are all going to the seaside on Saturday. I suppose you couldn't spare one of the girls—Ethel, or Molly, or Nesta?"

"I fear not. I wish we could, for their sakes. Our hope is that Mrs Aldworth may be better, and then we may be able to take her to the seaside."

There came a ring at the front door. Marcia coloured brightly. She felt her cheeks growing hot and then cold. Clara was watching her face.

"I think that is the ring of a friend of mine," she said, "and if you—"

Before she could finish her sentence the door was flung open and Susan announced Miss St. Just. Enter a tall girl in white, with a white muslin hat to match, and a face the like of which Clara had never seen before. The room seemed transfigured. Marcia herself sank into insignificance beside Angela.

Angela came up quickly and kissed her friend.

"You are surprised, Marcia? I want to take you back with me just for the day. If we are quick we can catch the next train."

"Won't you introduce me?" said Clara's voice, somewhat high-strained and mincing, at that moment.

"Oh, I beg your pardon. Angela, this is Miss Carter, Miss Clara Carter."

Angela turned. There was no false pride about her.

"You live at Court Prospect?" she said, "our old place. How do you do? I hope you like it."

"Very much indeed," said Clara, stammering in her eagerness. "It is a lovely place. We have, I think—and we'd be proud to show it to you—improved the place immensely."

"Improved it?" said Angela. "The cedar avenue, and the beech avenue, and the old Elizabethan garden?"

"We have altered the garden a good deal—I hope you don't mind. You know, it was very confined and old-fashioned, with its prim box hedges, and those quaint things that looked like animals cut out in box at each corner."

"And the sundial—you haven't destroyed that, have you!"

"If you mean that queer stone in the centre—well, yes, we have turned the whole garden into a tennis lawn. It is so delightful. If you could only come and see it."

"Some day, perhaps. Thank you very much." Angela turned again, to Marcia.

"Do run up and put on your things. I know you can be spared quite well. I want a whole day in the woods. We can catch the next train to Hurst Castle, and my little pony trap is waiting. Be quick, Marcia, be quick."

Marcia flew from the room. Now indeed was Clara's chance.

"I hope you're not hurt, Miss St. Just," she began. "If I'd known even for a single moment that you valued those things—"

"Thank you," said Angela, "I value their memory. Of course the place is no longer ours, and you have the right to do as you like with your own."

"Then you think we did wrong? You, who know so much better."

"I will try not to think so; but don't ask me about Court Prospect. Let us forget that you live there."

"Then you won't come to see us? We are so anxious to know you."

"How kind of you," said Angela sweetly. "What a hot day this is; don't you find it so?"

"Well, yes; but at Court Prospect it is much cooler."

"Of course; you are more in the country."

Angela wondered when Marcia would be ready.

"We are going to the seaside," continued Clara. "Of course, we cannot stand this great heat. I want to take one of the Aldworth girls with me; but Marcia—I mean Miss Aldworth, your friend—doesn't seem to approve of it."

"They couldn't leave home very well just now. The one who ought to go is Marcia herself."

"Indeed, yes. How sweet of you to confide in me. Don't you think she is looking very pale?"

"She has suffered a good deal. I am most anxious that she should have a fortnight or so at Hurst Castle."

"What a rapturous idea," thought Clara. "If only I could bring it about. What wouldn't I give to spend some days at Hurst Castle! If only that girl would get me to help her."

"But why won't she go?" said Clara. "It seems quite easy. Mrs Aldworth has three daughters of her own, and there is the nurse. I think she could."

"I quite agree with you," said Angela, and just then Marcia came into the room.

"I am ready," she said. "I am ever so sorry, Miss Carter, it does seem rude, but we shall miss our train."

"Marcia, Miss Carter and I have been having quite an interesting conversation about you. We both think you need a change, and Miss Carter thinks with me that your mother could be left with her own girls and the nurse."

The colour came into Marcia's cheeks.

"We can talk of that in the train," she said. "Good-bye, Miss Carter. Shall I call Nesta to you?"

"No, thank you, I must be going now. I am so glad to have seen you. Miss St. Just. It is a very great honour to make your acquaintance. I trust some day you will be induced to come to see us in our home. We should be so glad to get your opinion with regard to further improvements which we are anxious to make. You will come, won't you, come day? It would be such a very great pleasure."

Angela gave a dubious promise, and the next minute the girls were hurrying down the street.

"What a detestable creature!" said Marcia.

"Oh, no, she belongs to a type," said Angela. "But I don't want to think of the awful things they have done at Court Prospect. They think they have improved my garden—my dear, dear garden."

Chapter Fourteen

The Introduction

Meanwhile Nesta was in a state of wild excitement. No sooner had Marcia and Angela gone down the street than she darted into the drawing room.

"Well," she said, "is it all right? Did you really see her? Was she properly introduced to you? Can you say in future that you know her? When you meet her, will you be able to bow to her? Have you contrived to get her promise to come and see you? Tell me everything, everything."

"What affair is it of yours, child?" said Clara crossly. For although she had met Miss St. Just, it seemed to her that she had made but small way with that young lady.

"It means everything to me—everything possible. Do you know her?"

"Of course, I know her! Is it likely that your sister would be so rude, so fearfully rude as not to introduce me when I was in the room?"

"I don't know," replied Nesta. "Marcia can be rude enough when she likes."

"Well, anyhow, she wasn't. She did introduce us, and Miss St. Just was most pleasant. She has far nicer manners than your sister."

"That wouldn't be difficult," said Nesta. "Marcia is so very stand-offish."

"Ridiculously proud and prudish, I call her," said Clay.

"And do you think Miss St. Just as lovely as you always did?"

"Oh, far, far more lovely. She puts every one else into the shade. I invited her to Court Prospect, and I expect she'll come. I am going home now, and shall try to get up a grand party in her honour. After what she said to me she could hardly refuse. It is all delightful."

"Yes, delightful!" said Nesta. "Well, good-bye. Just mention to Penelope, will you, that you were introduced to her this morning."

"I wonder why I should do that?" said Clara, as she settled herself in the little pony trap which was standing outside the door.

"Oh, just to oblige me," said Nesta, and the next minute Clara Carter was out of sight.

Nesta skipped joyfully into the house.

"Now I've done it," she thought. "Penelope can't go back. We made a bet. How I was to fulfil my part I hadn't the least idea, but I am thankful to say I have won. She'll have to give me a whole sovereign. Yes, a whole, beautiful yellow-boy for my very own self; and if Clara contrives to get Miss St. Just to visit them at Court Prospect, Penelope is to give me two sovereigns. I shall be in luck! Why, a girl with two sovereigns can face the world. She has all before her. She has nothing left to wish for. It is splendid! Magnificent! Oh, I am in luck!"

Nesta danced into the garden. Notwithstanding the hot day she was determined to go at once to tell Flossie Griffiths the good news. Flossie had not been quite as nice as usual to Nesta of late. She had made the acquaintance of the Carters, and the Carters had not specially taken to her. Penelope Carter was also in some ways more fascinating to Nesta than her old friend Flossie, and in consequence Flossie was furiously jealous. But when you have a piece of good news to tell—something quite above the ordinary, you must confide it to some one, and if it is a jealous friend, who would long to have such a delightful thing happen to herself, why so much the better.

So Nesta pinned on her shabbiest hat and went down the narrow pathway, found the entrance to the woods, and by-and-by reached the Griffiths' house.

Flossie was in the garden; she was playing with her dogs. She had three, and was devoted to them. One was a black Pomeranian, another a pug, and the third a mongrel—something between an Irish setter and an Irish terrier. The mongrel was the most interesting dog of the three, and had been taught tricks by Flossie. His name was Jingo. He was now standing on his hind legs, while the other two dogs waltzed round and round. However strong his desire to pounce upon Ginger, the pug, and Blackberry, the Pomeranian, he had to restrain himself. They might yap and bite at his toes, and try to reach his ears, as much as they pleased, but he must remain like a statue. If he endured long enough he would have a lump of sugar for his pains, which he would eat deliberately in view of his tormentors; for this halcyon moment he endured the tortures which Flossie daily subjected him to. It was really time for his sugar now, he had been on his hind legs for quite two minutes; his back was aching; he hated the feel of the sun on his head, he wanted to get into the shade, and above all things he wanted to punish Blackberry and to snap at Ginger. Flossie's hand was in her pocket, the delicious moment had all but arrived, when Nesta's clear, ringing voice sounded on the breeze.

"I say, Floss, I'm just in time. Oh, do come away from those stupid dogs. I have something so heavenly to tell you—it's perfectly golloptious."

Flossie forgot all about her dogs. Jingo mournfully descended to all fours, bit Ginger, snapped at Blackberry, and retired sulking into a corner.

Meanwhile Flossie took the arm of her friend and led her into the shade.

"How red you look," she said. "You must have been running very fast."

"What does that matter? I have got it; I have won it."

"You don't mean to say you've won your bet?"

"Yes, I have though. This very morning she came over—Clay, you know, and soon afterwards the Fairy Princess, and my noble elder sister was present, and she had to introduce Clay to the Princess, and it's extremely likely that the Princess will be forced by circumstances to pay the Carters a visit at Court Prospect."

"I wish her joy of them," said Flossie sulkily.

"Oh, you needn't sulk, old Floss. I've got my yellow-boy all for myself. Now then, I'll tell you what. I know you're ever so cross, and as jealous as ever you can be, but I'm going to share some of it with you."

"You aren't! Not really? Then if you are, I will say you're a brick!"

Flossie's brow cleared, her shallow black eyes danced. She looked full at Nesta.

"You and I'll have a picnic all to ourselves," said Nesta.

"Then you must be very quick," replied Flossie, "for we are going to the seaside next week."

"And the Carters are going on Saturday. I do declare I'll have to look sharp after my yellow-boy. I tell you what—there's nothing on earth for us to do to-day; why shouldn't we go right away and see the Carters. I could get my money from Pen, and we'll have a treat. We can go to Simpson's and have ginger beer and chocolates. Wouldn't that be prime?"

"Rather!" said Flossie, "and I'm just in the humour, for the day is frightfully hot."

"But you don't mind the heat—I'm sure I don't."

"You're rather a show in that dress, Nesta."

"I don't care twopence about my dress," said Nesta. "What I want is my darling yellow-boy. I want him and I'll have him. We can go right away through the woods as far as our place; only perhaps that would be dangerous, for they might pounce upon me. They're always doing it now. Before mothery got so ill we had our stated times, but now we're never sure when we'll be wanted. It's Molly this, and Ethel that, and Nesta, Nesta, Nesta, all the time. I scarcely have a minute to myself. If it wasn't for my lessons I'd simply be deaved out of all patience; but it's hard now that there are holidays, that I can't get away."

"I wish you could come to the seaside with us," said Flossie suddenly, as she thought of the yellow-boy—twenty whole shillings. Perhaps her father and mother might be induced to take Nesta with them. Her father had said only that morning:

"I am sorry for you, my little girl; you will miss your companions."

Flossie's father was rather proud of her friendship for Nesta Aldworth. He thought a great deal of Mr Aldworth, and spoke of him as a rising man. Oh, yes, it might be worth while to get her father and mother to invite Nesta to join them, and Nesta would have her twenty shillings. Twenty, or nineteen at least, and they might have a great many sprees at Scarborough. It would be delightful.

"I tell you what it is," said Flossie. "There's no earthly reason why you should stay at home. I'll just run in this very minute and speak to mother. Why shouldn't you come with us for a week or fortnight?"

"Do you think there's any chance?" said Nesta, turning pale.

"There's every possible chance. Why in the world shouldn't you come with us? They can't want four of you at home, and it's downright selfish."

"The fact is," said Nesta, "they're all agog to get Marcia a holiday."

"Your elder sister—Miss Aldworth? The old maid?"

"Yes, indeed, she is that, but they all think she is looking pale, and they want her to go to those blessed St. Justs. She's hand in glove with them, you know. She thinks of no one else on earth but that Angela of hers."

"Well, I'm not surprised at that," said Flossie. "Every one thinks a lot of Angela St. Just. Now, don't keep me, I'll rush in and speak to mother."

She dashed into the house. The aggrieved mongrel raised a languid head and looked at her. How false she was, with that sugar in her pocket. He wagged a deprecating tail, but Flossie took no notice.

She found her mother busily engaged dusting the drawing room.

"What is it?" she said. "Are you inclined to come in and help me? This room is in a disgraceful state. I must really change Martha."

"Oh, mother, I'll help you another day, but I'm in such a hurry now. Nesta is outside."

"I wonder what you'll do without Nesta at the seaside," said the mother.

"Oh, mother, do you think you could coax father very hard to let me invite Nesta to come with us just for a week—or even for a fortnight? I wish—I wish you would! Do you think it could be managed?"

Mrs Griffiths paused in her work to consider. She was a very frowzy, commonplace woman. She looked out of the window. There stood Nesta, pretty, careless, débonnaire—untidy enough in all truth, but decidedly above the Griffiths in her personal appearance.

Chapter Fifteen

An Unwelcome Caller

"I wouldn't go near her now for all the world," said Flossie, shrinking back. "Oh, my word, Nesta, do get behind this tree. You're a perfect fright, you know, in your very oldest dress and your face as scarlet as a poppy. As to me—I wish I'd put on my Sunday-go-to-meeting frock; it isn't as grand as theirs, but at least it has some fashion about it. But I'm in this dreadful old muslin that I've had for three years, and have quite outgrown. It's awful, it really is. We can't say anything to them to-day, we must go away."

"Go away?" said Nesta. "That's not me. If you're a coward, I'm not. It's my way to strike when the iron's hot, I can tell you. I'll get into a scrape for this when I get home, and if there's one thing I've made up my mind about, it's this—that I won't get into a scrape for nothing. No, if you're frightened, say so, and sit down behind that haycock. Not a soul will see you there, and I'll walk up just as though I were one of the guests, and shame Penelope and the others into recognising me."

"Nesta! You haven't the courage!"

"Courage?" said Nesta, "catch me wanting courage. Stay where you are; I'll come back to you when I've got my yellow-boy. When that's in my pocket I'll come back and then you'll have a good time. Although," she added reflectively, "I don't know that you deserve it, for being such an arrant little coward."

Nesta disappeared; Flossie sat and mopped her face. She was trembling with nervousness. She had never been really at home with the Carters, and she disliked immensely her present position. She wondered, too, why she cared so much for Nesta. There was nothing wonderful about Nesta. But then there was the sovereign, a whole sovereign, capable of being divided into twenty beautiful silver shillings. Flossie's father was a very well-to-do tradesman, and could and would leave his child well off; but he was careful, and he never allowed her much pocket money. In the whole course of her life she had never possessed more than half-a-crown at a time, and to be able to have eight of those darlings, to feel that she could do what she liked with them, was a dream beyond the dreams of avarice. It is true the money would not be hers; it would be Nesta's; but Nesta, with all her faults, was generous enough, and Flossie felt that once she had the money and was away with her friend at the seaside they could really have a good time. Flossie was very fond of her food, and she imagined how the money could be spent on little treats—shrimps or doughnuts, and whatever fruit was in season. They could have endless little picnics all to themselves on the sands. It would be a time worth remembering.

Meanwhile where was Nesta? Flossie was afraid at first to venture to look round the other side of the haycock, but after a time, when she had quite cooled down, she did poke her head round. To her astonishment, envy and disgust, she saw that Nesta, in her shabby cotton frock, with her old hat on her head, was calmly walking up and down in the company of Penelope Carter. Penelope and her boy friend, and Nesta, were parading slowly up and down, up and down a corner of one of the lawns.

Penelope did all that an ordinary girl could to get rid of her friend; but Nesta stuck like a leech. At last Penelope was desperate.

"I am awfully sorry, Nesta, but you see we have all our sets marked out, and we—we didn't invite you to-day. You must be tired, and if you will go into the house, Mrs Johnson will give you a cup of tea."

"But I've brought Flossie, Flossie Griffiths. I cannot leave her out."

"Take Flossie with you, and both have a cup of tea."

"I'll go with pleasure, if you'll come with me."

"But I can't. Do speak for me, Bertie," she continued, turning to the boy. "Say that I cannot."

"Miss Penelope is engaged to play a set of tennis with me," said Bertie Pearson, trembling as he uttered the words, for Nesta's aggressive manner frightened him.

"She shall have her set with you as soon as I have said what I have come to say. It won't take long; I can say it if you will come as far as the house with me, Pen. You won't get rid of me in any other way."

Penelope fairly stamped her foot.

"If I must, I must," she said. "Bertie, keep a set open for me, like a good fellow. Come at once, Nesta." They turned down a shady walk.

"Oh, Nesta, how could you?" said Penelope, her anger breaking out the moment she found herself alone with her companion. "To come here to-day—to-day of all days, and to look like that, in your very shabbiest!"

"Oh, you're ashamed of me," said Nesta. "You're a nice friend!"

"I am not ashamed of you," said Penelope stoutly, "when you are fit to be seen. I like you for yourself. I always have; but I don't think it right for a girl to thrust herself on other girls uninvited. Now, what is it you want? I am busy entertaining friends."

"Flirting with Bertie, you mean."

"I don't flirt—how dare you say so? He is a very nice boy. He is a gentleman, and you are not a lady."

"Oh, indeed! I'm not a lady. My father's daughter is not a lady! Wait till I tell that to Marcia."

Penelope was alarmed. She knew that if this speech reached her father's ears he would be seriously displeased with her.

"I didn't mean that, of course, Nesta, you know I didn't I like you for yourself, and of course you are quite a lady. All the same you oughtn't to have come here now and—and force yourself on us."

"Well, I'll go if you give me what I have come for."

"What is that?"

They were now approaching the house by a side entrance.

"You needn't be bothered about your tea, for I don't want it," said Nesta. "I'm choking with thirst, but I don't want your tea—you who have said I'm not a lady. As to Flossie, she doesn't want your tea either. We'd rather choke than have it. There's a shop in the High Street where we can get ginger beer and chocolates. The ginger beer will go pop and we'll enjoy ourselves. It's fifty times nicer than your horrid tea. But I'll tell you what I do want—my yellow-boy."

"Your what?" said Penelope, looking at her in bewilderment.

"My beautiful, precious, darling twenty shillings. Only they must be given me in gold of the realm."

"Nesta, what do you mean? Your twenty shillings!"

"Come," said Nesta, "that's all very fine. But did you, or did you not make a bet with me?"

Penelope seemed to remember. She put her hand to her forehead.

"Oh, that," she said, with a laugh. "But that was pure nonsense!"

"It was a true bet; you wrote it down in your book and I wrote it down in mine. It's as true as true can be. You wrote—I remember the words quite well—'If Clay gets an introduction through Marcia Aldworth to Miss Angela St. Just, I will pay Nesta one sovereign; and if she fails, Nesta is to give me one sovereign.' Now did you, or did you not, make me that bet?"

"Oh, it was a bit of fun—a joke."

"It isn't a joke; it's real earnest. I tell you what; I'll go straight to your father and tell him before every one present what has really happened. I'll tell him that you made a bet and won't keep it, for I have won," said Nesta excitedly. "You ask Clay if I haven't. Clay was at our house this morning, and Angela called. Blessed thing! I see nothing in her. She was introduced to your Clay, and your Clay hopes to bring her here to Court Prospect, and if I haven't earned my sovereign, I want to know who has. So now."

"Really and truly, Nesta, I wish you wouldn't talk so loud. Oh, look at all those people coming this way. They'll see us, and Clay will call me. I see Clay with them."

"Let her call. I'd like her to. I'd like to explain before every one that you never kept your bet."

"Oh, do come into the house, Nesta. Do for pity's sake."

Penelope dragged the fierce and rebellious Nesta into the house by the side door.

"Now," she said, "sit down and cool yourself. What will Bertie say? and he came here specially on my invitation. He is my guest. I'm awfully sweet on him. I am really, and—oh dear, oh dear—I don't care about Angela St. Just, and I don't believe that she was introduced to Clay."

"Well, you ask Clara. I'll shout to her—I say, Clara!"

"Stop, Nesta! You must be mad!"

Penelope put her hand over Nesta's mouth.

"Give me my yellow-boy and I'll be off," she said, pushing back Penelope's hand as she tried to force her from the window.

"I haven't got it now; I'll bring it to-morrow."

"I won't stir from here till I get it," said Nesta. "I suppose with all your riches you can raise one sovereign. I want it and I'm not going away without it. Flossie and I are going to have ginger beer and chocolates at Simpson's, in the High Street, and we're not going to be docked of our pleasure because you are too fine a lady to care."

"Oh dear; oh dear!" said Penelope. "What is to be done? I haven't got the money—I really haven't."

"Well, I suppose some of you have. I see your father on the lawn; I'll run up to him and tell him. If I talk out loud enough he will give it to me. I know he will."

"Nesta, you are driving me nearly mad!"

"Let me have the money and I'll go."

"Pen, Pen! Where are you?" called Mabel's voice at that moment, from the garden.

"They want me. Bertie will think I've deserted him. Oh, Nesta, you are driving me distracted."

But Nesta stood her ground. Penelope stood and reflected. She had not much money of her own, and what money she got usually melted through her fingers like water. Her sisters had long ago discovered this and entrusted her with but little. Her father always said she could have what she pleased within reason, but he never gave her any sort of allowance.

"Time enough when you are grown up, Pussie," he used to say, as he pulled her long red-gold hair.

Now she looked out on the sunlit garden; on the pleasant scene, on Bertie's elegant young figure, on the boys and girls who were disporting themselves in the sunshine and under the trees. Then she glanced at her own really elegant little person, and then at Nesta, untidy, cross, and disagreeable. How could she by any possibility have liked such a girl? She must be got rid of somehow, for there was Mabel's voice again.

"Stay a minute," she said to Nesta. "Don't dare to go out. I'll get it for you somehow. You are the most horrid girl in the world."

She flew upstairs; Clara's door was open; Clara's room, as usual, was in disorder. Penelope frantically opened drawer after drawer. Could she find a loose sovereign anywhere? Clara often left them about; to her they meant very little. But she could find no loose money in Clara's room. She went from there to Mabel's; from Mabel's to Annie's. What possessed the girls? There wasn't even a shilling to be found amongst their possessions. Gold bracelets in plenty, necklaces, jewellery of all sorts, but the blessed money which would restore Penelope to the lawn, to the tennis court, to all her delights, was not forthcoming.

Her father's room came last. She rushed into it. Nesta was desperate; Nesta might confront her father on the lawn. She would tell him in the evening—he would forgive her. She ran in; she opened one of his drawers and took out a purse which he kept there to pay the men's wages on Saturday. Invariably each Monday morning he put the required sum into that special old purse. There were twenty sovereigns in it now. Penelope helped herself to one, snapped the purse to, shut the drawer, and ran downstairs.

"There!" she said to Nesta. "Now, for goodness' sake go. Don't worry me whatever happens. I've given it to you, and I'm free; but catch me ever making a bet with you again."

"Oh, I don't care!" said Nesta. "My darling little yellow-boy. Thank you, Penelope, thank you."

But Penelope had vanished.

Chapter Sixteen

Troublesome Consequences

On the whole Penelope Carter was a fairly good child. She had been very cross when disturbed by Nesta; but when she returned to the lawn her good humour immediately came back. She looked almost pretty, for there was much more character in her face than her sisters'. She ran about now, charming many people by her bright presence, and more than one visitor remarked that Penelope would be the best-looking of the Carters, and certainly had more character in her face than her sisters.

The gay party came to an end, and with it, some of Penelope's good spirits. When she had taken the sovereign from her father's purse, she had certainly not had the slightest idea of concealing the fact from him. A sovereign, as she knew, meant but little in that establishment. He would thank her for not allowing that wicked Nesta to disgrace him in public. He would pat her on the cheek and say: "Well done, little woman; I am glad you were good enough to confess!" and there would be an end of the matter.

This was Penelope's thought in cold blood; but when she reflected more over the matter, it seemed to her that the thing was not so easy as it had appeared when in the heat of the conflict with Nesta she had purloined the money. Mr Carter was very fond of his children; he was a very good-hearted, upright sort of man, ambitious, but without a scrap of taste; thoroughly upright and honest in all his dealings; he did not owe a penny in the world. He had made his money by honest toil, and he was proud of it. To rise in the opinion of the world seemed to him a very laudable thing to do. He hoped to establish his children well in the world. He hoped that his daughters would marry gentlemen, and his sons ladies. He hoped to die in a better position than that in which he was born. For this reason he encouraged the Aldworths, and rather snubbed the Griffiths; and for the same reason he was anxious to become acquainted with the St. Justs, not in a business capacity, but as a friend. He had none of the finer perceptions of character. It never occurred to him that it might be painful to Sir Edward to visit his old home under such changed conditions. On the contrary, he thought how agreeable it would be to show the ex-owner how much better the place looked since Clay had suggested the cutting down of those magnificent trees, and the opening up of that glade. What a beautiful tennis lawn that was, where the ancient garden used to stand. It never occurred to him for a single moment that the bric-à-brac, the beautiful furniture, the old pictures, the old oak which had belonged to the St. Justs, was not more than replaced by the modern splendours of modern and depraved taste. These things he knew nothing about. He was exceedingly anxious to know the St. Justs and their set, and would have given a good deal more than the sovereign which poor Penelope had taken to attain that object.

Nevertheless, Penelope felt that the whole thing had an ugly appearance on the present occasion. The sovereign, however, must be put back in the purse, or the truth confessed before Saturday morning, that was evident. This was Wednesday. There was all Thursday and Friday. There would be a little packing to do—not that Penelope would trouble herself about that—but there would be a little commotion in getting the family off to the sea. Her father was not going with them, at least not for the first few days, but he would follow.

That evening Penelope determined to make a confidante of her sister, Clara.

Clara was in a specially good humour. She had had, as she expressed it, a stunning day, one long series of triumphs, as she said now to her sisters, Mabel and Annie, as they clustered round her.

"Oh, and there's little Pen," she cried. "Come along, Penelope. You looked quite nice to-day. You'll take the shine out of us all when you are grown up. One or two people asked me who you were. Your hair is so pretty, and you will be taller than the rest of us."

"I don't care," said Penelope.

Clara pinched her cheek.

"You don't care? But you will care fast enough when you are older, and when you have several Berties walking with you, and other fellows anxious to get introductions to you. You wait and see."

Penelope looked what she felt, cross and discontented.

"What is it, Puss? What are you frowning about?"

"I'm only thinking. I want to have a talk with you all by myself."

"Oh, indeed, and so we're not to be with you?" said Mabel in some surprise.

"No, I want old Clay. Can't I go somewhere with you all by yourself, Clara?"

Now this sort of homage was sweet to Clara. She kissed the child, and said affectionately:

"Well, I'm a bit tired; what with running about all over the place and entertaining folks, I don't seem to have a leg to stand on; but I suppose we can just cross the lawn and get into the summerhouse and have a chat. Come along, Pen."

Penelope fastened herself on to her elder sister's arm and they went across to the summerhouse in question.

"Now, then," said Clara, somewhat severely, "they tell me that I spoil you."

"Oh, but you don't, Clay, you are ever so nice to me."

"Well, I don't mean to spoil you. Of course, these are holiday times; but when lessons begin again I am going to be ever so strict. It has just occurred to me that I might get an introduction for you through Miss Angela St. Just to that charming school at Frankfort."

"What charming school at Frankfort?" asked Penelope. "Frankfort—where's that?"

"Oh, you dreadful child! Don't you know?"

"I hate geography. I don't want to learn. I don't want to be a good, model, knowledgeable girl. And I hate Miss Just. I do; so there!"

"Well, Penelope, you are a good deal too young to choose for yourself, and if father can get an introduction to Mrs Silchester, I am sure he will avail himself of it. The school is most select; only the very nicest of girls go there."

"Isn't it the school where that horrid Marcia Aldworth was—that detestable old-maid thing."

"She is an exceedingly nice girl."

"Clay! As though she suited you one little bit! Why, I saw her one day, and she was as pokery as possible."

"But she is a friend of Miss St. Just's."

"Oh, Clay! Clay! I will be good; I will be good, and we needn't talk of that horrid school just now, need we, just when my long beautiful holidays are beginning. I will be good, I will, if you will only help me."

"Well, Puss, what can I do?"

"I did something to-day—it wasn't really wrong, but I am a bit frightened. I must tell you."

"You are a queer little thing—what can it be?" Penelope looked full up at her sister.

"You are as proud as Punch—you are, you old thing! And now I shall whisper to you why you are go proud?"

"Yes, do; whisper to me."

"You have got to know that Miss St. Just—that idol of yours, that angel up in the clouds that you are always thinking is too good for this world; you got to know her to-day at the Aldworths'."

"I did, and I find her not at all an angel up in the clouds, but a very pretty and sweet angel with her feet on the solid earth. And she is ever so pleased to know me; she showed it, and spoke about Court Prospect, and I described how we had improved it, and she was so interested. I asked her if she would come to see it, and I'm convinced she will come, and right gladly. I'm going to tell father all about it. Father will be pleased."

"Then, that's all right. If you tell father about that at the same time you are telling him about me, why it will be all right."

"About you? What in the world about you?"

"Oh, I'm coming to that. You remember that time when that Nesta was staying here?"

"That Nesta. I thought you adored her."

"I don't adore her; I dislike her very much. She is not a bit a nice girl. She is of the Flossie Griffiths style, and you know quite well father wouldn't like us to associate with the Griffiths."

"I should think not, indeed," said Clara.

She had visions, of herself as the special friend of Angela St. Just, of visiting Hurst Castle, of getting to know the county folks. She had visions of Angela reposing in the spare room at Court Prospect, with its gilt and ormolu and white paint, which used to be called the Cedar room in the days of the St. Justs. She had visions of Angela laying her head on the richly embroidered linen, and saying to herself, "What cannot money do to improve a place."

Among the many thoughts which flitted into her brain, she forgot Pen's anxious, little piquant face, and just at that moment Mr Carter came along. He paused, stared at his two daughters, and came deliberately in.

"There, now, Pen, if you want to say anything to father, you can say it yourself; here he is. Father, Penelope wants to speak to you about something."

"No, I don't—I don't," said Penelope, all her courage oozing out, as she expressed it, at her finger tips.

"Then if Penelope has nothing to say, I have," said Clara, who being quite selfish and commonplace, forgot the wistfulness which had gathered for a moment round her little sister's face.

Penelope stole away.

"I'll tell Clay in the morning," she said. "Father won't miss the money before Saturday. I'll tell old Clay to-morrow."

Meanwhile Clara poured the welcome news into her father's ears that the introduction to Miss St. Just had been accomplished. He was quite elated.

"That's capital," he said. "We must make much of that girl, the eldest Miss Aldworth. She is worth twenty of her sisters."

"Of course she is, father; I have always said so."

"Have you now, Clay? I shouldn't have guessed it. I thought you were entirely taken up with Miss Ethel and Miss Molly, and that little Nesta. Nesta seems to me to be the best of the bunch—a rollicking little thing, and full of daring. By the way, I saw her here to-day, and our Pen with her. What did she come about?"

"Nesta here to-day? I didn't see her," said Clara.

"Well, I did. She and Pen seemed to be having a sort of quarrel. You had best say nothing about it. Those sort of quarrels between girls soon melt into thin air when you take no notice of them. But I tell you what; this is good news. We'll have a big function after we have spent our month at the seaside. I know for a fact that the St. Justs are going to be at Hurst Castle for the entire season, and when you return, Clay, we'll just do the thing in topping style. I'll induce Sir Edward and his daughter to come here and stay for the night I think I can manage the old gentleman."

Here a peculiar knowing expression passed over Mr Carter's face. Clara watched him.

"What a clever old dad it is," she said.

"You'd like it, wouldn't you, Clay?" he said, putting his hand under her chin and turning her face round until he looked at her. "Upon my word you have a look of your mother, child. I was very fond of her," he continued, and then he stooped and printed an unlooked-for kiss on Clara's young cheek.

She was unaccustomed to special attentions from her parent.

"I'd be ever so glad if they came," she said. "And I'm sure if you wish it they will come."

"Yes, it's all right now that you've been introduced to Miss Angela. Now, look here; couldn't we send them a present of fruit—fruit from the garden? They'd like some fruit from their own old garden, wouldn't they now?"

Clara saw no impropriety in that.

"Fruit and vegetables; we'd send some vegetables, too," said Mr Carter. "Those marrowfat peas are just in their prime. We might send them a couple of pecks, and—and some peaches; they are just getting perfectly ripe now in the hothouses—peaches, nectarines, apricots, peas, and a few melons wouldn't be unacceptable, would they? What do you say, eh?"

"Just as you like, Dad, of course."

Clara went off to the house to inform her sisters of what was happening. Penelope had gone to bed.

"Why, where is Pen?" she said.

"I don't know; she seems to be sulky, and she said she had a headache. She'll sleep it off; don't bother about her," said Annie, with a yawn.

The elder sister sat down and divulged to the younger ones what was about to happen.

"We've got," she said, "rather to drop the Aldworths—they're all very well in their way, but with the exception of Marcia, father doesn't want us to see too much of them."

"I'm heartily glad," said Mabel; "I'm about sick of them."

"I call it beastly meant—" said Jim, raising his face from where he was apparently buried in the pages of a magazine.

"Hullo!" cried Clara. "You there? What are you listening to us for?"

"Well, I don't care—I call it beastly mean to drop people when you have once taken them up so strongly, more particularly when you have achieved your object."

"And pray what's that?"

"You know quite well you have been angling to get an introduction to Miss Angela St. Just. Well, I happen to know that you've got it, and now you want to drop the girls."

"Not Marcia," said Clay; "we are quite willing to be friends with her. She must come and stay with us—it is her turn. It will be delightful to have her here with Angela St. Just."

"I call it beastly free of you to call her by her Christian name."

"Jim, I wish you'd mind your manners. I'm sure I'm not half so rude in my speech as you are, and of course I wouldn't call her that to her face."

"I should hope not indeed," said Jim. "I don't understand girls, and that's the truth."

He marched away. The night was a dark one, but warm. He went down through the shrubbery; he passed a little arbour where Clara and Penelope had had their interrupted conference a little earlier in the evening. He thought he heard some one sobbing. The sound smote on his ear.

"Hullo," he said, "who's there?"

The sobs ceased; there was dead silence. He went in, struck a match, and saw Penelope crouched in a corner.

"Why you poor little wretch," he said, "what in the world is wrong with you? Why are you out here by yourself, and crying as though your heart would break? Why, a poacher might come across you, and then what a fright you'd get!"

"A poacher? You don't really think so, Jim?"

"Of course I don't; but you are as cold as charity. Here, snuggle up to me. What's the matter, old girl?"

"Oh, Jim, I stole a sovereign from father to-day; I took it out of his purse in his bedroom when all the visitors were here. I opened the drawer and took a sovereign out of the purse and slipped it into my pocket. At the time I thought I'd tell him, but now I haven't the courage. I thought perhaps Clay would tell him, but I couldn't get it out—Oh, I'm a very miserable girl. I don't know what to do—"

"But tell me," said Jim, "what in the world did you want with a sovereign? To think that my sister should steal just like the commonest, lowest-minded, most unprincipled girl."

"Oh, don't rub it in so hard, Jim. Don't, don't," said Penelope.

"Well, tell me all about it."

She did tell him.

"It was Nesta—we had a bet—it was about Clay and that horrid St. Just girl. We made a bet that if Clay got an introduction through Marcia Aldworth that Nesta should have a sovereign; but if it was the other way, I was to have the sovereign. I didn't think about it, for I knew she could never pay it if she lost, but somehow or other it all came about as she wished, and she came tearing over with that horrid friend of hers, Flossie Griffiths, and dashed into the middle of our party. She would speak to me, and she took me away and demanded the money. I did what I could to put her off; but she said she'd go straight to father and tell him before every one that I had made a bet and broken it. So I was desperate; I took the only money I could find. Oh, what am I to do; what am I to do? Do you think father will be frightfully angry?"

"I expect he won't much like it."

"Oh, Jim, what am I to do?"

"I'll see about it," said Jim. "Now, look here, Pen, I'm not going to let you off altogether; it would not be right; but you are a good, brave child to have told me, and I am glad to know: You might have done worse, and you might have done better. I didn't know that a sister of mine could be bullied by that sort of girl. I should like to give that Nesta a piece of my mind. I vow I should."

"But what will father say on Saturday?"

"You'll have to own up. I could give you the sovereign, of course, and you could put it back into his purse, but that wouldn't teach you a lesson. We fellows at school—we boys, wouldn't do a thing of that sort, and it wouldn't be straight for me to shield you, and let you put the money back without telling him anything about it. But I'll help you to tell father. Now, you can go straight off to bed. I'll help you, old girl, when you are telling him. Good-night, good-night."

"You are a brick! You are a dear," said Pen. She crushed her face against his cheek; he felt her tears and rubbed them away shamefacedly afterwards.

For some time he sat on in the little summerhouse in which Angela St. Just had sat when a child, and which had not yet been destroyed for a more elegant and modern edifice. When he went back to the house it was to ponder over many things. Jim was the most thoughtful of the family; he had grit in him, which was more than any of the other Carters, their father excepted, possessed.

Chapter Seventeen

Relief Intercepted

It is an old proverb that man proposes and God disposes. Certainly when Jim Carter went to bed that night he had not the most remote idea of not helping his little sister through her difficulties. But a very unexpected and strange thing happened. His father went up to him in the early hours of the morning and told him that young as he was he was about to send him on a very delicate mission, which no one else could execute so skilfully.

"You know, Jim," he said, "you are older than your years, and you are to leave school next term and enter my business. My clerk, Hanson, who ought to have attended to this business, has absconded, taking some money with him, and I have no one who can fill his place. I want you, my lad, to go over to Paris for me, and to deliver this letter in person to the firm, the address of which you will find on the back. You can talk French nearly as well as a native; you have never been there before, but I want you to catch the very earliest train, the one that leaves Newcastle at half-past six in the morning. You will then be in time to catch the mail to Paris. When you have done my commission, you may go to one of the hotels and amuse yourself for two or three days. You must stay there until I get my answer. I want the thing done privately. It is a very important piece of business, and I cannot attend to it myself, for I am so busy in Newcastle just now that I cannot possibly be spared. But you will do it, Jim, and if you manage it well I won't forget you, my lad. Here is forty pounds. You won't spend anything like that in Paris, but you may as well have the money in your pocket as not. You can go first-class, if you please; show yourself a gentleman, and act with discretion. You won't be questioned with regard to anything, and no one is to know where you are. Now then, up you get, and off you go. Here is my Gladstone bag; I'll pack your things and see you to the station."

Jim's heart had jumped into his mouth when his father began to speak, but before it came to an end he was aflame with excitement and delight. Here, truly, was an honour! Penelope and her small troubles were as completely forgotten as though they had never existed. He delighted in the sudden honour thrust upon him; he vowed that he would do it well, if his very life were demanded of him.

His quick dressing, his hurried getting downstairs; his father helping him and beseeching him not to make the slightest noise, made it all as mysterious as one of Henty's adventures. The breakfast which his father himself got for him; the quick walk to the station; the hurried good-bye, when he found himself in a first-class carriage in the train, and his father looking proud and confident, all dazzled his young head, and Penelope and her stolen sovereign were as though they had never been. But when Penelope awoke that morning, the very first person she thought of was Jim. She and Annie shared a room together. Annie was not particularly fond of Penelope; she was the least interesting of the Carter girls; she was a little more commonplace and a little more absorbed in herself than her elder sisters.

"There is one thing I'm going to ask father," said Annie, as they dressed that morning, "that is after we return from the seaside—if I may have a room to myself. I really can't stand the higgledy-piggledy way you keep your things in, Pen."

"Oh, I hate being tidy!" said Pen. "I wonder where Jim is. Jim is a brick of bricks; the dearest, darlingest, nicest fellow in the world."

"Oh, my word!" cried Annie, "why is Jim in such high favour? I never heard you go into raptures about him before."

"I never found him out until last night," said Penelope.

"And you found him out last night? Pray, in what way," said Annie.

"Ah, that's a secret," said Pen. "I'm not going to tell you."

"If there's a thing in this wide world I'd be deaved to death about, it would be one of your stupid secrets," said Annie. "Why, you're nothing but a child; and as to Jim, I don't believe he has made you his confidante."

"Yes, he has, though; yes, he has," said Penelope, and she dashed about the room, making the most of what she thought would tease her sister.

"You, indeed!" said Annie, as she brushed out her long hair and put it up in the most fashionable style—"you, with your Nesta and your Flossie Griffiths."

"With my what?" said Penelope—"My Flossie?"

"Yes, with that common girl. Half of us saw you yesterday, walking with Nesta. Really, it is too bad of her to come on our festive occasions in such a shabby dress."

"Well, that has nothing to do with Jim. Now, I'm going down to breakfast," said Pen.

But she felt a little nervous as she entered the breakfast room. Jim had given her to understand that he would meet her there, and before the rest of the party came down, he would get her to confide in their father. But Mr Carter, more red than usual in the face, and slightly disturbed in his mind, for he wondered if he had done right to put such confidence in his young son, was sitting alone at the breakfast table. He shouted to Penelope when he saw her.

"Come along, Lazybones, and pour out my coffee for me."

She obeyed; then she said, looking up and speaking, in spite of herself, a trifle uneasily:

"Where's Jim?"

"What do you want to know about Jim?" said her father, in some irritation. He had dreaded this inquiry, but had not thought it would come from little Shallow-pates, as he called his youngest daughter. However, he must account for Jim's absence in some sort of fashion.

"You won't see Jim for two or three days," he said. "Not for two or three days," said Penelope, and her small, round childish face looked almost haggard. "You mean that he won't be home before Saturday?"

"Bless you, no; he'll certainly be away till then. Now that's all about it. Why, good gracious, child; I didn't know you cared so much for him!"

She turned away to choke down the lump in her throat. The other girls came in but they did not even trouble to inquire for their brother. Mr Carter, however, thought it best to make his communication.

"Jim has gone to stay with one of his schoolfellows unexpectedly; a letter came for him last night. I thought it best he should accept. It is one of the Holroyds. Very respectable people the Holroyds are. Well, girls, what are you staring at?"

"I didn't know we were staring," said Clara. "I'm very glad Jim has gone. But what a violent hurry he went off in."

"Well, that's his affair, I suppose. Boys like your brother don't want the grass to grow under their feet. Anyhow, he's off, and he won't be back,"—Pen raised her face—"for a week or ten days; so you'll have to do without him at the seaside for a few days."

Pen slowly left the room.

"I don't believe he has gone to the Holroyds'," she said. She mounted the stairs and entered her brother's bedroom. She opened the drawers and peeped into his wardrobe.

"He has not taken his best clothes," she thought, "and if the Holroyds are swells, he'd want them. He hasn't gone to the Holroyds! Whatever is the matter?"

Then she sat down very moodily on a chair in the centre of the room.

"He promised he'd help me, and he hasn't. He has forgotten all about it, and he has gone away, and it's not to the Holroyds. He won't be back before Saturday, and whatever, whatever am I to do?"

Penelope was not left long to her own meditations. She was called downstairs by Clara, who gave the little girl several commissions to do for her.

"You have got to drive into Newcastle; the pony trap will be at the door in a quarter of an hour's time. You have got to get all these things at Johnson's, and then you are to go to Taylor's and ask them for my new things, and be sure you see that they have selected the right shade of blue for my ties. Then do—"

Here Clay thrust a long list of commissions into her sister's hand.

"All right," said Penelope.

"Be home as quick as ever you can; we are expecting some people here this afternoon, the Mauleverers and the Chelmsfords. It seems to me that we are getting to know all the county set. Go, the very last thing, to Theodor's and get the ices and the cakes that I ordered. Now, do look sharp, Pen. You have no time to lose."

Pen was quite agreeable. There was nothing to pay, for the Carters had accounts at the different shops where she was going. Just for the minute she looked wistfully into her sister's face.

"If I could but tell her," she thought. "But I don't suppose she'd understand. Well, I suppose if Jim doesn't come back, and there's no hope of that, and if he quite forgets to write, I'll have to confide in Clay before Saturday, for I couldn't face father if he found out without my telling him."

Penelope thought and thought during her drive. All of a sudden it flashed upon her that she might write a note to Jim. She could go to the post office—or still better she could stop at the Aldworths' on her way back, and ask for writing materials, and send a letter to him at the Holroyds'. The Holroyds did not live so very far away, only twenty miles at the furthest. Jim would probably get his letter that night; he would be certain to receive it the first thing in the morning.

Pen felt quite happy when she remembered this very easy way of reminding Jim of his promise. She knew the Holroyds' address quite well, for Jim had often spoken of it. There was George, and there was Tom, and they lived at a place called The Chase. Yes, she could easily get a letter to reach Jim at that address.

Accordingly she went through her commissions with ease and despatch, for she had, notwithstanding her youth, a wise little head on her shoulders. Then she desired the coachman to drive rapidly to the Aldworths' house.

Just at that moment a voice sounded on her ears, and looking round she saw Flossie Griffiths.

"Stop! stop! Pen! Do stop!" called out Flossie. Pen did not like being called by her Christian name by Flossie Griffiths; still less did she wish to have anything to do with that young lady, but she did not well know how to get rid of her. She accordingly desired the man to draw up the little carriage at the kerbstone, whereupon Flossie said eagerly:

"Oh, you are the very person—you are driving past the Aldworths', aren't you?"

"Yes; have you a message for them?"

"I want to go with you. I want to see Nesta in a very great hurry. It is most important."

"All right, if you must," said Pen not too cordially. Flossie's nature was far too blunt to be easily repressed. She jumped into the carriage and sat down, leaning back and feeling herself very important.

"It must be nice to be rich," she said. "I do envy folks with lots of money. I wish my father had made his pile the same as yours has. Oh, isn't it good to lie back against these soft cushions, instead of tramping and tramping on the hard road? Well, I'm going to have a jolly time at Scarborough. Are you going to the seaside, too?"

"Yes," said Pen, "we are going to Whitby."

"I'd much rather go to Scarborough; I went to Whitby once; it isn't half as jolly."

"Well, I like Whitby," said Pen, absolutely indifferent.

"You don't know what fun I'm going to have, and there's a great secret, too," said Flossie. "Oh, by the way, it was good of you to give Nesta that sovereign. She was nearly mad about it. I never saw anybody in such a fix. But when you had given it to her she got into the best of humours. We had a right good time at the pastrycook's, I can tell you. I never ate so many light cakes in the whole course of my life before. And we are going to have more fun, Nesta and I. By the way, I hope you're not jealous."

"Jealous!" said Pen. "What about?"

"Of me and Nesta."

Flossie giggled.

"No; I'm not jealous," said Pen. "I don't quite understand."

"I should think it was pretty easy to understand. Nesta and me—we've always been the primest friends—no husband and wife could love each other better than we do. But then you stepped in, and for a time I thought there was going to be a rift in the lute,"—Flossie was very fond of mixed metaphors,—"I really thought there was; but when Nesta saw us both in our true lights, she, of course, would never give me up just because you are the richest."

"I should hope not," said Pen. "It would be contemptible. But here we are at the Aldworths'. I am going in too."

"Are you? You don't want Nesta, I hope?"

"No; I don't care who I see. I just want a sheet of paper and a pen and some ink. I have a stamp in my pocket."

"Well, come along; I know the way better than you do," said Flossie.

They went up to the front entrance, and Flossie rang the bell. Then she pressed her face against the glass of the side window.

"Oh, dear," she said, "I see that dreadful, stately old-maidish Miss Aldworth coming downstairs. Don't let her see me. Just let me hide behind you. There, that's better."

Pen stood back a little stiffly. Presently the door was opened by Marcia herself.

"How do you do, Flossie?" she said. "How do you do, Miss Carter?"

"I have come," said Flossie, "to see Nesta. Where is she?"

"You cannot see her at present. She is engaged with her mother."

"But mayn't I just see her for the shortest of minutes?"

"I am sorry you cannot. Have you any message for me to take to her?"

"No; yes, that is if you are quite sure I can't see her."

"I am certain on the subject. She is very busy with her mother, and cannot possibly be disturbed until after the midday meal."

"Well, tell her—tell her—oh, no; don't tell her anything. You may just mention that I called, and, if she is free, I can be in the wood this afternoon."

"Very well; I'll remember," said Marcia with a grave smile.

Flossie was forced to take her departure, and Penelope, with a sigh of relief, turned to Marcia.

"I'd be so awfully obliged to you," she said. "I know it's a cool sort of thing to ask, but I want to write a letter—it's to Jim, my brother. He is staying with people of the name of Holroyd. They're very nice people; they're your sort, you know. He has gone off rather suddenly, and there's something he was going to do for me, and I want to remind him. Do you greatly object to my writing him a little note here?"

"Of course not, dear," said Marcia, in her kindest tone. "Come along into this room. I'll give you pen, ink, and paper."

She supplied Pen with the necessary materials, and the little girl wrote her note.

"My Darling Jim:

"Don't forget father and the big fat purse on Saturday morning. Your loving and distracted Pen.

"P.S.—You went off in such a hurry I suppose you forgot, you old darling. But please, please remember your most wildly distracted sister Pen."

This note was put into an envelope, and was addressed to Mr Jim Carter, care of the Holroyds, The Chase, Dewsbury. Pen took out her little purse, which alas! held little or no coins, produced a sticky stamp, put it on the letter, and prepared to leave the house.

In the hall she met Marcia.

"Is your letter ready?" she said. "I am just going to the post. I'll post it for you."

"When do you think it will get to Dewsbury?" asked Pen, raising an anxious face.

"Oh, that's no way off; it will get there to-night."

"Thank you, so very, very much."

"Good-bye, dear," said Marcia. "I don't seem to know you as well as the others."

"Good-bye. I'm ever so grateful," said Pen.

She wrung Marcia's hand.

"How nice she is. How kind she is—not a bit like the others," thought the child.

Marcia, as she dropped the letter into the post, glanced at the address. She smiled a little and then forgot all about it. Penelope went home in a far happier state of mind. Surely there was deliverance at hand. Jim, if he could not come back, and she did not expect him even for her sake, to leave such wonderfully grand people as the Holroyds, would at least write a long, explanatory letter to his father.

Chapter Eighteen

Seaside Anticipations

Meanwhile Nesta was very full of her own interests. Things were going in what might be considered a middling way at the Aldworths'. Mrs Aldworth was no worse, but she was not much better. She was suffering greatly from the heat, and yet she was not strong enough to be moved. Nurse Davenant still remained, and kept the invalid in comfort, and saw that she got the necessary food, and was not worried or neglected. Molly and Ethel were busy over their own concerns; they were forced to devote so much time, and Nesta was also required to be on duty for a certain time each day. The fright the girls had sustained when their mother was so seriously ill had not yet passed from their minds. Its memory still had power to move them. They were still alarmed when they thought of it.

But Nesta was less full of fear than her sisters, although her grief and terror had been greater at the time. Hers was the most elastic nature, perhaps in some ways the most unfaithful. She was now feverishly anxious to get away to Scarborough. She had ventured, on the morning after she had received her beloved yellow-boy, to sound Ethel on the subject of that visit.

"Do you think they'd let me go?" she said.

"Who are 'they'?" asked Ethel.

"Oh, you know—father, and Marcia—old Marcia, and Horace."

"If you ask me for my opinion," said Ethel, "I should once and for all advise you to put it right out of your head. You haven't the most remote chance of going away. You are required at home."

"I'm not much use, am I?"

"Frankly, you are not. You spilt mother's beef tea yesterday, and dropped the ink over that new fancy work which she takes so much pleasure in amusing herself with; and you screamed out and startled her frightfully when you were in the garden and thought you were stung by a wasp when you weren't. I don't see what particular use you are to anybody."

"Then, if that is the case," said Nesta, "why can't I go away and enjoy myself? I can't help being alive, you know. I must be somewhere in the world, and if I'm such a bother here, why shouldn't I go off with old Floss and have a good time? Floss doesn't think me a worry. Floss and I could have a good time."

"By what possible right ought you to have a good time? There's Molly, the eldest of us, and there's me, and what chance have we of going into the country or to the seaside, or having any fun? There's nobody at all in this hateful Newcastle, or in its suburbs, in the summer. There's nothing but the horrible coal-dust in the air, and the whole place is choking at times."

"But really not out where we live," said Nesta, who must be honest at any cost.

"Well, anyhow, we're not in the most charming part of the country, and that you know quite well. But if you ask me, I should say that you had best give up the idea of going. You can do as you please, of course."

"Yes, I can do what I please; but I can't see, even if mother is ill, why four girls should be kept to wait on her."

"There won't be four. Marcia is going to the St. Justs' next week. She's going away for a whole month. The doctor has ordered it. He says she isn't well."

"Just because she looks pale. You know that she is quite well; she is the strongest of us all."

"I don't know anything about that—she is going; that's all. She has the doctor's orders and it is arranged."

"And it's because of her I have to stay at home?"

"Don't keep me any longer now, Nesta. Put it out of your head, once and for all."

Ethel marched out of the room; but Nesta had no idea of putting the tempting subject out of her head. She went upstairs to her own room. She counted over the shillings left of her darling yellow-boy. She had eighteen shillings and sixpence. Nesta was careful with regard to money and had not indulged Flossie beyond eighteen-pence worth of good things at Simpson's shop. With eighteen and sixpence, what could she not do? What pleasures could she not enjoy? Oh, she must go. She slipped her little purse under a pile of handkerchiefs on one of her drawers, tidied herself as well as she could, and went into her mother's room. How hot and dull it all was. Her mother's face looked more fagged and tired than usual; but the girl, full of her own thoughts, had none for her mother.

"Mothery," she said suddenly, "when do you think you'll be well enough to go to the seaside?"

"Oh, I should love it," said poor Mrs Aldworth, and she stretched out her arms wearily. "I am so hot and so tired; I'm sure if once I could get there, it would do me a world of good."

"If you do everything the doctor says, and keep on taking your tonics, you will be able to go in a fortnight's time, or so," said Nurse Davenant. "Now, here is a delicious blancmange, you must eat it, and you must take this cream with it. Come, now, dear, eat it up."

"It does look good," said Mrs Aldworth; "but I get so tired of these sort of things, and I am so hot—so hot!"

This was her constant complaint. "Anybody would be hot," said Nesta, "who stayed in this stifling room."

She went out and stood on the balcony. From there she saw, to her intense annoyance, Flossie and Penelope coming up the path towards the house, side by side. She wished she dared ask leave to go down; her face turned scarlet, and her heart beat quickly. What was to be done? She would have given anything at that moment to see Flossie. Of course, Flossie had come to arrange about the visit to Scarborough, and there was so little time to spare.

Mrs Aldworth's weak voice called her.

"Dear, little girl, come in and sit on this stool at mother's feet, and tell me something funny."

"I'll tell you a fairy story," said Nesta, sitting down. "It is all about a poor fairy princess, who was all covered with coal-dust and grime, and she wanted to bathe in the cool sea, and she couldn't because—because—"

"Why?" said Mrs Aldworth.

"Because there was a horrid dragon—rather, a dragoness, who took all the pleasures for herself, and left the poor little fairy princess to pine, and pine—"

"That doesn't sound at all a nice story," said Nurse Davenant. "There's no sense in it either," she said, as she saw Mrs Aldworth's mouth quiver. "Now, get your book and read something. Here's 'John Halifax.' Go on with that."

Nesta was forced to comply. Mrs Aldworth had been interested in the beautiful story when read aloud by Marcia, but Nesta's rendering of it was not agreeable. "You gabble so, dear," she said, "and you drop your words so that I cannot always catch your meaning. What was that about Ursula?"

"Oh, mother, it's so hot, and I can't read. I expect, mothery, I'm the fairy princess, the poor begrimed little princess."

"You?" said Mrs Aldworth.

"Yes, mothery."

"Then who is the dragon?"

"Old Marcia," said the child.

She had scarcely uttered the words before Marcia herself came in.

"Marcia," said Mrs Aldworth, her blue eyes brightening for a minute, "this naughty Nesta says you are a dragon, and she is a begrimed fairy princess."

"I don't understand," said Marcia. She looked at Nesta, giving her a long glance, under which the girl had the grace to colour.

Chapter Nineteen

Nesta's Cunning Scheme

Marcia never gave herself away. Nesta sincerely longed that she would, but there was not the most remote chance. She seemed, when dinner time came, to have quite forgotten Nesta's spiteful speech. As a matter of fact she had forgotten it. She was sorry for the child. She was sorry for all her sisters; but still she was firmly convinced in her own mind that they ought to look after their mother.

Nesta, however, had no special duties that afternoon, and Marcia repeated Flossie's message that they were to meet in the middle of the wood.

"Don't be too long away," she said, "but if you greatly wish to go to have tea with the Griffiths, why you may. I understood from Flossie that they were going to the seaside on Saturday."

"Thank you, Marcia," said Nesta.

She ran out of the room. Dress was indeed a matter of total indifference to her. Once again, she flew down the path, entered the wood, and in a very short time she and Flossie were embracing each other. Flossie was smartly dressed.

"You are just as untidy as ever," she said. "But never mind. What about the day after to-morrow? Are you prepared to come with us?"

"I'm prepared," said Nesta, "but they're not."

"Who are 'they'?"

"Oh, you know—all of them. I spoke to Ethel this morning, and she said I hadn't a chance."

"But it does seem cruel—you can't be cooped up in this hot place when everybody else is away enjoying themselves. You really must come with us— besides, I want you."

"I want to go most awfully," said Nesta. "I've got my eighteen and sixpence, and we could have no end of fun."

"Mother gave me five shillings this morning," said Flossie. "That, with your eighteen and sixpence, would make twenty-three and sixpence—one pound, three shillings and sixpence. Think of it."

"But it wouldn't be that way at all," said Nesta. "My eighteen and sixpence would be in my pocket, and your five shillings would stay in your pocket. I'd treat you when I pleased, and you'd treat me when you pleased. Do you understand?"

"Oh, yes," said Flossie, "of course." She really bore a great deal from Nesta, who could be quite unpleasant when she liked. "But the thing is how to get you to the seaside. Do you think it would be any use for father to go over and see your father, and tell him what a splendid chance it would be for you?"

"No," replied Nesta, "there's only one way for me to go—I must run away. I must meet you at the station, and when I get to Scarborough, I don't suppose they'll bother about getting me back, and I can spend sixpence on a telegram and tell them where I am. I wouldn't sent it till pretty late in the day, and then they couldn't get me back for a day or two. That would be the best thing—it's the only thing to do."

Flossie sat down under a wide-spreading oak tree and considered Nesta's proposal.

"That would be right enough," she said, "as far as I am concerned, but you have to think of father. He wouldn't take you for all the world if he knew you were coming in that sort of fashion."

"Wouldn't he, Flossie? Why not?"

"Because—although I dare say you think my father common enough—I have often seen that you do—he is very strict in his ideas, and he wouldn't think it right for you to come. If you manage your running away, you must let father think you have got leave."

"Well, can't you help me, Flossie? You are so clever in inventing things. Even if I could have two whole days at the seaside I'd come back better, and really and truly mother is quite convalescent, and there are Molly and Ethel, and they have Nurse Davenant—they could manage her for the time being. Can't you help me, Flossie?"

"I'll think," said Flossie. She remembered those stories which she loved—those stories of naughty heroines and princes and princesses, when the princes always rescued the princesses, when the naughty heroines were brought to see the error of their ways, although they had a dreadful time at first following their own devices. Flossie quite longed to have a sort of affair going on in which Nesta should be on tenter-hooks, and very much obliged to her for all that she was doing for her, and in consequence inclined to spend her money for Flossie's delectation.

"Well," she said, after a pause, "if I can manage it I will. I'll just get father to understand, without telling too big a tarradiddle, you perceive, that it is all right, and that you are coming. Then you must be at the station, and you must bring a box with you. You must on no account come without luggage, or he'd be up in arms at once."

"What train are you going by?" asked Nesta, whose cheeks were very bright.

"We're leaving Newcastle by the 12:15. There'll be a crowd of people, because so many go away from Saturday to Monday, and just now it is holiday time, and the crowd will be worse than ever. We are going third-class, of course; you won't mind that, will you?"

"Not a bit."

"Well, father will have taken four tickets—one for himself, one for mother, one for me and one for you, and all you have to do is to hide yourself as much as possible behind me. But what about your box? Whatever will you do about getting it there?"

"I could come with quite a small box. Could not you put some of my things in with yours? I could get them to you to-morrow evening. I know I could."

"That's a good idea; I'll ask mother to give me a larger trunk than I really want for myself, and I'll put your best things on the top. I'll tell mother that you haven't a great lot of trunks at home, and that I am helping you by packing some of your things. That will do; only be sure you don't come in too shabby a frock, Nesta. We must be at least a little smart at Scarborough. Mother is making me a blue gingham frock, and a red gingham, and a bright blue voille for Sunday. I wonder how many nice dresses you have?"

"I don't care—I've got something, and I'll rummage the other girls' drawers for ribbons and a pair of gloves. I'll manage somehow. I can take just a little box, that can be easily managed."

"You had best be going back now," said Flossie.

"Oh, I can go home with you to tea, Marcia said I could if you liked."

"Well, that's all right—I'm very glad, because if you meet father you can tell your own tarradiddle. I'd much rather keep my own conscience clear. I have never told a downright absolute lie in my life."

"Very well," said Nesta. She wondered what was the matter with her; why she cared less and less to be good, and why she felt so reckless and indifferent to all that most girls would have considered sacred. She was puzzled about herself, and yet at the same time she did not care.

She went back with Flossie to the home of the latter and enjoyed the excellent meal, and when, in the course of it, Mr Griffiths appeared, she ran up to him and clapped her hands.

"I'm going, it's all right," she said. "Isn't it prime!"

"I'm as pleased as anything," he said, his honest face beaming all over. "So your father don't mind. I thought perhaps Aldworth would be too proud—I mistook him, didn't I?"

"Father?" said Nesta; "oh, father's all right, and I'm going; it's splendid. And what do you think?" she added. "Flossie is going to take some of my things in her trunk. You don't mind that, do you, Mrs Griffiths?"

"For goodness' sake," cried Mr Griffiths, "don't bring too much finery, girls, too much toggery and all that sort of thing. The place will be chock full, and we haven't taken expensive rooms. Mother and me, we didn't see the sense of it. You are heartily welcome to come with us, Nesta, and if we can give you a good time—why, we will. It'll be about a week or ten days you'll be staying, won't it?"

"Yes, that will be nice," said Nesta.

"And you don't mind, dear, sharing the same room with Flossie," said Mrs Griffiths.

"I don't mind a bit," said Nesta.

"Of course, she doesn't, wife. We always pack up like herrings in a barrel at the seaside, don't we?"

"That's true enough," said Mrs Griffiths, "and I must own sometimes I find it a bit stuffy—that is, when I'm indoors."

"But you don't when you're on the seashore, wife, when you're looking at the merry-go-rounds and listening to the bands, and watching the niggers dancing, and seeing the Punch and Judy shows."

Mrs Griffiths smiled and her face relaxed.

"We'll wade and we'll bathe and we'll go out in boats, and we'll have no end of fun!" said Flossie. "Oh, it will be prime."

She and Nesta wandered away by themselves when the meal came to an end.

"I didn't even tell him a lie. Didn't I manage splendidly?" said Nesta.

Flossie replied that she did.

"Now, I must really be going home. I'll have to be as good as gold; butter won't melt in my mouth between now and Saturday," said Nesta.

She flew home. In the garden she met Molly and Ethel, who were walking up and down, having a rather dull time, poor girls, and were anything but contented. When they saw Nesta they pounced upon her.

"Now, Nesta, it's all arranged. Marcia has been planning everything. She goes to the St. Justs on Saturday."

"On Saturday?" said Nesta, starting and colouring very deeply.

"Yes, I thought you knew."

"I knew she was going, but I didn't know the day. You needn't look at me as though you wanted to eat me."

"You're so horribly disagreeable, Nesta, ever since you got that bedroom to yourself," said Ethel. "I hope you've put out of your mind, once and for ever, that selfish plan of yours of going away to the seaside with Flossie Griffiths."

"Am I likely to think much more about it after the way you snubbed me this morning?" replied Nesta.

"Well, that's all the better, for you will be kept very much occupied. Marcia is a martinet, I will say. Mule Selfish is no word for her. The way she has planned everything—all our time taken up—Molly is to house-keep, and I am to look after the house linen, and Nurse Davenant is to superintend every scrap that mother eats, and mother is to have all her time planned so that she is to be as cheerful as possible, and Marcia will come to see her once a week, and if there is any change for the worse, Marcia will come right back, and won't we have a time of it, if that happens?"

"I do think," said Nesta, "that if we ever made a mistake in our lives, it was that time when we begged and implored father and Horace to bring Marcia back."

"Well, there's more to come. Father and Horace are also going away on Saturday."

Nesta's face very perceptibly brightened. If Marcia was away, as well as her father, and also her brother, why, there would be nobody to make much fuss about her having absented herself. When she was at Scarborough, she would be allowed to stay there, for there would be no one to force her back. How delightful.

"I'm glad they're going to have a holiday," she said. "I really am; and they're going on Saturday?"

"Yes, by the 12:15 train. They're going through Scarborough right on to—why, how pale you are."

"It's so horribly hot," said Nesta, sinking into a chair.

"Well, that's about it; they're going by the 12:15 train, but they're not going to stop at Scarborough, they're going to a little place about twenty miles further on. They're going to have a lot of fishing and yachting. Father says that he doesn't want to be too far away from mother in her present state, and, of course, Horace loves his fishing. There, Nesta, you do look white. Hadn't you better go into the house?"

"No, I'm all right; don't bother me," said Nesta.

Chapter Twenty

The Missing Sovereign

It was Saturday morning; the Carters were going to Whitby, the Griffiths to Scarborough, Mr Aldworth and his son to a place called Anchorville, on the coast, a remote little fishing hamlet, far away from railways, or any direct communication. Nevertheless a telegram could bring Mr Aldworth back to his wife if necessity arose, within six or seven hours.

The whole place seemed to be redolent of paper and string and trunks and labels and all the rest of it, thought Penelope Carter. Penelope was watching eagerly for the post, and that letter from Jim, which never came. She was really working herself into a fever, and when Saturday arrived and the sun shone brilliantly, and the whole world—or at least, all their world—was full of confusion, she could scarcely eat her breakfast. At each sound she started, and Clara came to the conclusion that the child was not well. In reality, Pen, having given up all hope of Jim's coming to the rescue, was struggling to make up her mind. If, by any chance, her father did not miss the sovereign, she would not tell, but if he missed it, and if he began to suspect any one of having stolen it; why, tell him she must.

She ran up to Jim's room; shut the door and fell on her knees by Jim's bedside.

"Give me strength," she murmured. "Give me strength. I am awfully frightened. Please, God, give me strength. I won't let any one else be suspected."

Just then Clara's voice was heard calling her.

"Come along, Pen, what are you hiding for? And in Jim's room of all places! We want every hand that we can get; we'll never be in time for the train."

"Where's father?" said Pen wildly.

"How do I know where father is? Pen, you must be mad. What do you want with father of all people?"

"Oh, nothing, nothing?" said Pen. "Nothing at all." She felt frightened at Clara's manner.

"Now, do bustle up," continued Clara. "Look here, we want a lot of peaches to eat by the way. There are some peaches in the hothouse at the end of the garden, you can pick some of those; never mind how cross old Archer is. Tell him that I want them. He won't dare to keep anything back from me."

Pen started on her errand. She was glad to be out, but when she reached the place where the peaches were, she stood for a long time in contemplation. Then she suddenly roused herself.

"I haven't a bit of strength; I don't know how I can do it," she thought.

She went in and picked some peaches, without giving much thought to the fact that they were not ripe, and she was presently aware that old Archer was standing over her. Archer was rather a terrible personage; he began to scold Pen. How dare she take his peaches? and she had not taken the ripe ones. Here were ten lovely peaches absolutely destroyed, good for nothing.

"You can't have 'em," he said. "I'll lay 'em in the sun. Maybe they'll ripen. It's a sinful shame to have a tree with its fruit torn off in this fashion. Why, Miss Pen, haven't you got any sense at all? Don't you know by this time when a peach is ripe and when it isn't? Miss Clara'll be in a fine tantrum when she sees these sort of things. Here, give me yer basket, you stand by me, and I'll select 'em."

Pen did not seem to care. Archer made a careful choice. He picked seven or eight peaches, then chose some nectarines, then some apricots, and then some grapes; the basket was packed, and he was proud of its appearance when he handed it to Pen.

She went back to the house. Clara was in the hall, her face was scarlet.

"What a time you've been," she said. "I do declare you've been away three-quarters of an hour. But oh, that fruit does look good. Put it there in the hall; I'll tell James to cover it over. Pen, what do you think has happened?"

"What?" asked Pen faintly.

"Why, father went to his room, as usual, to get his purse to pay the men, and he found a sovereign short. He's in a thundering rage. Who in the world can have taken it? He has made up his mind that it is Betty, that new under-housemaid. She's not been with us a month yet. He says he'll dismiss her; nothing will induce him to keep her unless she confesses."

"Has he—has he—accused her?" asked Pen.

"Of course, he has; he went to her and spoke to her, and she's crying fit to break her heart, but I suppose all the same she has done it. There, there, Pen, it's no affair of yours. Father would be fit to kill anybody who did such a mean thing. Fancy going to his room and taking a sovereign out of his drawer."

"He—he wouldn't be likely to forgive very easily?" said Pen.

"Forgive! I wouldn't like to be in Betty's shoes." Penelope went slowly upstairs.

"Now do hurry; the carriage will be at the door in twenty minutes. And, Pen, do change your dress. We may meet smart people going to Whitby, we may indeed."

Pen turned an angle in the staircase. She walked more and more slowly. Clara's words kept echoing in her brain. "Father would half kill anybody who had done this. She wouldn't like to be in Betty's shoes." Pen went straight into Jim's room. When she had shut the door, she said aloud:

"You might have helped me out of this awful mess; oh, you might, I wrote you such a distracted letter. Oh, I can't see Betty. I can't, I can't! Oh, what am I to do? Well, I won't go to Whitby, on that point I have quite made up my mind."

Before her resolution could falter she ran downstairs again.

"My dear Pen, not ready yet?" said Mabel, who was now in the hall.

"No, I'm not, and what is more, I'm not going."

"Not going, Penelope? Not going?"

"No, I'm not well, and I'm not going."

"You do look hot, we all noticed it this morning; but you are not so bad as all that."

"Yes, I am, but you needn't stay, I can get nursey to look after me. I will go when I am better; anyhow, I am not going to-day, so there."

Mabel rushed at her sister, and felt her brow, and took her hot hand.

"I don't believe you are so bad you can't go. I wonder where father is? Oh, here you are, Clara. What do you think this tiresome Pen has gone and done?"

"What now?" said Clara. "Does she want father? He is at Newcastle. He won't be back until late this evening. He bade us all good-bye. He asked for Pen, but as she was not about he sent his love to her."

"I don't want to go," said Pen, "that's all. I'm going to stay behind. I'm—I'm not well."

"But what ails you? A headache?"

"Splitting," said Pen.

"Pain in your back?"

"A bit."

"Sore throat?"

"A bit."

"Good gracious! What else have you got a bit of?"

"I don't know—a bit of everything. Anyhow, I'm not going."

"Hadn't we better take her temperature?" said Clay. "It seems frightfully wrong to leave her."

"No, no, I won't put that horrid little thing into my mouth," said Pen. "I'll stay with nursey. Nursey shall look after me. You can all go, and if nursey wants to send for the doctor she can. But I'm not bad enough for that, only I can't stand the train. Do let me stay, please, please. If you don't, you'll have to take me by force, for I'll scream and shriek all the way."

The waggonette appeared at the door. The coachman bent down.

"Young ladies," he said, "it's about time to go."

"Our luggage has gone," said Clara, "and yours too, Pen."

"Perhaps I'll come to-morrow," said Pen. "I can't—I can't go now."

"We'll have to leave her," said Clara. "I'll just run up and tell old Richardson to look after her."

Clara rushed upstairs, and found Nurse Richardson, who told her there was not the slightest occasion for any of them to stay with Pen, for she could nurse her and fifty more like her, if it were necessary. Clara, therefore, returned to the hall.

"Where is the child?" she asked.

"I don't know," said Mabel. "Isn't the here!"

"You'll miss your train, Miss," said the coachman. "So we will. Clara, do get in!" called out Mabel. "Here you are, Annie, we are both waiting for you." Clara jumped into the waggonette; the door was slammed to, the delicious fruit lay in a basket on the seat, and the horses started forward. They went down the avenue at a spanking pace. Pen was watching them from behind the house. She gave one glad cry, a cry almost of ecstasy, and then she burst into tears.

"Oh, I'm glad and yet I'm sorry," she said. "Both glad and sorry! both glad and sorry!"

Mrs Richardson called and called in vain for Pen; there was no sign of her darling young lady. What in the world had become of her?

But Pen was determined to stay out. She had got to make up her mind. There was just a vague hope within her that perhaps Jim might yet return. Perhaps he was coming back in person; he was answering her letter in that best of all ways. Still, it was scarcely likely, for he must know that by Saturday morning his father would have discovered the missing sovereign. There was Betty, too. Pen had scarcely given Betty a thought. She was a very common, rather untidy little girl. She had never in the least attracted Pen; but she hardly thought of any one else that day. And yet, after a fashion, she quite envied Betty, for Betty at least was innocent.

"She hasn't my guilty conscience," thought Pen. "Oh dear, oh dear, what is to become of me?"

By-and-by Pen heard the sound of crying. It came nearer and nearer. A girl with her apron over her head was coming down the shady path where Pen herself was sitting. Pen started to her feet. That was Betty; she could not meet Betty, she would not see her for all the world.

But Betty had caught sight of Pen. She ran up to her, removed her apron, and said:

"Oh, Miss Pen, couldn't you save me? Won't you speak for me to Mr Carter? I ain't done it, Miss. I ain't done it. I wouldn't touch what don't belong to me. He says I'm the only one that could ha' done it, and if I don't confess I'm to go, but if I confess he'll forgive me. But I ain't done it, and I'll have to go, and he won't give me a character, and mother—mother, she'll never forgive me. She'll believe as I done it."

"But—but—" said Pen, bringing out her words with difficulty, "didn't you take it?"

"Oh, no, Miss Pen. Oh, that you should think that! All my people are as honest as honest can be. I never took it, I never knew anything about that purse, and I never, never opened a drawer in my master's room, not since I came to the house. But there, I see you don't believe me."

Betty did not waste any more time with Pen. She walked on, her sobs grew louder, and then fainter; she was perfectly distracted, she did not know what to do with herself.

Chapter Twenty One

Nurse Comforter

When Betty had left her, Pen sat very still in the hammock where she had perched herself. Once or twice she swung herself backwards and forwards, but most times she sat motionless. She had come to the first real grave problem in her young life. She had always been a careless, never-may-care, somewhat untidy, reckless little girl. She had had no special training. Being the youngest she had been petted now and then, and scolded now and then; fussed over occasionally, bullied occasionally; allowed to grow up in any sort of fashion. She had had some sort of teachers, but they had never had much influence over her. Nurse Richardson thought more of her than of all the other girls, for was she not her darling, her baby? Her father, too, was fond of pinching her rosy cheeks, and calling her his little dear, or his little pet, just as fancy took him. Her elder sisters made her their messenger, and partly their slave. She did not mind; she was contented. She had a few friends, but not any very special ones. When Nesta and her sisters had come to stay at Court Prospect during their great trouble, Pen had at first taken warmly to Nesta; but she was tired of her now. She had never liked Flossie Griffiths, and Flossie was really Nesta's friend.

As to the affair of the sovereign, Pen had made a bet without giving it a serious consideration. She had never for one moment supposed that Nesta considered it a serious affair. Then Pen had begun to long to be grown up like her sisters, to wear dresses which would cover her somewhat ungainly feet, to walk about with boys, and to receive compliments from them; never to do any tiresome French or German, or any unpleasant practising on the school-room piano, or any grammar, or any English history, or any of those things which she called school work, and hated accordingly. She wanted these things to cease, and she hoped to have a right good time when Clay and Mabel and Annie were getting passée. She considered that Clay would be quite passée when she was one and twenty, and by that time surely Pen, who would be about seventeen, would be in her first charming bloom.

By this it will be seen that Pen was quite an ordinary little girl, but she was a girl with a conscience. She had inherited a sturdy sense of honour from her father, who was a good business man, and Pen, had circumstances been different, might have been a good business woman. He had won his present enviable position by the strongest code of honour; he had piled up his gold without injuring any man. To be honest—honest at any cost—was his motto, and he had instilled these ideas into his sons, and had talked about them in the presence of his daughters. The elder girls had never listened, but Pen had. Her conscience now was stirred to its depths. Nothing but fear would have kept her from confessing the truth. She struggled hard with herself for some time.

It was the middle of the day, however, and Nurse Richardson, after many fruitless searches, found Pen just at the time when luncheon was to be served. She pounced upon the little girl, and took her hand somewhat roughly.

"There now," she said, "a nice state of things you have been and gone and done. I've been the whole morning searching for you. Why, Miss Clara said you were that feverish and sore-throaty and head-achy as never was. Why, what has come to you, Miss Pen? What's wrong?"

Pen sprang from the hammock, ran up to old Richardson, and embraced her.

"I'm not a bit head-achy, nor a bit sore-throaty, nor a bit of anything, but just that I didn't want to go," she said.

"And you made up all that story?"

"I'd rather stay with you, nursey," said Pen, rubbing her cheek against the old woman's.

Nurse was by no means a strict moralist; she was soothed by Pen's attitude.

"Then you will come right in and have a beautiful little bit of dinner," she said. "Roast duck and green peas, and afterwards a plum tart, and cream and peaches."

Pen was, notwithstanding her perturbation of mind, somewhat hungry.

"And you'll have it up in the old nursery with me," said Richardson.

"All right, nursey, if you'll eat your dinner with me."

"If you don't mind, my pretty."

"Mind?" said Pen. "I'd love it."

For the time she was in quite good spirits. She went into the house with the old nurse. They visited the nursery, and the dinner in question was soon brought on the board, and the two ate with hearty good appetite.

"I'm that relieved that you ain't a bit sore-throaty nor head-achy," said the nurse.

"No. I'm as right as possible," said Pen, "as well as possible," she repeated. "It isn't that."

"You'll go to-morrow? Miss Clara was in a state."

"I don't know—I don't know when I'll go."

Having satisfied her appetite her nervous fears began again.

"I want to go back to the garden—I want to be alone," she said.

But as she was leaving the room she turned.

"Where's Betty?" she said.

"Betty, the bad little thing! To think of her doing it," said nurse.

"Oh, nursey, do you think she did it?"

"You have heard, then, my pet?"

"Yes, I have heard."

"Of course, she done it," said the nurse. "Who else would? All of us old trusted servants, and she just fresh in the place. But I've heard before now that the Wren family are just about—well, to say the least of it, not all they might be. She'll have to go back to Mrs Wren."

"What sort of a woman is Mrs Wren?" asked Penelope.

"Oh, a decent body enough; but they do say the husband was a poacher. Well, he's dead, and Betty's the eldest of the family. She wouldn't have got in here if I hadn't spoke for her, and I'm ashamed of her, that I am."

"Nursey, I do wish you'd tell father that you know she hasn't done it, and beg and beseech of him not to send her away."

"I, tell the master that?" said nurse, holding up her hands. "Much good it would be. He'd say back to me—'Nurse, who has done it? Until I find out who has done it, I shall suspect Betty Wren and Betty Wren must go out of the house. If she confesses I may forgive her, but if she sticks to it that she hasn't done it, out she goes, and without a character.' That's the master all over, and I must say he's about right. A thief ought to be punished awfully severe."

Pen went and stood by the window.

"I believe I have a bit of a headache," she said, after a pause. "I'll just go down to the garden and sit there in the shade. What time is father coming back, nurse?"

"I suppose the usual time, about six. He'll be took up to see you, and he'll be pleased enough, I take it. You may as well stay with him now until next Saturday, when I understand he is going to join the young ladies."

Pen made no reply to this. When she got into the passage she gave a deep sigh. When would Jim be back? Why had he not answered her letter? She passed his room, the door was ajar, but she did not go in this time. Jim was faithless, he was no better than the others. Indeed, he was worse. He had promised to help her, and then had not done so.

She went into the garden and chose a shady seat under a tree, took up a book which she could not read, and then pressed her hand to her eyes.

Perhaps she had fallen asleep; at any rate she found herself sitting bolt upright, and gazing straight before her. A great trembling took possession of her, and just for a moment she did not know what had happened. But coming down the path to meet her, was some one who looked very like a vision—some one slender, marvellously graceful, and all in white; a white dress, a white hat, everything white. The hat was tilted back from a broad brow, and the dark hair under it was rendered darker by the shade of the hat, and the eyes were large and misty and very beautiful, and the face was pale. The girl, for Pen soon discovered that it was only a girl, and not an angel, hurried when she saw Pen, and went towards her with outstretched hand. Pen rose, confused and puzzled.

"Don't you know me? I have seen you before. I am Angela St. Just. May I sit down for a little?"

"Oh, please do," said Pen. How delighted Clay would be! How overpowered Mabel would be! Even Annie would be confused, and a little off her guard; but Pen was not confused, nor off her guard in the least. "Would you like the hammock?" she said, "or this seat? The hammock is most comfortable."

"I will take the seat," said the young lady.

She leant back and looked across the garden.

"That is our tennis lawn," said Pen, pointing in the distance. "It used to be the old garden, with the queer dragons and beasts and birds cut out of the box trees. Doesn't it make a beautiful tennis lawn? Wouldn't you like to see it? Clay is so proud of it."

"No, I shouldn't like to see it," said Angela very gently.

She turned those misty, unfathomable eyes of hers towards the little girl.

"Don't you understand," she said impulsively, and she laid her slender hand on Pen's arm, "that the old garden was more to me than the tennis lawn is to you?" Pen felt a vague, very vague sort of flutter at her heart. She did not know that she understood, but she felt puzzled and uneasy.

"Why have you come here to-day?" was her next question.

"I am waiting for my friend, Marcia Aldworth. I hope to take her back with me to-night—that is if Mrs Aldworth's mind is relieved."

"But what has happened?" said Pen. "Is Mrs Aldworth ill again?"

"Not exactly, but she is anxious. Perhaps you can tell us something. It is Nesta."

"What about Nesta?" asked Pen.

"She cannot be found. Since early this morning no one has seen her. They are searching for her everywhere, and are making inquiries, but no one knows anything about her. Mrs Aldworth hasn't been told exactly what has happened, but she particularly misses Nesta, and dear Marcia will not be able to come to me unless Nesta turns up. Do you know anything about her?"

"No," said Pen, a little wearily. She was not deeply interested in Nesta, nor particularly interested in Mrs Aldworth.

"I half hoped you might, or some of you. You were so kind to the Aldworths when they were in such trouble about their mother."

"No, I wasn't kind," said Pen abruptly, "I didn't like them."

Angela did not smile; she looked grave.

"Still, I don't know why you came here?" was Pen's next remark.

"Your sister wanted me to come; she invited me, and I thought I would come to see her. Is she at home?"

"I'm the only one at home. They have all gone to Whitby to have a spree. I didn't want to go."

"But why? You are the youngest, are you not?"

"Yes, I'm the youngest."

"Why didn't you want to go?"

Pen coloured. There was nothing at all inquisitive in the visitor's voice, but there was a note of sympathy in it as though in some indescribable, marvellous way she could guess that Pen was in trouble, and that Pen had something on her mind that was worrying her a good deal. Insensibly Pen drew a little nearer to the white-robed visitor.

"I say," she exclaimed, "shall I tell you what I thought you were when I saw you coming down the path?"

"What?" asked Angela.

"Well, perhaps I had been asleep, I can't quite tell, but I opened my eyes with a start, and there was an angel coming along; I really thought for a minute that you were an angel; and that is your name, isn't it?"

"Angela is my name."

"Now that I come to look at you more closely, Angela," said Pen, bringing out the word without the slightest hesitation, "I think you are very like an angel. Have you ever seen them?"

"I have never seen them, but I have often thought about them."

"I don't quite know why you are different from others," said Pen. "It's that far-away sort of look, and yet it isn't the far-away look—you are different, anyhow."

Angela laid her hand again on Pen's arm.

"Tell me your name," she said.

"Pen, Penelope."

"Penelope, what a grand old name. Have you got that wonderful perseverance that the real Penelope had? Will you be as faithful as she was?"

But Pen did not know the story of the real Penelope, nor did she ask. Angela's hand seemed to draw her in some marvellous way.

"Look at me," said Angela very gravely. "I must go in a few minutes. I wonder why I came to you instead of going straight to the front door. Your servant would have sent me away. But as I drew up my ponies at the front entrance, I saw a girl in the garden, and I thought I could bear this visit to the old place best if I came across the garden and spoke to the girl. And do you know, what is more, I hoped the girl would be you?"

"Did you?" said Pen, her black eyes dancing with a look of intense pleasure.

"I did, for you have such an honest face."

"No, no; if you knew you wouldn't say that. You wouldn't speak to me. Angels would have nothing to do with me; but I can't help it—oh, why did you come?"

"Tell me, dear; tell me."

Pen struggled and struggled. Give herself away to this girl, to Angela St. Just, whom all the neighbourhood worshipped from afar; tell this girl what she had done? She could not! But just as little as though Angela were a real angel could Pen withstand the matchless sympathy which Angela could throw into her voice, with which she could fill her eyes, with which she could wrap the sore heart of the puzzled little sufferer.

"It was Jim," said Pen at last in a stricken voice. "Jim—he's my brother; he's not a bit like others. Jim has thoughts, you know, thoughts, and he is splendid, and full of honour. He said he would help me out. He promised faithfully, but he went away, he went to a place called The Chase, to some people of the name of Holroyd. He went quite suddenly. I had a talk with him one evening, and I told him; and he said there was only one thing to do, and he'd put it right, and be with me when I did it. But he's away. Oh dear, oh dear!"

"Was the thing you had to do very difficult?"

"Awfully. But oh, Angela, you don't know."

It never occurred to Pen to call this fascinating visitor by any other name.

"I am sure I can partly guess; it is exceedingly difficult for any one to own himself or herself in the wrong, and we all do wrong at times. Your brother must be a very nice boy."

"Oh, he's grand, only I don't know why he forsook me."

"Tell me more. I think I must have been guided to go down the garden path and have a talk with you."

"But you will never speak to me again."

"Does that really matter, Penelope? The one thing for you to do is to put wrong right."

"I will tell you more," said Penelope suddenly.

"You won't always be in the house to stare at me as Clay would do, and as Mabel and Annie would do, thinking that perhaps I'd do it again, and always taunting me with it. Oh, no, you won't be there."

"Only in spirit, and my spirit will be very tender, and full of love to you."

"Love to me?" said Pen.

"Of course, Penelope. Can you doubt it?"

Penelope could not look in those eyes, which were full of matchless love, eyes such as she had never before encountered. She burst into a torrent of tears, struggled with her emotions, and finally laid her curly head with its wealth of red-gold hair on Miss St. Just's white dress. The slender hand touched the head once or twice, but Pen was allowed to cry until the pain in her heart was eased a little.

"It was this way," she said, and then she told her story.

"I spoke to Jim first, I was driven to it, and—and Nesta was so persistent. But I don't want to excuse myself."

"I wouldn't," said Angela, "for of course you have no excuse."

Her words were perfectly gentle, perfectly firm. Pen looked up at her.

"Ah," she said, "you and my conscience say the same thing."

"I hope so; your conscience is sure to tell you the right thing."

"Well, anyhow, I told Jim, and Jim agreed with me. He said there was only one thing to do. Only, you see, it was like this; he had promised to help me, and he didn't. He went away instead. I wrote to him, and he took no notice of my letter, no notice at all. I know he must have got it, and I couldn't speak, although I tried. Then Saturday came, and father has discovered all about the lost sovereign, and Clay said he was in a thundering rage, quite wild with rage. She said he was fit to kill any one who had done it, and he accuses Betty, our new under-housemaid, Betty Wren is her name, and of course, Betty is innocent. He says unless she confesses she will be sent away; that's quite awful. I don't know how I am to tell him; I can't imagine how I am to do it, for he'll half kill me, and I shall die, die, if Betty Wren is sent away. Oh, I am so frightened. I wish Jim were here. What shall I do?"

"You must do this," said Angela, "you must give your fears to God, he will take care of them, and of you. You must not think of what your father will do, you must simply think of what is right. The very moment he comes in you must go and tell him what you have told me, that in a moment of impulse you took the money, that afterwards you were afraid to tell him, that all the week you have been frightened, that this morning your fears kept you away from him, but that now you wish him to know the truth, and he—but never mind about him; he must know the truth."

"I can't, Angela, I can't. Oh, if only Jim were here!"

"Do you think I should do instead of Jim?"

"You?" exclaimed Penelope. "Oh, Angela! Angela!"

Chapter Twenty Two

Wrong Set Right

Mr Carter hurried home about six o'clock. He had spent a busy day in Newcastle, and had gone through a few worries. He took the worries of life hard. He was exacting on all nice points of honour, and one of his clerks had deceived him. His mind, therefore, was especially sore as he sank back in the luxurious carriage which was to convey him back to Court Prospect. Halfway back he also remembered the affair of the sovereign. The loss of the sovereign was a mere nothing, but the fact that one of his dependents could steal from a private purse kept in one of his drawers, meant a great deal.

"Of course, it's that girl," he thought. "She's as bad in her way as young Hanson is in his. I am sorry for them both, of course, but as I said to Hanson, if he had told me that he was in money difficulties, I would have helped him out; but instead of that he thought he'd help himself. Well, he has helped himself out of my service for ever; that's plain, that's only justice, and that girl, Betty Wren, if she doesn't confess, she'll go the same road; I vow it, and I'm a man who never yet broke my word."

But as he got nearer to the house, more pleasurable thoughts succeeded the dismal ones. There was Jim—his eldest son, his pride, his boy. He had had a business letter from Jim that morning which had not arrived at Court Prospect, but had been sent to his father's big offices in Newcastle, and in that letter it turned out that Jim had done splendidly. He had acted with tact and diplomacy, and would soon be back again.

"Won't I give him a good time for this?" thought the father. "He is a lad to be proud of. Hullo, though, who's that?"

He had turned into the avenue now; the horses were going under the beautiful beech trees at a spanking trot, and a girl was coming slowly to meet him.

"Why, if that isn't my own Pen," he said.

He was so amazed and startled that he pulled the check string, and the carriage stopped.

"Hullo, Pen!" he said. "What in the name of wonder are you doing here? What is the matter? Here, jump in, child."

Pen obeyed.

"I want you, father," she spoke in a tremulous voice—"I want you to come into the study the very minute you get home. I have something to say to you."

Mr Carter turned round and gazed at Pen in surprise.

"Have you been ill?" he asked. "Why didn't you go with the others to Whitby?"

"I'll tell you when we get in the study."

He looked at her again, and a frown came between his brows. He did not know why he was suddenly reminded of young Hanson and of Betty Wren, but he was. Oh, of course it was all nonsense, his little Pen—and yet she kept her face averted.

Presently they reached the house. Her father helped her out of the carriage.

"Now, come along, child," he said with a sort of gentle roughness. "I guess by your manner that you have got into a bit of a scrape. I cannot make out what it is, but you are right to come to the old father; the old father will help you, if he can. What on earth are you trembling for?"

"Oh, come at once to the study, father."

Pen pulled him along. He was tired, he had gone through a hard day; he wanted his customary cup of tea; he wanted to go into the garden and talk to Archer. He loved his garden, he enjoyed counting his peaches and gloating over his fruit trees, and considering how he could make more and more money out of the old place. He was terribly keen about money making. He was interested in money, it was a power, and he meant to have it whatever else he failed in.

But there was Pen, why had she not gone with the others to Whitby? Something ailed her; she was his youngest. He was fonder of Penelope than of any of his other children, except Jim. Jim, of course, was altogether on a different platform; there was no one like Jim in the world. It was worth struggling hard to make a fortune for a boy like Jim.

So he hurried as fast as Pen could wish, and presently she burst open the door of his study. There, standing by the window, was the white-robed vision which had so startled, so stirred, so moved Pen herself a few hours ago. The white vision came forward slowly, and Mr Carter looked with dazzled eyes at the girl he most wished to know, Angela St. Just. She was in his study, she was coming to meet him.

"I must introduce myself," she said. "You have, of course, met my father in business matters, Mr Carter, but I want to see you on quite a different subject."

"Miss St. Just," said the startled man.

"Yes, I am Angela St. Just, Penelope's friend."

Mr Carter turned and looked at Pen as though he suddenly loved her passionately.

"Penelope's friend; and I trust I may be able to help her through a rather difficult matter."

"Now, what in the name of fortune does this mean?" said Mr Carter. "You here, Miss St. Just, you here in your old home, when they said that neither you nor your father could abide to come near the place, and yet you are here! What does it mean? I don't understand."

"Penelope will explain," said Angela very gently. Then Penelope came forward. She made a valiant struggle, and after a minute or two some words came to her lips.

"Clay says that perhaps you will kill me. I don't think you can forgive me. Father, it was I who took that sovereign out of your purse—the purse you always put money in to pay the men's wages. I took it in the middle of the week, father."

Mr Carter had forgotten Angela by this time. What was this—what was the matter? He was so absorbed, so stunned by Pen's words that he could scarcely contain himself. He made one step forward, seized her hand, drew her to the light.

"What?" he said. "Say those words again."

"I took your sovereign."

"You—you, my child, stole my money!"

Angela now moved slowly across the room and put her hand on Pen's shoulder.

"She is very, very sorry," said Angela. "She feels heartbroken; she failed just in the one thing, she had not the courage to confess. But because you discovered the theft she would not go to Whitby to-day; she was determined to stay and brave it out."

"And she came," said Pen, "and she told me that I ought to tell you."

There was no word about Jim. Pen had determined that Jim was to be left out of the matter.

But just at that moment there was a noise in the hall, a hurried step, a cheerful tone, and Jim himself burst into the room.

"Oh, father! You here, Pen? Oh, my darling, I am ever so sorry! Father, I forgot all about it in the other excitement, but it's all right, it's all right. We're all right, everything is all right, and—and Pen told me. I said I would speak to you, but when you sent me away in such a hurry, I forgot, and Pen, I suppose she was frightened. Pen, can you forgive me?"

"Then you never got my letter?" said Pen. "I sent it to the Holroyds', I knew you were there."

Mr Carter looked troubled. He went up and took Jim's hand.

"I am ever so puzzled," he said. "I accused that girl, Betty Wren, and it seems—but tell me the whole story, Pen. I must hear it from beginning to end. Then I shall be able to decide."

So Pen told him the story. Angela stood very gravely by. She stood a little bit in the background, and the shadow of the great curtain partly concealed her face, but the light of evening fell across her white dress, so that her whole appearance was like that of a pitying angel, who was waiting for the moment when the sinner was to be forgiven. Mr Carter looked from one of his children to the other, then at Angela.

"You have pretty high ideas of honour," he said. "You know what this sort of thing means. Now, tell me what you would do if you were in my shoes."

"There is no doubt whatever about what you will do," said Angela.

"You think, don't you—I believe saints always do—that sin ought to be punished."

"We have the Divine Example," said Angela in a low tone.

Mr Carter looked at her.

"You said a strange thing a minute ago; you said you were Penelope's friend," he remarked.

"So I am, from this day forward, as long as we both live."

"You are in rare luck," said Carter, looking gloomily at Pen, "to have a friend like that." He walked to the other end of the room and began to stride up and down. He was hurt beyond anything he could have imagined. What was he to do? How was he to endure his own misery? It was bad enough to have a servant in the house who could be dishonest, bad enough to have a clerk who could steal, but here was his own child.

"Did I ever deny you anything?" he said.

"No, father."

"Couldn't you come to me and ask me for the money?"

"I was so terrified and afraid—oh, I have no excuse."

"That is it," said Angela. "She has no excuse whatever. It is not a case of excuse, it is a case of a girl having done wrong, and being bitterly sorry, and having confessed her fault. Now you come in, sir."

"I come in, pray?" he said.

He forgot that the speaker was Miss St. Just, she was just a girl addressing him. But there was wonderful power in her voice.

"Of course you come in. What would God do in such a case?"

Carter turned away.

"Oh, father, you will, you will forgive me."

"I come in, forsooth!" said the man. "I, who made a fool of myself this morning, and told that poor girl that she certainly had done it, but that if she confessed I would forgive her!"

"Then there is a similar case," said Angela. "Penelope has confessed, so you ought to forgive her."

"I don't know—I don't know," he said.

"Oh, father, mayn't I bring Betty down, and may I tell her that I was the real thief?"

"No good in that, child. No good in making it public."

"Of course, father, you'll have to forgive Pen," said Jim's sturdy young voice at that moment.

"If you wish it, Jim—if you wish it, of course there is nothing more to be said. What do you feel about it? You have metal in you; you're made of the right stuff. What do you feel about this matter?"

"I feel that I have never loved Pen more than I do at this moment. I never was so proud of her. She has grit in her, she is worth all the rest of us, to my way of thinking."

"No, that is not so; but if you wish it, Jim, and you, Miss St. Just."

"I do wish it," said Angela.

"Then I will say nothing more. Pen, I am disappointed; I am bitterly hurt, but I will say nothing more."

He took the child's hand, held it for a minute, looked into her face, and said:

"Why, I do believe you have suffered, you poor bit of a thing."

Then he abruptly kissed her on her forehead and left the room.

Chapter Twenty Three

Nesta Lost Again

The Aldworths were in a state of confusion. Mrs Aldworth was anxious; Nurse Davenant was keeping the worst from her, but nevertheless she was anxious. Molly and Ethel were so firmly desired on no account to give themselves away, that they were absolutely excluded from the room. They were loud in their denunciations of Nesta.

"Catch old Nesta getting herself into trouble," they said. "She has just gone off on one of her sprees."

That was their first idea, but when they went to the Griffiths' house, as the most likely place for the naughty Nesta to have taken herself to, and were greeted by the news that Mr, Mrs, and Miss Griffiths had started for Scarborough that morning, and that certainly no one else had gone with them, their ideas were somewhat shaken; they really did not know what to think. What was to be done? There was Mrs Aldworth wanting Nesta, and asking for her from time to time.

"Where is the child?" she said.

Now, Mrs Aldworth was herself, with her own delicate fingers, making a new blouse for Nesta. It was a very pretty one, of delicate pink silk, with embroidery trimming it all round the neck and round the pretty fancy sleeves. Mrs Aldworth wanted to try it on, and there was no Nesta to be found. The other girls were slighter than Nesta, who was a very buxom young woman for her years.

What was the matter? What was to be done? Still she was not seriously alarmed, for Marcia managed to keep her mind at rest. Nesta was out, she would be in soon.

But when lunch time came, and no Nesta appeared, Marcia sent a hurried line to Angela to tell her that she might, after all, not be able to go to Hurst Castle that day. She certainly would not leave the Aldworths while they were in anxiety.

Angela had replied that she was coming into Newcastle, and would go and pay the Carters a visit. She would wait for Marcia, and take her back.

It was late that evening when Angela did call for Marcia. She drew up her little pony carriage outside the door; she had driven all the way from Hurst Castle, but the ponies were fresh from their long rest in the old Court Prospect stables. Angela waited in the porch.

"I won't come in to-night," she said to Susan. "Just go up and say that Miss St. Just is waiting."

Marcia came down. Her face was very pale.

"Oh, my dear Angela," she said. "Whatever will you think of me? What is to be done? I have spent such a miserable day. We are all most anxious."

"What?" said Angela, "haven't you found the truant yet?"

"No; we have searched high and low, all over the place. We don't want to alarm people. We could, of course, send a telegram to father and Horace, but we don't want to do that."

"She is evidently a very naughty girl," said Angela.

"I am afraid she is; she is terribly self-willed," said Marcia with a sigh.

"I'm not a scrap uneasy about her," said Angela. "She is quite certain to have taken care of herself. But what frets me is that you are looking so white, dear. You want your holiday so badly."

"I can't really go with you to-night; I am ever so sorry, Angela, but it is quite impossible."

"Then let me stay and help you."

"Oh, I can't do that!" but Marcia's eyes expressed a longing.

"Now, why shouldn't I stay?" said Angela. "I have always longed to see Mrs Aldworth. You might bring me up to her, mightn't you?"

"I wonder if I dare?"

"Of course, you can, dear. Have I ever tired or frightened any one in the whole course of my life?"

"You have been so shamefully neglected, dear, and what will your father say?"

"I'll send him a wire telling him not to expect us to-night. Or, better still, I'll send the carriage home with a note. He'll get it just when he is expecting me, and he will be quite contented in his mind."

"Well, then, if you will, you can share my room."

"Certainly," said Angela lightly.

"You have been a long time at the Carters'," said Marcia.

"Yes, I have had a most interesting time."

"Your first visit to your old home."

"I hadn't much time to think of that, and I'm glad it is over. I shall go there very often. What nice young people the Carters are."

Marcia opened her eyes.

"The two I saw—Jim and Penelope."

"Penelope—yes, there is a good deal in that child."

"I am her friend; I will tell you presently something, but not all, about her. I am truly glad I went to-day. Now, if only I can help you."

"You can, you shall; I think God must have sent you."

Marcia and her friend entered the house. They went into the library, where Marcia ordered a meal for Angela, and then went upstairs. Molly and Ethel were ready to dart upon her in the passage.

"What a long time you've been. Mother is beginning to cry. She says that Nesta has deserted her shamefully. We daren't say that she is not in the house. I was thinking," continued Molly, "of making up a little story, and saying that she was in her bedroom with a headache; mother couldn't be very anxious about that, could she?"

"You mustn't make up any such story. It wouldn't be right."

"Marcia, you are so over particular. Of course, you are not going to Hurst Castle to-night."

"I am not."

"Is Miss St. Just very sorry?"

"She is rather; but by the way, Molly, you might help me; Miss St. Just is spending the night here."

"Good gracious!" said Ethel, drawing herself up. "Yes; won't you two go down and have a chat with her? I wish you would. She is going to see mother presently. I think she will do mother a lot of good. Anyhow, she is staying, and I must make up my mind what is to be done about Nesta. If there are no tidings of her within the next hour or so, I must send a telegram to father."

"We must make ourselves smart, first," said Ethel, turning to Molly.

"I suppose so," answered Molly.

They both went into their bedroom, the nice room which Marcia had prepared for them, and considered.

"My white dress," said Molly—"oh, but there's that horrid stain on it. I got it yesterday."

"Our pink muslins are quite fresh; we look very nice in pink, and two dressed alike have always a good effect," was Ethel's suggestion.

Accordingly the pink muslins were donned, the raffled but pretty hair was put into immaculate order, and the girls, their hearts beating a little, went downstairs to entertain their distinguished guest. Of course, she was distinguished. But she was going to stay in their house—she was to be with them for a whole long, beautiful night. How lovely! They could look at her and study her, and furtively copy her little ways, her little graciousnesses, her easy manners, her politeness, which never descended to familiarity, and yet put people immediately at their ease. And better still, they could talk to their friends about her and about what had occurred. When those upstart, disagreeable Carters came back, what a crow they would have over them.

They were both in good spirits and forgot Nesta. Nesta was nothing but a trouble-the-house. She would turn up when she pleased. She deserved a sound whipping, and an early putting to bed; that was what she deserved.

Molly entered the room first; Ethel followed behind. Susan had lit a lamp, and the drawing room looked fairly comfortable. Angela was standing by the open window. She turned when she saw the girls and came forward to meet them.

"We're so pleased and proud to know you," began Molly.

"You are Molly, of course—or are you Molly?" said Angela, glancing from one girl to the other.

"We're awfully alike, you know," laughed Molly, "aren't we, Ethel? Yes, I am Molly, and this is Ethel. We're not twins, but there's only about a year between us. We're very glad to know you. Have you heard much about us?"

"Of course I have, from Marcia, my greatest friend." Molly's eyes were fixed in fascinated wonder and open admiration on her distinguished guest. There was something intangible about Angela, something quite impossible to define; she was made for adoration; she was made for a sort of worship. Girls could never feel about her in the ordinary way. These girls certainly did not. They looked at one another, and then looked back again at Angela.

"Are you tired? Are you really going to stay the night here?" said Molly at last.

"I will sit down if you don't mind. No, I am not tired."

"But you look so pale."

"I am always pale; I never remember having a scrap of colour in my life."

"I think pale people look so interesting," said Ethel. "I wish Molly and I were pale; but we flush up so when we are excited. I know I shall have scarlet cheeks in a minute or two."

"That is because we are so glad to see you," said Molly.

"That is a very pretty compliment," laughed Angela. "But although I'm not tired, I shouldn't mind going up to Marcia's room just to wash my hands and take my hat off."

"We'll both take you," said Molly.

They were immensely flattered; they were highly pleased. Angela ran upstairs as though she were another girl Aldworth, and had known the place all her days. Marcia's room was immaculately neat, but it was shabbily furnished; it was one of the poorest rooms in the house. Molly earnestly wished that she could have introduced her guest into her own room.

"I wonder," she said suddenly, "where you are going to sleep to-night?"

"With Marcia; she said so."

"Oh, but her bed is so small, you would not be comfortable. We'd be ever so pleased if you—"

"But I prefer to sleep with Marcia, and this room is quite nice."

Molly ran to fetch hot water, and Ethel remembered that she had a silver brush and comb which she always kept for visits which seldom occurred. She rushed away to fetch it. Angela brushed her hair, washed her hands, said that she felt as though she had been living with the Aldworths for years, and ran downstairs again.

"How nice you are," said Molly; "we don't feel now as though we were afraid of you."

"Afraid of me," said Angela. "Why should you be that?"

"Only, somehow, you belong to a better set."

"Please, don't talk nonsense," said Angela, with the first note of wounded dignity in her voice. "I have come here to make myself useful. Can I be useful?"

"It is so delightful to have you—"

"That's not the point; can I be useful?"

Molly looked puzzled.

"We'll have supper presently," she said. "I'll go and speak to Susan. I'll be back in a minute."

She turned away. Of course, Angela could not be useful—the mere thought was profanation. She had come there to be waited on, to be worshipped, to be looked at, to be adored, Angela St. Just, the most beautiful, the most aristocratic girl in the entire neighbourhood!

Ethel drew nearer to Angela.

"I have been at Court Prospect to-day," said Angela.

"Why, that was your old place."

"It was."

"Did you find it much changed—bourgeois, and all that?" said Ethel.

"Nothing could really change the old place to me; but I would rather not talk of what the Carters have done."

"I am sure it must have given you profound agony," said Ethel.

Angela faintly coloured, and then she said:

"Tell me about your little sister, the one about whom you are so anxious."

"Oh, Nesta! Nesta's all right."

"Then she has come back?"

"No; she hasn't come back; we can't imagine where she is."

"Then how can you say she is all right?"

"She is always all right; she is the sort that turns up when you least expect her. She is not specially good," continued Ethel, who felt that she might revenge herself on Nesta's many slights by giving Angela as poor an opinion of her as possible. She did not want Angela to like Nesta better than her. She had dim ideas of possible visits for herself to Hurst Castle. Could she possibly manage the dress part? She was intensely anxious now to lead the conversation away from Nesta to more profitable themes.

"You must have a good many people staying at Hurst Castle," she said.

"My uncle has some guests, naturally. But tell me about your sister. When did she go?"

"I wish I could tell you. I don't know."

"You don't know? But surely you can guess!"

Molly came in at that moment. She had made a frantic effort to order a supper which would be proper to set before so distinguished a guest. A fowl had been hastily popped into the oven—that would be something. People in Angela's class, for all Molly knew to the contrary, lived on fowls.

"Molly, when did we see Nesta last?" asked Ethel.

"She was here at breakfast. I just saw her when she was rushing out of the room. I was rather late. Why do you ask?"

"Miss St. Just was anxious to know."

"We are all troubled about your sister," said Angela.

"Oh, I'm not troubled," said Molly.

"Nor I," said Ethel.

But Ethel was quick to read disapproval in Angela's soft eyes.

"I suppose we ought to be," she said abruptly. "Do you think there is any danger?"

She opened her eyes wide as she spoke.

"I hope not; but, of course, she ought to be found. Then there is your mother—the great thing is to keep your mother from fretting."

"We have managed that, for Marcia, old Marcia—I mean dear Marcia,—is so clever about mother."

"She is clever about everything. I wonder if you know what a very remarkable sister you have got." Marcia rose by leaps and bounds in both the girls' estimation. If she was remarkable, and if Angela, beautiful, bewitching Angela, said so, then indeed there must be something to be proud of, even in old Marcia. Ethel remembered how she had nicknamed her Miss Mule Selfish, and a nervous desire to giggle took possession of her, but she suppressed it.

"I wish I could tell you," said Angela, "all that Marcia has been to me; how she has helped me. And then she is such a wonderful teacher. My aunt, Mrs Silchester, never ceases to lament her having left the school at Frankfort, I understand that she came here to help you girls."

"Oh, no; she didn't," said Molly, her face becoming crimson, "she came home to look after mother."

"You mean to help you to look after her, isn't that so?"

"Yes, of course. Oh, dear Miss St. Just, aren't you very tired? I know you are, even though you say in that pretty way that you are always pale, I know you are weary."

"I'm all right, thank you; I really am."

Just then Marcia entered the room.

"Angela," she said, "we shall have supper presently, and afterwards you shall come up and see mother."

"Oh, Marcia, do you think it well?" said Ethel, who looked very pretty with her flushed cheeks and bright eyes.

"I should like to go," said Angela. "Do you think I should harm her?"

No; it would be impossible for such a creature as Angela to harm any one, even if that person were seriously ill; there was repose all over her, sweetness, tenderness, sympathy, where sympathy was possible. But Ethel and Molly, notwithstanding their efforts, did not feel that Angela truly sympathised with them. The moment Marcia came in they began to see this more clearly.

"What are you doing about Nesta?" she said immediately.

"If we don't know by nine o'clock, I must wire to father."

It was just at that moment that there came a ring at the front door, a sharp ring. Ethel felt her heart beating; Molly also turned first red and then pale.

"That sounds like a telegram," said Molly, and she rushed into the hall.

It was; it was addressed to Marcia Aldworth. She tore it open and read the contents.

"I'm all right; expect me when you see me. Nesta."

There was no address; but it was plain that the telegram had been sent from Scarborough. Marcia sank on to the sofa. Molly bent over her; Ethel peered at the telegram from the other side.

"There, didn't I say she was about the—"

"Please, Angela, will you come with me into the next room?" said Marcia.

She left the telegram for her two sisters to devour between them, and took Angela away. The moment they were alone, Marcia sank down on a chair; tears rose to her eyes—she did not know that they were there—one overflowed and rolled down her cheek. Angela looked at her steadily.

"It is quite hopeless," she said. "Think of her doing that!"

"Doing what? Remember I have not seen the telegram."

"She says she is all right, and we are to expect her when we see her. She has gone to Scarborough; she has run away. She is with the Griffiths, of course. What is to be done with a girl of that sort?"

"Marcia, you are wearing yourself out for them."

"I am, and it is hopeless. What am I to say to mother? How am I to put it to her?"

"You must tell her that Nesta will not be back until the morning; that she is quite safe. In the morning you must tell her the truth."

"How can I possibly tell her the truth?"

"You must."

"Oh, Angela! it is hopeless; those girls seem to have no hearts. I did think after mother was so ill that they had turned over a new leaf; I was full of hope, and Nesta seemed the most impressed; but see what this means. She has gone away; she has left us all in misery. What a day we have had! and now, at the eleventh hour, when she thought we could not possibly send for her, she sends this. What am I to do?"

"You must just go on hoping and praying, and trusting and believing," said Angela. "My dear Marcia, twenty things ought not to shake a faith like yours."

"Well, at any rate, she is not in bodily danger; but what a terrible revelation of her character! She must have planned all this. She knew that father was away, and that Horace was away, and she fully expected that I should also be away. She had a kind of vague hope that the girls would not open the telegram. You see how she has laid her plans. She knows in the end she must be recalled, but she is determined to have as much pleasure as she can."

"Marcia," said Molly, putting in her head at that moment, "supper is ready. Shall we go in?"

They went into the dining-room. Angela ate little; she did not perceive the efforts the two younger Aldworths had made in her honour; the presence of the best dinner service, the best glass, the fact that the coffee—real Mocha coffee—was served in real Sèvres china. She ate little, thinking all the time of Marcia, who was as unobservant of external things as her friend.

"Now, you will come up to see mother," said Marcia, when the meal was over.

"Yes; let me. I will tell her about Nesta—I mean as much as she need know to-night."

Marcia took her friend upstairs. Mrs Aldworth was tired. Her day had not been satisfactory, and she still wanted that one thing which she could not get—the presence of her round, fair, apparently good-natured youngest daughter. When Marcia opened the door, she called out to her:

"Dear me, Marcia! I thought you were going?"

"No, mother; I am not going to-night."

"Has Nesta come back? We should have plenty of time, if you light that pretty lamp and put it near me, to try the effect of the new blouse. I am so anxious to see if it will fit."

"I have just got an account of Nesta; she is all right, mother; she will be back to-morrow," said Marcia. "So I am going to stay with you; and, mother, may I introduce you to my friend, Angela St. Just? Angela, this way, please. Mother, this is Angela, my great friend." Mrs Aldworth had been on the eve of crying; on the eve of a fit of nervous anxiety with regard to Nesta; but the appearance of Angela seemed to swallow up every other thought. She flushed, then turned pale, then held out her hand.

"I am glad to see you," she said.

Angela dropped into a chair.

"Just run away, Marcia," she said. "Leave me with Mrs Aldworth. Oh, Mrs Aldworth, I'm so glad Marcia let me come in. I have been longing to come to you—often and often. I have been so sorry for you; I have been thinking what a weary time you must have; I hope you will let me come often as long as I am near; I should like it so much."

The sweet eyes looked down into the faded face of the elder woman. They seemed somehow to have a magical power to arrest the finger of time, to erase the wrinkles, to smooth out some of the constant pain. Mrs Aldworth smiled quite gladly.

"How nice you are," she said, "and not a bit—not a bit stuck-up. I am so glad to make your acquaintance. Sit there and talk to me."

Angela took a chair and she did talk—all about nothings, perhaps about nothings; but she still talked and Mrs Aldworth listened.

Chapter Twenty Four

An Uneasy Conscience

Nesta's first day at Scarborough had been full of intense enjoyment. She had managed her escapade with great cleverness. The Griffiths were quite sure that she was going away with the consent of her parents. Mr Griffiths was kind, and pleased to have her; Mrs Griffiths was motherly; Flossie was all delight. First had come the journey; what a delicious sensation of excitement had she felt whenever the train stopped; with what more than a delicious sensation of importance she had owned to a thrill through her being at the thought that the others were anxious about her. That her own people would be trying to get her back as soon as possible but added to the sense of enjoyment.

The day was a brilliant one; the sea breezes were exhilarating, and Nesta's conscience did not awaken. She enjoyed the lodgings, and the room she was to share with Flossie, and the shrimps for tea, and the wading when the tide was down. She enjoyed listening to the band; in short, she enjoyed everything. Her constant smiles were always wreathing her lips; Mr and Mrs Griffiths thought her quite a delightful girl.

So passed the first day. Nesta had even managed, with Flossie's aid, to send a telegram without either Mr or Mrs Griffiths knowing anything about it. Those magical shillings, which had been produced by her yellow-boy, were so useful. She went to bed that night without any unpleasant telegram, or any unpleasant person coming from Newcastle to disturb her pleasure.

But the next morning she woke with a sigh. It would be all over to-day; she could not expect it to last longer than the middle of the day. Pleasure would be followed by retribution. She had made up her mind to this. She thought, however, that she would have a good morning. Immediately after breakfast she got away with Flossie.

"Floss, it will be all up to-day; they are quite certain to send for me. Even if Molly and Ethel did not open the telegram last night, they will at least send it on to old Marcia, and do you suppose that Miss Mule Selfish will not use every bit of her influence to get me back, and to have me well punished? There's no doubt on that point whatever."

"I know all that," said Flossie. "But, perhaps, they won't want you back."

"Not want me back?" said Nesta.

This comment, delightful as it sounded, was scarcely flattering.

"Mothery will want me," said Nesta.

"If you thought that, I wonder you came."

"Oh, don't begin to reproach me," said Nesta. "Let us go and have a long, long morning all by ourselves."

"But I want to bathe. Mother is going to bathe, and she said we two could go with her. You didn't, of course, bring a bathing dress, but we can hire them here."

Nesta was not inclined to bathe. It would, she protested, take up too much time. She wanted to go for a long walk alone with her friend. She suggested that they should go first of all to a pastrycook's, supply themselves with a good, large bag of edibles, and then wander away on the cliffs. Flossie; after due consideration, was nothing loath.

"That horrid telegram is sure to come, and then the fat will be in the fire," said Nesta.

"That's true enough," replied Flossie, "and I expect I'll be scolded too. You'll have to stand the blame—you'll have to tell them that it was more your fault than mine."

"Oh, I like that!" said Nesta. "You mean to tell me that you won't take my part, when I get into a beastly row all on account of you?"

The girls had a little tiff, as was their way; but their real affection for each other soon smoothed it over. Mrs Griffiths was talked round to see the expediency of Nesta and Flossie putting off their bathe until the next day, and accordingly the two girls started off for their walk.

There was no doubt whatever in Nesta's mind that retribution must come that day. It was the right day for Nemesis. She had enjoyed Saturday, but she had not enjoyed Sunday quite so much, for there was the possibility that somebody would come to fetch her back. On Sunday the girls might have sent the telegram to Marcia by special messenger, but on the other hand, Molly and Ethel were very careless; they did not care whether Nesta was in the house or not. They had probably not sent it on. But of course, there was not the least doubt that Marcia would receive it on Monday morning. What was to be done? She resolved to enjoy her walk even if it was the last. She spent a shilling of her precious money, secured a most unwholesome meal, which the two girls ate on the high cliffs just outside Scarborough, and then returned home in time for lunch.

"I'm not a bit hungry," said Nesta, "and I know there'll be a fearful row when we go upstairs. Do go first, Flossie; I'll wait here. If there's anything awful, I'll run down by the shore until it has blown over. Do go, Floss."

Flossie was cajoled into doing what Nesta wished. She went upstairs. Her father and mother were both waiting for them. They looked tranquil, as tranquil could be.

"Where's Nesta!" called out Mrs Griffiths from the landing. "Tell her to take off her hat and come in at once. Our dinner is getting cold."

Flossie flew downstairs.

"You needn't be a bit uneasy. Father and mother look as contented as though they never had a trouble in the world."

Wondering somewhat, Nesta did go upstairs. She ate her dinner, but all the time she was watching the door. Any minute either Marcia herself, stern, uncompromising, unyielding, unforgiving, might appear, or a horrible telegram addressed to Mrs Griffiths might be thrust into her hand. In any case her disgrace must be near at hand.

But strange as it may seem, the whole day passed, and there was no sort of telegram for Nesta. She wondered and wondered.

"This is quite lucky," she said to Flossie, as she was undressing for the night. "I really can't understand it. Of course, it's those girls; they never sent my telegram on to Marcia."

"Well, you know, you didn't send any address," said Flossie.

"Of course I didn't; but don't you suppose that they'd immediately rush off to your house, and get your address from your servants?"

"I never thought of that," said Flossie.

"They could find me if they wished. It's all that Miss Mule Selfish; she's so absorbed in her own pleasure she has forgotten all about me."

The next day passed without any notice being taken of Nesta, and the next, and the next. Nesta was quite bewildered. At first she was delighted, then she began to consider herself a slightly aggrieved person, particularly when Flossie taunted her with the fact that she did not seem to be missed much at home.

This was gall and wormwood to the little girl.

On the fifth day of her visit, Mr Griffiths, who had received some letters, said to Nesta:

"You don't seem to be hearing from your people—at least I have not seen any letters addressed to you. I hope they are all right."

"Oh, of course they are, no news is good news," said Nesta.

He took no notice of her remark, being absorbed in his own affairs. When he had read one of his letters he looked at his wife.

"I must go back to Newcastle this afternoon, but I'll return to-morrow," he said. "I'll call in, if you like, Nesta, and find out how your mother is."

"Oh, please don't—I mean you really needn't," said Nesta.

He raised his brows in some surprise.

"I should think," he said slowly, "that a girl who has an invalid mother, would like to know how she is."

Nesta coloured. She did not dare to say any more. She and Flossie had been having what she called a ripping time, that is, Nesta could enjoy herself in spite of her anxiety. But now things were changing. The yellow-boy had his limits; he was reduced in bulk until he had come down to a few pence. Between Nesta and that which made her so valuable in Flossie's eyes there was now but eleven-pence halfpenny. Nearly a shilling, a whole beautiful silver shilling, but not quite. When that was spent—and it would be spent that very day—Nesta would be of no special importance to Flossie Griffiths.

Flossie was making friends, too, on her own account. There was a family of young people also staying at Scarborough, whom the Griffiths used to know. They boasted of the name of Brown. They were all good-natured, hearty, friendly young folks. But in the beginning Nesta had chosen to turn up her nose at them. In consequence they devoted themselves to Flossie, and left Nesta very much out in the cold.

On the very day that Nesta was forced to spend her last pence on a feast for Flossie, Flossie calmly informed her that she was going early the next morning on a picnic with the Browns.

"They haven't invited you—I'm sorry," said Flossie. "They might have done it, but I said you were going away. This is Friday, you know. You will have been with us a week to-morrow. I know father and mother will want you to stay until the middle of next week, at any rate, but, of course, you and I—knowing what we do—" Flossie giggled—"thought you would be gone long ago."

"Well, I'm here," said Nesta, "and I wish I weren't."

"Why do you say that? I'm sure we have done all we could to give you a real good time."

"I think you hate me," said Nesta, in a passion.

"Well, Nesta, I do call that ungrateful! But there, you're in the sulks, poor old girl. You thought you'd be awfully missed at home, and you see you are not one little bit."

"I'm anxious about mother," said Nesta. "It's so queer none of them writing."

She burst into tears. Flossie was soft-hearted enough, and she comforted her friend, and said that she would not hurt her for the world, and would do her very best to get her an invitation to the picnic the next day. At this intimation Nesta immediately wiped her eyes.

"I'd like it," she said; "it would be horrid to be left at home with only your old mother."

"You needn't call mother old—she's no older than yours."

"Well, anyhow, mine's the prettiest," said Nesta.

"And my mother is the strongest," retorted Flossie. "Oh, there, don't let us quarrel," said Nesta. "If I hadn't you for my friend now, Floss, I'd be the most miserable girl in the world. To tell the truth, I'm rather terrified at the way they're taking things at home—not a word—not a line, nothing whatever. It does seem odd, doesn't it?"

Flossie made no remark. Just then Henrietta Brown was seen passing the window. Flossie put out her head and called to Henrietta to stop, and then dashed downstairs.

"Oh, Henny," she gasped, "I'm ever so sorry, but Nesta Aldworth, my friend, she is still with us. I wonder—"

"We really couldn't," said Henny, who was downright, and not quite as refined as even the Griffiths themselves. "We haven't a seat left. Either you must come, or your friend. We can't fit in the two of you. It's impossible. We might have done so at the beginning, but you said your stuck-up Miss Aldworth would be gone away."

"Well, she has not gone," said Flossie. "Of course, if you like I can give up my seat if you are sure you couldn't squeeze us both in."

"I'm certain, positive on the subject. And, Flossie, you mustn't give up your seat," said Henny, linking her arm inside Flossie's arm, "for we don't like her one little bit. She's not pretty like von, and she has no go in her. You must come. Why, Tom and Jack and Robert—they'd be just mad if you weren't there."

Flossie was pleased to hear that the Brown boys—Tom, Jack, and Robert— wished for her society.

"Well, of course, it's her own fault," she said aloud, and then she went back to Nesta.

"It's no go," she said. "You must stay with mother—or—or do anything you like. Ah, there's father—he's off. Good-bye, Dad."

Flossie's voice sounded on the summer breeze. Mr Griffiths looked up and kissed his hand to her.

"Good-bye to you both," he said. "I'll be back to-morrow, and if I can, Nesta, I'll look in and see how your mother is getting on. Are you sure you have no message?"

"None; please, don't trouble," said Nesta.

She was feeling now most frantically wretched. That last feast with Flossie was scarcely a success. She did not know how she was to live through the next day. If she had money enough she would return home. She would boldly declare that she had a right to her own home, the home that no longer seemed to want her. There was no telegram that day—no letter, no message of any sort.

The next morning rose bright and glorious. Flossie, dressed in her very best, went off for the picnic with the Browns. They had two waggonettes packed full of people, and Flossie squeezed herself in amid peals of laughter. Nesta watched her from behind the curtain of the drawing room window; Mrs Griffiths was well to the front, bowing and smiling, and kissing her hand.

"There," she said, when the waggonettes passed out of sight, "I'm glad my Floss is going to have a good time. Sorry for you, Nesta, but then you gave us to understand that you'd be sent for so soon."

"I thought so," said Nesta.

"Well, dear, it's all the better for you, you have the advantage of the sea. You must put up with an old woman for once. I'm going for a dip in the briny this morning. What do you say to coming with me?"

Nesta acquiesced. She might as well do that as anything else. She didn't care about it, of course.

Mrs Griffiths was energetic when she was at the seaside, and she took her dip and then a long walk, and then she waded for a time, and Nesta had to wade with her. They were both tired when they returned to the house in the middle of the day.

And now, at last, there was a telegram. It lay on the table in its little yellow envelope. Nesta felt suddenly sick and faint. Mrs Griffiths took it up.

"It's for me," she said. "It's to say that my man is coming back this evening—or maybe not until to-morrow, or Monday."

She read the telegram. Nesta watched her with parted lips, as Mrs Griffiths slowly acquainted herself with the contents. She was a quick, energetic woman, but as regarded matters relating to the mind she slow. The telegram puzzled her.

"It's queer," she said. "Can you make anything of it?"

She handed it to Nesta. Nesta road the contents.

"'Coming back sooner than I expected. Have been to the Aldworths'—a very queer business; will tell you when we meet.'"

"I wonder if your mother is worse," said Mrs Griffiths, looking with her kind eyes at the girl. "Why, Nesta, you are as white as a sheet! Is anything wrong?"

"No," said Nesta. She let the telegram flutter to the floor; it was Mrs Griffiths who picked it up. Nemesis had come—Nemesis with a vengeance.

"I don't expect it is anything. Your father—I mean Flossie's father, is always fond of making mountains out of molehills. It is nothing special, it really isn't; you may be sure on that point," said the good woman. "Anyhow, he will tell us when he comes, and not all the guessing in the world will spoil our appetites, will it, Nesta? See this pigeon pie, the very best that could be got; I ordered it from the pastrycook's, for I don't much like some of our landlady's cooking."

Nesta could have enjoyed that pigeon pie, but the telegram, Nemesis, in short, had crushed what appetite she possessed out of her. She fiddled with her food, then sprang up.

"I am so anxious," she said.

"Why, what is it, child?"

Mrs Griffiths looked at her; Nesta looked full at Mrs Griffiths.

"I must tell you something; I know you will hate me; I know you will, but if you would be kind just for once—"

"Goodness me, child! Of course I'll be kind. What is troubling you? Anything wrong with the mother?"

"It isn't that—it is that when I came with you I ran away."

"You did what?" said Mrs Griffiths.

Nesta mumbled out her miserable story. She told it dismally. Mrs Griffiths had, as she averred afterwards, to drag the words from the child. At last the ugly facts were made plain to her. Nesta had deliberately left her home without saying one word to anybody. She had been aided and abetted by Flossie, Mrs Griffiths' good, honourable, open-hearted Flossie—at least that is what Mrs Griffiths had considered her child. Yes, Flossie had helped her friend, and her friend had gone; she had not said a word to any one at home; she had only sent off a telegram. The telegram, of course, must bear the Scarborough mark, but they had taken no notice.

"Of course, Mr Griffiths went to see them, and of course they told him, and of course—of course, he will be just mad," said Mrs Griffiths. "He will be in a towering rage; I don't know what he won't do. There'll be a split between us; he'll never let our Flossie speak to you again, that's plain."

"Oh, Mrs Griffiths, if you would be good, if you would but just lend me enough money to get home before—before he comes."

"Well, now, that wouldn't be a bad idea," said Mrs Griffiths. "You can make off, I will see you into the tram; you don't mind travelling third-class, do you?"

"I'd travel on the top of the train—I'd travel in the guard's van—I'd travel anywhere only to get away," said Nesta.

"Well, child, I'll just look up the trains, and put you into one myself—or no, perhaps I'd better not. You might give us the slip, as it were. If he thought that I'd let you go home before he came, he'd give me a piece of his mind, and there'd be the mischief to pay again. You can find your own way to the station."

"I can. I can."

"I'll look out the very next train, the very next."

"Oh, do, please do. And please lend me some money."

Mrs Griffiths produced half a sovereign, which she put into Nesta's palm. Nesta hardly waited to thank her.

"Good-bye. Oh, I am grateful—I will write. Explain to Flossie. Try to forgive me—it was so dull at home, only Miss Mule Selfish, you know, and Molly and Ethel."

"And your mother," said Mrs Griffiths, a little severely, for it was the thought of the anxiety that Nesta had given her mother which touched Mrs Griffiths' heart most nearly.

"Mothery wouldn't be cross, that is certain sure," said poor Nesta.

She was putting on her hat as she uttered the words, and a few minutes later she was toiling through the hot sun and blinding dust, for the day was a windy one, to the railway station en route for Newcastle.

Chapter Twenty Five

Nemesis

It was late that evening when two men entered Mrs Griffiths' drawing room at Scarborough. One was Mr Griffiths, and the other Horace Aldworth, Nesta's half-brother. Mrs Griffiths was overpowered by Horace's presence. She had spent a wretched time since Nesta had gone. The girl was scarcely out of the house before the elder woman decided that she had done very wrong to lend her money; there was no saying what she might do, nor how she would spend it. She might not go home at all. She was a queer girl—unlike her Flossie. She had done a strange, a most unaccountable thing; just for the sake of a bit of pleasure, she had left her own friends, her mother, her sisters—she had planned it all cleverly, but—and here lay the sting—she had not planned it alone. Flossie was in the thick of the mischief.

Mrs Griffiths' uneasiness with regard to Nesta presently melted down into a tender sort of regret. Her real sorrow was for her Flossie, her little black-eyed, dancing, mischievous girl, Flossie, who had always been fond of her father and mother, and who had never given herself airs, but had just delighted in Nesta because she must have some friend, but who would not do what Nesta had done for the wide world. And yet, try as she would, Mrs Griffiths could not get over the fact that Flossie had aided and abetted Nesta; that she knew all about it. Mrs Griffiths thought she could understand. She had recourse to her favourite adage—"Girls will be girls." She remembered the time when she was at school. Girls' schools were somewhat common sort of places in Mrs Griffiths' early days. She remembered how she had smuggled in cakes, how she had secreted sticky sweetmeats in her pockets, how she had defied her teachers, and copied her themes from other girls, and what romps they had had in the attics, and how they had laughed at the teachers behind their backs. All these things Mrs Griffiths had done in the days of her youth; but nevertheless these things did not seem so grave or serious as what Flossie had done. Of course, she would forgive her; catch a mother being long angry with her only child; but then Griffiths—Mrs Griffiths always called her husband by that name—he would be wild.

"Griffiths will give it to her, and she's that saucy she'll answer him back, and there'll be no end of a row," thought the poor woman.

So it was an anxious-faced, wrinkled, rather elderly woman who started up now to receive the two men. Griffiths came in first.

"I have brought Mr Horace Aldworth back with me, wife. Did you receive my telegram?"

"I did, dear. You will be wanting a bit of supper. How do you do, Mr Aldworth? I hope your poor mother is easier—suffering less, getting stronger by degrees."

Horace bowed and murmured something in reply, and took a seat with his back to the light. Griffiths strutted over to the hearthrug, put his hands behind him, swelled out,—as Mrs Griffiths afterwards expressed it,—looked as red as a turkey-cock, and demanded the presence of the two girls.

"The girls," said Mrs Griffiths—"they are out."

Her first impulse was to hide the fact that she had lent Nesta money; but second thoughts rejected this. Griffiths would worm it out of her. Griffiths could get any secret out of her—he was terrible when he reached his turkey-cock stage.

"The girls," she said timidly, "they're not in."

"Neither of them?"

"Neither of them."

"Then where in the name of all that is good are they?" thundered the angry man.

"Flossie is away on a picnic with the Browns."

"I'm not inquiring for Flossie in particular at present. I want that other hussy—I want Miss Nesta Aldworth. Where is she?"

"I have come," said Horace, breaking in at this juncture, and speaking in a most self-restrained voice—"to take my sister Nesta home with me, and to thank you most sincerely, Mrs Griffiths, for your kindness."

"It's the most dastardly, disgraceful thing that ever occurred, and to think that I should have had a hand in it," said Griffiths. "I have been done as neatly as ever man was. I, paying all the expenses and treating the girl as though she were my own child, and thinking that Aldworth, there, and his father, would be pleased, and believe that I meant well by his family, and all the time I was doing them a base injury. It's a wonder that girl's mother isn't in her grave, and so she would be if it wasn't for—"

"My mother is all right, thank you," said Horace. "But I am most anxious to catch the last train back to Newcastle. Is Nesta upstairs? Can she come down? I want to take her away."

"She is not," said Mrs Griffiths, and now she trembled exceedingly, and edged nearer to Horace, as though for protection. "It is my fault, you mustn't blame her. I got the telegram—I'd rather not say anything about it, but I can't hide the truth from you, Griffiths. You are so masterful when you get red in the face like that—I'm just terrified of you, and I must out with the truth. The poor child was so frightened that she told me what she had done. She owned up handsome, I must say, and then she said: 'Lend me a little money to take me home—I will go home at once.' She was frightfully cut up at nobody really missing her. She had evidently thought she would be sent for at once. I own that she did wrong."

"Of course, she did wrong," shouted Griffiths. "I never heard of a meaner thing to do, a meaner and a lower, and if I thought that my child—"

It was on this scene that Flossie, radiant with the success of her happy day, broke. She opened the door wide, rushed in, and said:

"Oh, if I haven't had—where are you, Nesta? Why, whatever is the matter?"

"You come along here, Flossie," said Griffiths. "There's no end of a row, that's the truth. Come and stand by me. Tell me what you know of this Nesta business—this runaway business, this daring to deceive an honest man, this creeping off, so to speak, in the dark. Tell me what you know. Own up, child, own up, and be quick."

"Yes, tell us what you know," said Horace. His voice was kind; Flossie turned to him.

"I—it was my fault as much as hers."

"Your fault?" bellowed her father. "Your fault?"

"Oh, for goodness' sake, Griffiths, don't frighten the wits out of the poor child; let her speak," exclaimed the mother.

But when all was said and done, Flossie had grit in her. She was not going on this day of calamity to let her friend bear the brunt alone.

"We did it between us," she said. "Poor old Nesta, she was having such a bad time, and I wanted her so much. We planned it together. We knew that if father knew it he would not take her, so we planned it, and you never guessed, father, and, and—Oh, I suppose you will give me an awful punishment—send me to a terrible school or something of that sort."

But Griffiths was past himself.

"You knew it—you planned it! Why, you are as bad as she is!"

He took her by her shoulders and shook her. Her black eyes blazed up into his face.

"Yes, I am quite as bad as she is," she said.

"Then go out of the room. Go upstairs."

"Griffiths, Griffiths," moaned the mother.

"You must do just as you please with regard to your daughter," said Horace then. "I am sorry for Miss Griffiths; I don't think, notwithstanding her confession, that she can be as bad as Nesta; but what I want to know is, where is Nesta?"

"I will tell you, Mr Aldworth. If my poor child was brave enough to fight her father when he was in the turkey-cock stage, I'm not going to be a whit behind her. We may be bad, Floss and I, but we're not cowards. The poor child was so cowed by the tone of Griffiths' telegram that she begged and implored of me to lend her money to go home before Griffiths got back. That is the long and short of it, and she's safe back at Newcastle by this time, and safe in your house, and doubtless her mother has forgiven her. I lent her the money to go."

"How much?" said Horace sternly.

"Not a penny more than ten shillings. The poor child said she would let me have it back again. Not that I want it—indeed I don't."

Horace put his hand into his pocket, took out half a sovereign and laid it on the table.

"I have to thank you both," he said, turning to Griffiths, "for your great kindness to my sister. You meant well, however ill she meant. I have nothing to say with regard to your daughter's conduct except that I would not be too hard on her, Mr Griffiths, if I were you. The girl might have tried to get out of it, but she did not; there is always something in that. Now I shall just have time to catch my train."

"You won't take bite nor sup, Mr Aldworth? We're so honoured to have you in the house, sir, so pleased, so delighted. You are sure you won't take bite nor sup?"

"I am sorry, but I must catch my train; it leaves at 9:10."

"And how, if I might venture to ask you, is your poor mother, Mr Aldworth?"

"My mother is better. She is not at home at present. She is at Hurst Castle with Miss Angela St. Just. Miss St. Just has had a wonderful effect upon her, and has managed to get her over there, and I trust she may come back a very different woman."

"Then after all," said Mrs Griffiths, "poor little Nesta did not injure her mother; that is something to be thankful for, and when you are scolding her, sir, I hope you will bear it in mind. And I hope, Griffiths, you will also bear it in mind, and act handsome by our child, and take her in the true spirit and forgive her."

"I am disgusted," said Griffiths, "disgusted."

He stalked to the door, pushed it wide open, let it bang behind him, and went down the stairs.

"There!" said Mrs Griffiths, bursting into tears, "he will be unmanageable, not only to-night, but to-morrow, and the day after, and the day after. A pretty time Floss and I'll have—a pretty time truly. But I'm glad you spoke up, Mr Aldworth. You are not offended with us, forsooth?"

"Offended with you, madam," said the young man; "how can I do anything but thank you for your kindness to my poor silly young sister? But now I must really be off."

Chapter Twenty Six

In Hiding

When Nesta reached the railway station she was almost beside herself with fear. She went to the ticket office to get a third-class single ticket for Newcastle. There was a girl standing just in front of her, a commonplace, respectable looking girl, who asked for a ticket to a place which she pronounced as Souchester. The ticket only cost one and sixpence. It flashed through Nesta's mind that she might just as well go to Souchester as anywhere else. It had not before entered into her brain that here lay an immediate source of relief. Perhaps her family would be really frightened when they knew nothing about her, so frightened that when they saw her again, they would forgive her.

Scarcely knowing what she did, and with no previous intention of going anywhere but straight home, she too asked for a ticket to Souchester. The man handed it to her.

"One and sixpence, please," he said.

She pushed in her half-sovereign, received back eight and sixpence change, which she thought great riches, slipped the money into her purse, put the purse into her pocket, and went on the platform. The man directed her which way to go to catch the Souchester train. She followed the girl who had first put the idea into her mind. This girl looked of the servant class. She was respectably dressed, she carried a parcel wrapped up in brown paper. Nesta felt that between her and that girl there was a sort of link; she could not quite account for it, but she was anxious not to lose sight of her.

"Souchester," said the man who stood on the platform, taking Nesta's ticket and examining it, "there you are, Miss, right ahead, that train, that train, Miss, it's just starting, you be quick if you want to catch it." Nesta hurried. The girl with the brown paper parcel got into a third-class carriage, Nesta followed her, and a minute later the train was in motion. At first it went slowly, then quickly, and soon the gay town of Scarborough was out of sight, and they were going rapidly between fields full of waving corn, with the blue sea still close at hand.

It so happened that Nesta and the girl with the brown paper parcel were the only two in this special compartment. Nesta looked at her companion; she did not exchange a single word with her, but nevertheless, she was for the time being her guiding star. The girl was essentially commonplace; she was stout, very dumpy in figure, she had a large, full-moon face, small eyes, a wide mouth, and high cheek bones. She wore no gloves, and her hands were coarse and red. Presently she pulled a coarse sandwich, made of two hunches of bread with a piece of bacon in the middle, from her brown paper parcel, and began to eat it deliberately. When she had eaten half, she looked at Nesta. Then taking a knife out of her pocket, she cut a piece from her sandwich and offered it awkwardly, and yet with a good-natured smile, to her fellow traveller. Nesta thanked her, and said she was not hungry.

This incident, however, opened the ball, and Nesta was able to ask what sort of place Souchester was.

"Oh, just a country place," said the girl. "Be yer going there, Miss?"

"I'm a poor girl just like yourself," said Nesta. She became suddenly interested. If this was not a real adventure, a real proper running away, she did not know what was.

"I am a poor girl like you," repeated Nesta, "and I am going to Souchester."

"Now I wonder what for?" said the girl. "My name is Mary Hogg. I'm in a place— it's a big house, and I'm under kitchenmaid. I have had a week's holiday to see my aunt, who lives in a poor part of Scarborough, not where the rich folks live. I've had a jolly week and now I'm going back to my place. There are very few poor at Souchester, it's just a little bit of a village, and it's owned by the St. Just family."

Nesta suddenly felt she had been entrapped once more. "What St. Justs?" she asked.

"Why, the St. Justs," answered the girl. "Miss Angela's folks. You must have heard of Miss Angela St. Just."

"Yes," said Nesta, then she added petulantly—"They seem to be everywhere."

"Oh, no, they ain't," said Mary Hogg. "Sir Edward and his daughter, they've had what you call reverses, but the rest of the family is rich, very rich. They owns Hurst Castle, and my place. I belong to 'em, so to speak. I'm at Castle

Walworth. I'm under kitchenmaid. They keep a power of servants; you can scarce count 'em on your fingers."

Nesta was interested.

"Have you very hard work to do?" she asked.

"Oh, no; nothing to speak of, and I gets rare good living, and no end of pickings, too, which I takes to my mother, whenever I has time to go and see her. She lives in a bit of a cottage just outside of the village. She's very poor, indeed, is mother. She's a widdy. Father died five years ago, and left her with me and two boys. The boys is still at school. The St. Just family is very good to mother, and it was through Miss Angela asking, that I got a place as kitchenmaid at the Castle. I'm proud of my place."

"You must be," said Nesta.

"It's real respectable," said the girl. "You can't be like ordinary servants; you mustn't consider yourself an ordinary servant there. Just think of me—a bit of a girl like me—I ain't seventeen yet—having to wear a little tight bonnet with strings fastened under my chin, and a regular livery. Grey, it is, with red pipings. That's the livery the servants at Castle Walworth wear. The bonnets are black, with a bit of red just bordering them inside. We look very nice when we go to church, all in our livery. But when I goes to see mother, then I can wear just what I like, and when I'm with my aunt—oh, my word, I did have a good time at Scarborough—but here we be, Miss, here we be. I'll wish you good-day, Miss."

The train stopped and the two girls alighted on the platform. Nesta walked hurriedly by her companion's side. The girl with the brown paper parcel did not seem to want anything more to do with her. The tickets were taken by the ticket collector, and then they found themselves side by side in a narrow road, a road branching off to right and left. It was a winding road, quite pretty and very countrified indeed. If there was a village, there seemed to be no trace of one.

"Where's the village?" asked Nesta, doing her best to detain the sole person in all the world whom she thought she had a right to speak to.

"Why, there—down in the valley, nestling among all them trees," said Mary Hogg. "This is my way," she added, "straight up this steep hill, and there's the Castle, and the flag is flying; that shows the family are at home. They'll be waiting for me. If Mrs Gaskell, that's our housekeeper, finds I'm five minutes late, why she'll blow my nose off."

"How awful!" said Nesta.

"Oh, she ain't really so bad; she's quite a kind sort; but the family is at home, and I'm due back now, so I'll wish you good-evening, Miss."

"Stay one minute, just one minute."

"I can't really, Miss; I must hurry; time's up, and time's everything at Castle Walworth. We, none of us, dare be one minute late, not one blessed minute. There's the family has their pleasure, and they must have time for that, and we servants, we has our work, and we must have time for that. That's the way of the world, Miss. I can't stay to talk, really, Miss."

"Then I'll walk with you," said Nesta.

"It's a steep hill, Miss, and if you've come to see your friends—"

"That's just what I haven't—I have come to—Oh, Mary Hogg, I must confide in you. I have come here because I want to—to hide for a little."

"My word! To hide!" said Mary Hogg. She really quite interested at last. She forgot the awful Mrs Gaskell and all the terrors that punctuality caused in the St. Just establishment. Her eyes became round as the letter "O," and her mouth formed itself into much the same shape.

"You be a bad 'un!" she said. "So you've run away?"

"Yes, I have. I haven't time to tell you my story, but I want to stay at Souchester just for a little! you must help me, for I wouldn't have come to Souchester but for you."

"There now; didn't I say you were bad? What in the name of wonder have I to do with it?"

"I was going in quite another direction, and I heard you ask for a ticket to Souchester, and I thought I'd come too, and I got into the same carriage with you because I thought you looked kind and—and respectable. I've got some money," continued Nesta, speaking with sudden dignity. "I'm not a beggar, but I want to go to a very cheap place just to spend the night. Do you know of any place? It won't do you any harm to tell me if there's anybody in the village who would give me a bed."

"But, do you mean a very, very cheap place?" asked Mary Hogg, who thought on the spot that she might do a good deal for her mother. Mrs Hogg was so poor that she was glad even of stray sixpences and pence.

"I don't mind how poor it is, if it is only cheap; that is what I want—something very cheap."

"There's mother's house. Would you mind going there?"

"Of course I wouldn't. Where is it?"

"I must be quick; I really must. You had better come a little way up the hill with me, and I'll tell you. It's rather steep, but there, I'll go a little slower. I'll tell Mrs Gaskell that I met a fellow creature in distress. She's a very Christian woman, is Mrs Gaskell, and that, perhaps, will make her more inclined to be lenient with me. I'll tell her that."

"But you won't tell her my name, will you?"

"In course not, seeing as I don't know it."

"That's true," said Nesta, with a relieved laugh.

"And I don't want to," said Mary Hogg.

"Better not," said Nesta.

"Well, if you think mother'll give you a bed—"

"I don't know—it was you who said it."

"She will, if you pay her. You may have to give her fourpence—can you afford that?"

"Yes, I think so."

"She'll give you your breakfast for three ha'pence, and a sort of dinner meal for threepence. Can you manage that?"

"Yes, quite well."

Nesta made a mental calculation. If Mrs Hogg was really so very reasonable, she might stay with her for several days. Eight and sixpence would last a long time at that rate.

"You are very kind," she said, with rapture. "That will do beautifully. Now, just tell me where she lives, will you?"

"You say as Mary Hogg told you to come. Mother'll know what that means. It's a very small house; 'tain't in no way the sort as you're used to."

"I don't mind. Tell me where it is."

"Well; there's the village yonder. You foller your nose and you'll get it. By-and-by you'll cross the stream over a little bridge, but still foller after your nose, and you'll come to a cottage just at the side of the road, standing all alone. You can go up the path and knock at the door, and when you knock, mother'll say, 'Come right in,' and you'll go right in, and mother 'll say, 'What do you want?' and you'll say, 'Mary Hogg sent me.' Then you'll manage the rest. Good-bye to you; I really must run."

Mary put wings to her feet, and toiling and panting with her brown paper parcel, she hurried up the steep hill towards that spot where Castle Walworth reflected from its many windows the gleam of the now westering sun.

Nesta stood for a minute just where her new friend had left her, and then went down towards the village. She felt in her pocket for her little purse; she took it out and opened it. Yes, there was the money that Mrs Griffiths had lent her—eight shillings and sixpence. She felt herself quite wealthy. At the Hogg establishment she might really manage to live for several days.

Following Mary's directions she reached the little village street, found the rustic bridge, crossed it and went along a pretty shady road. Some people passed her, poor people returning from their work, people of her own class, some well dressed, some the reverse. They all looked at her, for people will stare at a stranger in country villages. Then a carriage passed by with several gaily dressed ladies in it, and they also turned and looked at Nesta. Nesta hurried after that. How awful it would be if she suddenly met Angela St. Just Angela would know her, of course, and she would know Angela. But no one in the carriage seemed to recognise her, and the prancing horses soon bowled out of sight.

Then she came to a cottage covered with ivy, roof and all; it almost seemed weighted down by the evergreens. She saw a tiny porch made of latticework, which was also covered with evergreens. The porch was so small and so entirely covered that Nesta had slightly to stoop to get within. There was a little door which was shut; she knocked, and a voice said, "Come right in."

Nesta felt for a moment as though she were Red Riding Hood, and the wolf were within. She lifted the latch and went in. The first person she saw was a sandy-haired middle-aged woman, with a strong likeness to Mary Hogg. The woman said, "Oh, my!" then she gave a little curtsey, then she said, "Oh, my!" again. Nesta stood and stared at her. A small boy who had been lying face downward on the floor, started to his feet, thrust his hands into his trouser pockets, and stared also. Another boy, who had been bending over a book, and who was a little older, flung the book on the floor, and added to the group of starers.

"Mary Hogg sent me," said Nesta.

She used the words wondering if they would be a talisman, the "open sesame" which her hungry soul desired. They certainly had an immediate effect, but not the effect she expected. Mrs Hogg darted forward, dusted a chair, and said:

"Honoured Miss, be seated."

Nesta dropped into the chair, for she was really very tired.

"If you are one of the young ladies from the Castle, I'm sorry I ain't got all the sewing done yet, but I will to-morrow."

"No," said Nesta, "it isn't that. I'm not one of the young ladies from the Castle; I'm just a girl, a stranger, and I want a bed for the night. I travelled in the same train with your daughter, Mary Hogg, and she sent me on here. She said you would give me a bed, and that you'd expect me to pay. I can pay you. I have got eight and sixpence. I hope you won't charge me a great deal, for that is all the money I have in the wide world. But I can pay you; will you give me a bed?"

Now this was most exciting to Mrs Hogg. It was still more exciting to the two boys, whose names were Ben and Dan. They stood now side by side, each with his hands in his pockets, and his glowing eyes fixed on Nesta's face. Mrs Hogg stood silent; she was considering deeply.

"There's but two rooms," she said, at last. "This room, and the bedroom beyond; but there's the scullery."

"I could sleep anywhere," said Nesta, who was terrified at the thought of being thrust out of this humble habitation.

"There's only one thing to be done," said Mrs Hogg, "you must share my bed."

This was scarcely agreeable, but any port in a storm, Nesta thought.

"Very well."

"I'll charge you twopence a night."

"Thank you," said Nesta.

"The boys will have to leave the room and sleep in the scullery."

"Hooray!" said Dan.

"Hurroa!" cried Ben.

"Quiet, lads, quiet," said the mother. "You go right out of the way and let the young lady rest herself."

"I'm just a girl," said Nesta. "I'd best not be a young lady; I'm just a girl, and I'm very glad to come and stay with you. I shall be rather hungry presently," she continued; "could you give me any supper?"

"If it's anything special, I'll charge you what it costs," said Mrs Hogg; "but if it's anything, why, it'll be three ha'pence for supper, twopence for breakfast, threepence for dinner. Them's my terms."

"It must be anything," said Nesta.

Mrs Hogg nodded. She whispered to her eldest boy, who, with another "Hooray!" rushed out of the cottage, followed by his brother. Nesta sank down in the shadow; she had found a refuge. For the present she was safe. Even Horace, with all his penetration, could not possibly find her in Mrs Hogg's kitchen, in Souchester. She made a hurried calculation. She might live here for over a week quite comfortably. In her present terrible plight a week seemed like forever.

Chapter Twenty Seven

Unaccustomed Fare

Mrs Hogg's bedroom was choky and Mrs Hogg herself snored loudly. But the place was really clean, and Nesta was too tired to lie long awake. When she did open her eyes in the morning, it was to the pleasant perfume of fried herring. A small boy was standing gazing at her out of two of the roundest eyes Nesta had ever seen. She came to the conclusion that the eyes of the entire Hogg family were not made like other people's; they were as round as marbles, and protruded very slightly from the head. The boy said:

"Red herrings!" thrust his tongue into his cheek, winked at her, and vanished.

Nesta proceeded to dress herself, and went into the living room. The place of honour was reserved for her. There was bread for breakfast, but no butter. There was, however, a sort of lard, which the children much appreciated. There was tea, but very little milk, and coarse brown sugar. Mrs Hogg helped the boys liberally, but she did not give them any of the red herring. Nesta noticed that Ben's eyes watered when he glanced at it. She herself could not touch it, so she transferred the morsel which had been put on her plate to that of the little boy. The boy shouted; he did not seem to be able to speak quietly. He said "Hurra!" The moment he said "Hurra!" the eldest boy said "Hooray!" and stretched out his hand and snatched a piece of herring from the dish. Mrs Hogg rose and smacked both the boys on their ears, whereupon they fell to crying bitterly.

"Oh, don't," said Nesta. "How can you? It seems so cruel."

"Crool?" said Mrs Hogg; "crool to smack yer own children? Why, don't Bible Solomon say, 'Spare the rod and spoil the child'? There's no spoiling of my children in this house. Put back that fish, you greedy boy. Ain't it got to do for Missie's dinner and supper, as well as for her breakfast; you put it back this blessed minute."

Nesta felt a sudden sense of dismay. To be obliged to eat red herring as her sole sustenance for one whole day did seem dreadful, but she reflected that anything was better than her father's and brother's wrath, and the sneers of her two sisters, and better than Marcia's gracious, and yet most intolerable forgiveness. Nesta was not at all sorry yet, for what she had done, but she was sorry for the sense of discomfort which now surrounded her. She had borne with her supper, which consisted of porridge and milk, the night before, but her breakfast was by no means to her taste. When the boys had gone to Sunday school, she said almost timidly:

"If I can't help you in any way can't I go out?"

"Oh, for goodness' sake do, my dear. I don't want to see you except when you want to see me. You're welcome to half my bed, although I was half perished in the night, for you would take all the clothes and wrap yourself in them. I've got rheumatics in my back, and I could have cried out with the pain. You're a selfish young miss, I take it."

Nesta was accustomed to home truths, but Mrs Hogg's home truths hurt her more than most. She felt something like tears burning at the back of her eyes.

"Perhaps I am," she said. "I know I'm not at all happy."

She went out of the house, and wandered down the summer road. Soon she got into an enchanting lane where wild flowers of all sorts grew in wild profusion. Here also was a distant, a very distant glimpse of the blue, blue sea. She was glad to be away from it; she was glad, of course, to be here. She had not an idea what would become of her in the end. She felt as though all her life had suddenly been drawn up short, as though the thread of her existence had been snapped. It was her own doing; she had done it herself.

She heard the church bells ringing in the distance, but she knew it was impossible for her to go to church. She began to wonder what they were doing at home, and to wonder what the Griffiths were doing. She found she did not like to think either of her home or of the Griffiths. What could she do when her eight and sixpence was gone? Mrs Hogg was not at all an affectionate woman; she would exact her pence to the uttermost farthing. Nesta felt that if she were to live on red herrings for a week, she would feel very thin at the end of it. She detested red herrings She sincerely hoped there would be a variety in the Hogg menu. But Mrs Hogg's emphatic statement did not seem to point that way. At least for to-day she was to be supported on butterless bread and red herrings.

Still she wandered on, the country air fanning her cheeks. There was peace everywhere except in her own troubled heart. As yet she was not at all sorry, there was only sorrow for herself, she was not sorry for the pain she was giving others. Had the temptation come to her again she would have succumbed.

"The people at home don't love me much," she thought, "or they'd have sent for me. I gave them every chance. It might have been naughty of me to run away, but I gave them the chance of sending for me. But they never sent a line or a message; they never would have done it, if Mr Griffiths had not gone to see mother and found out the truth. Oh, to think of what he would say when he came in. I wonder what he did say. I wonder what Flossie is doing. I wonder— oh, I wonder!"

She went on until she was tired, then she sat down by the edge of a babbling brook, dipped her hand into the water, and amused herself watching the minnows and other small fish as they floated past her in the bed of the stream. There were forget-me-nots growing on the edge of the bank; she picked some and tore them to pieces. Then she started up impatiently. What was she to do when the eight and sixpence was out? She began to think of Mary Hogg up at the Castle. It must be nice to have something to do. She wondered if the St. Justs would take her on as one of their servants. They kept such a lot, perhaps they might have room for her. She did not relish the idea. She had some pride, and she did not care to sink to the position of a domestic servant. Nevertheless, she thought it would be better than doing nothing at all; better than going back to her family; better than starving. But then the St. Justs might not have her. She could not honestly say she would make a good servant. She felt certain in her heart that she would be unpardonably careless, thoughtless, unable to do any one thing properly. Why, she could not even make a bed! She used to try at home, sometimes, and always failed miserably.

Then she began to consider another fact. The St. Justs would very quickly discover who she was. Oh, no, she must not go there; she must go to somebody else. But who else? She had really no time to lose. Perhaps she could go as reader or companion. That was much better. That would be quite nice. There must surely be a blind lady in the village, and blind old ladies always wanted companions to read to them. Nesta could read—how often she had read to her mother. Oh, yes, she would really do that part quite nicely. She was the quickest reader she knew. She could gabble through a story at breathless speed; it did not matter whether she pronounced her words right or wrong. Yes, a blind old lady was the very thing.

She began to feel hungry, for her breakfast had not been very satisfying. Whatever happened she must be in time for the Hogg dinner. This was the principal meal of the day; it would cost her threepence. She began to think that she was paying dear for the sort of food she got at the Hoggs'.

She walked back without meeting any one, and entered her new home. She was right; they were preparing for dinner. Mrs Hogg was stirring something over the fire; the boys were in their old attitude of rapt attention, their hands in their pockets. There was a cloth on the table which had once been white; it was certainly that no longer. There were coarse knives and forks and very coarse plates, with the thickest glasses to drink out of that Nesta had ever seen. Mrs Hogg said:

"If you'll take your 'at off, Miss, dinner'll be ready in a twinkle."

Nesta retired into the bedroom; she came back in a few minutes. When she did so the youngest boy came up to her, and whispered in her ear:

"Pease pudding for dinner." He then said, looking round at his brother, "Hurra!" and the brother, as was his invariable habit, cried "Hooray!"

The pease pudding was lifted out of the pot in a bag; the bag was opened, the boys looking on with breathless interest. It was put in the centre of the table on a round dish, and the family sat down.

"Your grace, Dan," said Mrs Hogg.

Dan said:

"For all your mercies—" He closed his eyes and mumbled the rest.

Then Mrs Hogg cut liberal slices of the pease pudding and helped Nesta and the two children. She gave Nesta the largest share. Nesta disliked pease pudding as much as she disliked fried herring, but that did not matter; she was so hungry now that she ate it. The pease pudding was followed by a dumpling, which the boys greatly appreciated. There were currants in it, so few that to search for them was most exciting and caused "Hurras!" and "Hoorays!" to sound through the cottage. This was a dinner which was, as the boys expressed it, "filling."

"Seems to puff you out," said Ben.

"Seems to stuff you up," said Dan.

"Out you both go now," said Mrs Hogg, and she and Nesta were alone. Mrs Hogg washed up and put the place in perfect order. She then sat down by the table, put on her spectacles, and opened her Bible.

"Ain't you got a Bible with you?" she said.

"No," replied Nesta, "I haven't got anything with me."

"Shall I read aloud to you, Miss?"

"No, thank you," replied Nesta.

Mrs Hogg glanced up at Nesta with small favour in her face.

"Please," said Nesta, coming close to her, "I want to get something to do. I am a young lady, you know."

"Maybe you be; but you took all the clothes off me last night, and that ain't young-ladyish to my way o' thinking."

"I'm sorry," said Nesta, who thought it best to propitiate Mrs Hogg, "Please," she continued, in a coaxing tone, "do you happen to know a blind lady in the village?"

"A blind lady—what do you mean?"

"Isn't there one?" cried Nesta, in a tone of distress. "Why, you talk as though you wanted some one to be blind. What do you mean?"

"Well, I do; I want to read to her."

"Sakes alive! what a queer child."

"But is there one?"

"There ain't as far as I'm aware. There's old Mrs Johnston, but she ain't blind; she has the very sharpest of eyes that were ever set into anybody's head. She's crool, too, crool, the way she snaps you up. She used to have a lady to read to her, but that lady has gone to Ameriky to be married. She went a week ago, and they say Mrs Johnston almost cried, crool as she used to be to Miss Palliser. Now, if you really wanted to—"

"But I do; I do," said Nesta. "I want to very badly indeed. May I go to see her? What is her address?"

"What ails her is rheumatism. She can't stir without screeching out loud, and she wants some one to bolster her up. Not that I think much of you myself, but anyhow you might as well go and see."

"Would she like me to go and see her to-day?"

"Bless you!" said Mrs Hogg, "on the Sawbath? Not a bit of it. She'd never give you nothing to do if you went and broke in on her Sunday rest. It's church with her, as far as church indoors can be church, and she wouldn't see you if you called fifty times. But you might go to-morrow, if you so liked it."

Chapter Twenty Eight

Applying for a Situation

On the morrow between twelve and one o'clock, Nesta, who had no best clothes to put on, but who had to make the best of what she stood up in, as Mrs Hogg expressed it, started on her mission of inquiry to Mrs Johnston's. Mrs Johnston lived in the high street. It was not much of a street, for Souchester was quite a tiny place; but still there were a few houses, and three or four shops, and amongst those houses was one with a hall door painted yellow, and pillars painted green. In that house lived Mrs Johnston. Nesta's whole horizon, every scrap of her future, seemed now to be centred in Mrs Johnston. She had lain awake a good part of the night thinking about her, and making her plans. If Mrs Johnston would pay her—say ten shillings a week, she could easily manage to live quite well. She would still board with the Hoggs and take her food with them. She would soon get accustomed to the red herrings and to the half of Mrs Hogg's bed. She would soon get accustomed to the boys, who could only articulate, as far as she was concerned, the words "Hooray" and "Hurroa." In fact she would get accustomed to anything, and she would stay there until her family, tired out with looking for her, would cease to trouble their heads. By-and-by perhaps they would be sorry, and they would hold out the olive branch, and she would go home, but that time was a long way off.

Meanwhile all her future would depend on Mrs Johnston. She reached the house and rang the bell.

The house was not pretty, but it seemed to be immaculately neat. A girl as neat as the house itself presently opened the door. When she saw Nesta, she said:

"My missus can't see anybody to-day," and was about to slam the door in Nesta's face, when that young lady adroitly slipped her foot in.

"I must see her. It is most important. It has something to do with the St. Justs," said Nesta.

She was desperate and had to make up an excuse to secure her interview at any cost. The servant girl was impressed by the word St. Just, and telling Nesta she might stay in the hall and she would inquire, she went away to find her mistress.

Mrs Johnston's celebrated rheumatism was at its worst that day. She was consequently more cranky than usual, and less inclined to be civil to any who wanted her.

"A girl, did you say, Mercy? Speak out, my lass. What sort of a girl?"

"A kind of lady girl, ma'am."

"A stranger?"

"Yes; I never seen her before."

"Did she say what she wanted?"

"I think the people from the Castle sent her, ma'am. She said it was to do with the St. Justs."

"Why, then, for goodness' sake show her in. I am expecting Miss Angela, and perhaps she will call some time to-day. We must have the place in apple-pie order. I hope to goodness that girl hasn't come to say that Miss Angela can't come. I've been counting on her visit more than anything."

"In course, you have, ma'am, and no wonder. She's a beautiful young lady."

"Well, show the other young lady in, Mercy," said Mrs Johnston; "but tell her that I'm bad with the rheumatics and I can't entertain her long. If I ring the bell twice, Mercy, you will bring up the gingerbread and milk; but if I ring it three times, it will be for the gingerbread and cowslip wine, and if I don't ring it at all, why, you are to bring up nothing. It all depends on what the young lady wants."

How poor Nesta would have enjoyed the gingerbread and milk, let alone the gingerbread and cowslip wine which she was never to taste, for her diet at the Hoggs' was the reverse of appetising. Try as she would she could scarcely manage it; hunger would, of course, bring her to it in time. But although she was nearly starving for her ordinary food, she was not hungry enough yet for the food which the Hoggs consumed. Mercy came back to her.

"You may come in, Miss," she said. "It is entirely because you are a young lady from the Castle; but my missis wishes to tell you that her rheumatics are awful bad to-day. You'll be as gentle as you can with her, Miss."

Nesta nodded, and entered the room, the door of which Mercy held open for her.

Now, Nesta could never be remarked for her graceful or gentle movements, and she managed, in coming into the room, to excite Mrs Johnston's quickly aroused ire, by knocking violently against a little table which held a tray full of some pretty silver ornaments. One of them was knocked down, and the whole arrangement was destroyed.

"Clumsy girl!" muttered Mrs Johnston under her breath. She looked up with a frown on her face as Nesta approached.

Mercy stooped to rearrange the silver ornaments.

"Go away, Mercy, for goodness' sake!" snapped the old lady. "Shut the door, and remember about the bell. If I don't ring, bring nothing whatever, Mercy. You understand?"

"Yes, ma'am," said Mercy.

Nesta went and stood in front of Mrs Johnston.

"Take a seat, my dear," said the good lady, for she recalled that even a clumsy visitor from the Castle was worth propitiating. "So you have come from Miss Angela St. Just. I do trust and hope that the sweet young lady isn't going to disappoint me?"

"But I haven't," said Nesta, "and she didn't send you a message."

"But you are staying there?"

"No; I'm not."

"Then what message have you from the St. Justs, may I ask?"

Mrs Johnston held herself very upright. Even her rheumatism gave way to her anger.

"What has brought you here, may I ask, young girl?"

"I came," said Nesta, "because Mrs Hogg sent me."

"Mrs Hogg? Hogg? You don't mean Mary Hogg, the laundress?"

"I don't know whether she's a laundress or whether she's not, but I am lodging there."

Mrs Johnston sat still more upright. "I am lodging there for the present I know the St. Justs, but I am lodging there, and I want something to do in this place, and I thought perhaps you'd let me—oh, please don't get so red in the face! Please don't! Please hear me out. I thought perhaps you'd let me come and read to you, the same as the girl who went to America. Mrs Hogg said you wanted some one."

"Mary Hogg shall never have one scrap of my washing again. What does she mean by sending me a total stranger? I shall request Mary Hogg to mind her own business."

"Please, it isn't her fault. I wanted a blind one, but when there wasn't one, I thought, perhaps, you'd do."

"What?" said Mrs Johnston.

"Some one who is blind; but you aren't blind."

"Thank Heavens, no! I can see quite well, and I don't much admire your face, Miss."

"But I could read to you. I can read, oh, so well. I have an invalid mother, and I've read to her, oh, stories upon stories out of the penny papers. I can read ever so quickly. I wish you'd try me. What I want is ten shillings a week, and, and—oh, not my food. I could have my food at Mrs Hogg's. It is awfully plain—pease pudding and herrings mostly; but I don't mind that if only you'd pay me ten shillings a week and let me come to you every day."

"You are the most audacious girl! I really never heard of anything quite so extraordinary in the whole course of my life. And, pray, may I ask why you said you had come from the St. Justs?"

"I know them, you see, and I thought your maid wouldn't let me in, so I made up an excuse."

"Then you are a liar as well. Now, let me give you my answer. I don't know you or anything about you. I don't like your appearance. I don't intend to employ you as my reader. You are exceedingly awkward and your dress is untidy. If you are a lady you scarcely look like one, and ladies don't go to lodge with women like Mary Hogg."

"If they are very poor they do," said Nesta. "I have got very little money."

"What is your name?"

"Oh, please, don't ask me. I would rather not say."

"Indeed! You'd rather not say. And do you suppose that I'd take a girl into my employment—a girl who cannot give me her name?"

"I'd rather not. What is the use? You are very cruel. I wish there had been a blind one about; she wouldn't be so cruel."

"Will you please go. Just go straight out by that door. Don't knock yourself against my silver again. The hall is very short, and the front door within a few feet away. Open it; get to the other side; shut it firmly after you and depart. Don't let me see you again."

Nesta did depart. She felt as though some one had beaten her. She had never, perhaps, in all her pampered existence, received so many blows in such a short time as that terrible old Mrs Johnston had managed to inflict. At first, she was too angry to feel all the misery that such treatment could cause; but when she entered the Hogg establishment and found in very truth from the moist atmosphere of the place, from the absence of any preparations for a meal, and from the worried expression on Mrs Hogg's face, that she was indeed a laundress, she burst into tears.

"Highty tighty!" said Mrs Hogg. "I can't have any more of this. Out you go. Did you see her?"

"Oh, don't ask me. She's a perfect terror!"

"She has a sharp bark, but what I say is that her bark's worse nor her bite. She pays regular. Now, why couldn't you bring yourself to mind her and to soothe her down a bit? Maybe she'd do well by you."

"She wouldn't have me on any terms. She turned me right out. She didn't like me at all."

"I'm not surprised at that. I don't much like von, either. But there's your dinner in the corner there. I wropt it up in a bit o' paper. You'd best take it out and eat it in the fields. It'll be all mess and moither and soapsuds and steaming water here for the rest of the day."

"And when may I come back again?"

"I don't want you back at all."

"But I suppose you won't turn me out?"

"No, you may share my bed. You behaved better last night. Come back when you can't bear yourself any longer, and if you can buy yourself a draught of milk and a hunch of bread for supper it would give less trouble getting anything ready. The boys'll have cold porridge to-night, without any milk, and that's all I can give you. I can never be bothered with cooking on a washing day."

Nesta took up her dinner, which was wrapped up in a piece of old newspaper, and disappeared. She walked far, far until she was tired. Then she sat down and opened the little parcel. Within was the rind of a very hard cheese and a lump of very stale bread. But Nesta's hunger was now so strong that she ate up the bread and devoured the cheese and felt better afterwards.

Chapter Twenty Nine

Making Sunshine All Round

It was between three and four o'clock on that same day when Angela St. Just stepped out of her pretty carriage and went up the neatly kept path which led to Mrs Johnston's house. Mrs Johnston was not a favourite of hers, nor, for that matter, of anybody else. How Mercy, her nice little maidservant, managed her so wonderfully; how Miss Palliser, the girl who had lately been married and gone to America, had put up with her, was a marvel to most people. But then, Angela rather liked people whom others disliked, and she generally managed to give them a ray of brightness. She entered the little parlour now, and was received by the old lady with outstretched hand.

"My dear, my dear! this is good," she said. "I am so delighted, Angela; sit dawn, and tell me all about yourself."

Angela pushed back her hat and looked at old Mrs Johnston, then she said quietly:

"I was determined to give you a whole hour, and here I am, and you must make the most of me, for I am leaving Castle Walworth to-day. I am going back to Hurst Castle."

"Oh, dear, what a pity. Just when I thought you'd stay here for a good while."

"I am sorry, but it can't be helped. My friend, Marcia—you have heard me speak of Marcia."

"Of course, I have, my dear, and a wonderful young lady she is."

"Well, she is in trouble. All the Aldworths are in trouble."

"Are they indeed?" said Mrs Johnston. She could be sympathetic enough where anybody in the most remote degree connected with the St. Justs was concerned, in especial with Angela, whom she worshipped.

"I am sorry for that," she said, "if it worries you. You ought to have no worries."

"But why not? But I'm not exactly worried, only, of course, I want to help them, and I am quite sure it will all come right in the end. I feel like that about everything."

"You are a very blessed girl," said the old lady.

Angela smiled.

"God is so good to me," she said.

"Well, tell me all about it—what has put you out?"

"I have told you, have I not, about Mrs Aldworth? Well, you know, she is getting better. We managed to get her to Hurst Castle last week, and she is enjoying herself very much. Marcia is looking after her, and she is gradually getting more and more the use of her limbs, and a great specialist is coming from London to see her, and to give advice as to her future treatment. Everything except one now points to the possibility of a complete recovery."

"And what is the one thing, my dear?"

"The one thing that is making us all so anxious is this. You know I told you that there are three young Aldworth girls. Molly is one, Ethel another, and Nesta, the third. Nesta has been very difficult and very troublesome, and the fact is she has run away." Mrs Johnston did not know why she suddenly gave a little jump, but the next minute she said quickly:

"How old is she?"

"About fifteen, I think."

"Rather big for her age?"

"I should say she was; she is unformed; she is rather untidy."

"Awkward, I should say. Shouldn't you now pronounce her awkward?"

"I think I should. I don't know her very well, you see. I have only seen her once, and Marcia has told me about her. She is a very difficult girl."

"And how long is it since she left home?"

"She left home last Saturday week. She ran away first to Scarborough to stay with some friends. We were all distressed about that, and we had to tell a story to Mrs Aldworth which partly satisfied her. We didn't tell her anything that wasn't true. We said Nesta had gone to stay with the Griffiths, and we thought it best that she should stay there for a few days. Then we got Mrs Aldworth to Hurst Castle, and she has been doing splendidly ever since. But the difficulty is that we shall have to tell her soon that we really don't know where Nesta is. We don't know, and we are in great trouble."

"Oh, my dear, I am sure trouble is very bad for you, you look so frail. There now, I wonder when Mercy will bring the tea."

Mrs Johnston had scarcely uttered these words before the room door was opened, and Mercy, her cheeks crimson with excitement at the greatness of the honour conferred upon her, laid a delicately prepared tea on the centre table. There was silver of the oldest and quaintest pattern; there was china thin as an eggshell; there was a little silver teapot, in short everything was perfection. There were cakes of the very lightest that Mercy's skilful hands could make. Angela was the last person to despise such a meal; on the contrary, she received it with marked appreciation.

"How delicious! How much, much nicer than the meal I should have had at Castle Walworth. Oh, how good of you, how good of you to get it for me. But you must let me pour out the tea, and give you a cup."

The radiant face, the shining eyes, the sympathetic manner, all did their work on cross old Mrs Johnston. Why couldn't other people come in like Angela and make sunshine all round them? What was the matter with Mrs Johnston that she forgot her ailments and her crotchets, and her disagreeablenesses? She was only anxious now to please her young guest.

"There now," she said, "it is good for sair een to look at you. You have cheered me and heartened me up wonderfully. But as I was saying, troubles aren't good for you, dear, you are fretting yourself, I'm sure."

"I am really anxious, though I know I oughtn't to be. I am sure things will come right, I have always thought so. They do come right in the long run, but still

Mrs Aldworth is so delicate, and Nesta has run away again from the people she was staying with at Scarborough."

"Well," said Mrs Johnston, "you say you believe things will come right. I've not been at all of that way of thinking. I don't pretend that I have. It has been, my idea that things were much more likely to go wrong than right. I have found it so in life. But there, what ever possessed you, in the midst of all your anxieties, to write me a little note last night and say that you would come to see me this afternoon, and that perhaps you'd come about tea time, and that perhaps Mercy would make some of her scones, for you could never forget how delicious they tasted last time? I can tell you, Miss Angela, I awoke this morning feeling as cross and as bad and as sour as an old woman could feel, for I was aching from head to foot with the rheumatism, and I was thinking how lonely it was not to have chick nor child belonging to me, and Miss Palliser, who had her faults, poor thing, but who knew my ways, gone to America, and had it not been for your note, I don't know what I should have done, but that cheered me, and I got downstairs. But what do you think?—even with the hope of seeing you, I couldn't help having the grumps. But to go on with my story, I was grumbling and grumbling inside me—not that I said a word, for there wasn't any one to say it to; Mercy was in the kitchen, with her heart in her month at the thought of seeing you, and I was by the window wondering how I could pass the hours and bear the pain in my back and down my legs, when there came a loud, impertinent sort of ring at the bell of the front door, and I wondered who that could be. I heard Mercy parleying with some one in the hall, and after a bit, in she walked and said that a girl wanted to see me, and that she knew you. Oh, dear, I thought for sure she'd come to tell me that you couldn't come, and the same thought must have been in Mercy's mind, for her eyes looked quite dazed. So I said: 'Mercy, show her in,' and in she came, as awkward a creature as you could clap your eyes on. Will you believe me, my dear, she wasn't more than half inside the room before she bumped against my little table with my precious silver ornaments, and knocked some of them over, and it was a providence that they weren't injured. Then, she came right in front of me, and asked me if I didn't want some one to read to me. Never was there a queerer creature. When I questioned her whether she had brought a message from you, she said she hadn't, and that she came herself, to see me, and that she was living in Mrs Hogg's cottage—Mary Hogg's cottage; that widow that I have so often told you about, the one who does my washing, by the way. You may be quite sure I was pretty well excited and angry when she said that, and I sent her away double quick; but it's my certain sure opinion that she is the very girl you are looking for. I am as sure of it as that my name is Margaret Johnston."

Chapter Thirty

Found at last

Angela did not quite know how she got out of the house. There was some fuss and some regret on the part of Mrs Johnston, and Mercy very nearly cried, but at last she did get away. She stepped into her little carriage, and drove down the road and went straight as fast as she possibly could to Mrs Hogg's cottage.

Mrs Hogg was still busy over her washing, but she had come to the wringing stage, and the steam was not quite so thick in the kitchen, and certainly her face, flushed and tired as it was, quite beamed when she saw Angela.

"Dear, dear, Miss Angela, you mustn't come in. 'Tain't a fit place to put your dainty, beautiful feet into, 'tain't really, Miss."

"Will you come and speak to me here for a minute, Mrs Hogg?" said Angela, and she waited in the tiny porch.

Mrs Hogg came out.

"You have a girl staying with you, haven't you?"

"Oh, dear me, Miss, so I have, a young girl—I don't know nothing about her, not even her name, nor a single thing. It was Mary, my daughter, sent her. She's nothing but a fuss and a worry, and that touchy about her food as never was, turning up her nose at good red herring and at pease pudding, and dumplings, and what more can a poor woman give, I'd like to know?"

"You are sure you don't know her name?"

"No, Miss. She's a very queer girl."

"Is she—you understand those sort of things, Mrs Hogg—is she, in your opinion, a young lady?"

"Handsome is as handsome does," was Mrs Hogg's rejoinder, "and to my way o' thinking—to be frank with you—Miss, she ain't."

This was rather a damper to Angela's hopes, but after a minute she reflected that probably Nesta was a rough specimen of the genus Lady, and that at any rate it was her duty to follow up this clue to the end.

"I should like to see her," she said. "Where is she now?"

"Oh, Miss, if I thought, even for a single moment, that she was a friend of yourn, I'd treat her very different; but all she did was to stand in the middle of my kitchen on Saturday—"

"On Saturday?" said Angela.

"Yes; Miss, on Saturday, and she says as bold as brass—'Mary Hogg sent me.' That was her; but if I'd known—"

"Where is she now?" said Angela:

"I gave her a bit of dinner when she came in all flustered and angry, forsooth, because poor old Mrs Johnston hadn't been given a stroke of blindness—that seemed to put her out more than anything else. She must have a most malicious mind—that is, according to my way of thinking. Well, anyhow, Miss, I gave her a bit of dinner when she came in, and I told her to take it out and eat it. I don't know from Adam where she is now."

"She would go, perhaps, into the country?"

"Well, Miss, perhaps she would. Would you like Ben and Dan to go along and look for her!"

"I wish they would," said Angela.

Ben and Dan were rotated out of their lairs in the back part of the premises, and were only too charmed to do Angela's bidding. They flew off, fleet as a pair of little hares, down the shady lanes, looking in vain for Nesta.

But it was Angela herself who at last found her. She had decided not to drive in her carriage, for the sound of wheels, and the rhythmic beat of the ponies' feet might startle the girl, and if she really meant to hide, might make her hide all the more securely. No, she would walk. So she gathered up her white skirt and walked down the summer lanes. By-and-by she thought she heard a noise which was different from the song of the birds, and the rushing of the waters, and the varied hum of innumerable bees. She stood quite still. It was the sound of distress, it was a sob, and the sob seemed to come from the throat of a girl. Angela stepped very softly. She went over the long grass and came to a tree, and at the foot of that tree lay a girl, her face downward, her whole figure shaken with sobs. Angela laid her hand on her.

"Why, Nesta!" she said. "How silly of Nesta to be afraid."

The words were so unexpected that Nesta jumped to her feet; then covered her face, then flung herself face downwards again and sobbed more piteously than ever.

"I have found you, Nesta, and nobody is going to be in the least bit angry with you. May I sit by you for a little?"

"You are Miss St. Just—you are the person everybody worships and makes a fuss over. I don't want you. Go away."

"I am sorry you don't want me, but I am not going away. I am going to stay by you; may I?"

Nesta could not refuse. Angela sat down. Ben and Dan peeped their round childish faces over the top of the hedge and saw Angela sitting by Nesta's side.

"Hooray!" said Ben.

"Hurroa!" said Dan.

Angela turned.

"Go back to your mother, boys. Here is a penny for you, Dan, and another for you, Ben. Go back to your mother, and say that I have found my friend, Miss Nesta Aldworth, and am taking her back to Castle Walworth."

This was a most awe-inspiring message; the boys, young as they were, understood some of its grand import. They rushed presently into their mother's cottage.

"You be a little flat, mammy!" they said. "Why, the gel you give red herrings to, and no butter, is a friend of our Miss Angela's."

"The Lord forgive me!" said Mrs Hogg, and she forgot all about her washing, and sat down on the first chair she could find, and let her broad toil-worn hands spread themselves out one on each knee.

"The Lord forgive me!" she said at intervals.

Ben was deeply touched. He went and bought some fruit with his penny and pressed it on his mother, but she scarcely seemed to see it.

"To think as I complained to her of robbing me of half my rightful bedclothes," was her next remark. "May I see myself in my true light in the future. How could I tell? How could I tell?"

But down by the stream a very different scene was being enacted; for Angela, having given her message to the boys, did not say anything more for a long time. Nesta waited for her to speak. At first Nesta was angry at being, as she expressed it, caught. She had not that worshipful attitude towards Angela St. Just that all the other girls of the neighbourhood seemed to feel. She rather despised her, and did not at all wish to be in her company. But then that was because she had never before been in close contact with Angela. But now that Angela gave that remarkable message, that respect-restoring message to the boys, it seemed to Nesta that a healing balm, sweet as honey itself, had been poured over her troubled heart. She could not help liking it; she could not help reflecting over it. A friend of Angela's, and she was to go back with her to Castle Walworth.

After a little she raised her head again and peeped at her companion. How pretty Angela looked in her white dress, with her perfect little profile, the dark lashes partly shading her cheeks. She was looking down; she was thinking. Her lips were moving. Perhaps she was a real angel—perhaps she was praying. Very much the same sort of feeling as she had inspired in the breast of Penelope Carter, began now to dawn in that of Nesta, and yet Nesta had a far harder and more difficult nature than Penelope. All the same Nesta was touched. She reflected on the difference between herself and this young lady, and yet Angela had spoken of her as her friend. Then suddenly, she did not know why—Nesta touched Angela on the arm. The moment she did this Angela turned. Quick as thought her soft eyes looked full into Nesta's face.

"Oh, you poor child, you poor child!" she said, and then she swept her arms round the girl and kissed her several times on her cheek.

"Now, Nesta," she said, "we won't ask you for any motives. I am not going to put a single question to you, but I want you just to come straight back with me to the Castle. I will tell you after dinner what I am going to do next; but there is no scolding, nothing of that sort, you are just to come back with me."

"Am I?" said Nesta. "I can't believe it."

"You will believe it when you see it. Come, we must be quick, it is getting late."

She took Nesta's hand and led her down the road. There was the pretty carriage, there were the ponies with the silver bells; there was the smartly dressed little groom.

"Harold, get up behind," said Angela, "I am in a great hurry to get back to Castle Walworth."

Nesta found herself seated beside Angela, and quick as thought, it seemed to her, they were flashing through the summer air, past Mrs Hogg's cottage, where the boys, Ben and Dan, raised the loudest and heartiest "Hooray!" and "Hurroa!" that Angela had ever heard. The ponies pricked up their ears at the sound, and flew faster than ever, up the village high street, past the station, and up and up, a little slower now, the steep hill where Nesta and Mary Hogg had walked side by side; then through the portcullis, and into the courtyard of the castle.

Then indeed a new shyness came over Nesta. It was like a troubled, hopeless, despairing sinner, so she thought, being led into heaven by an angel.

"I'm not fit—I'm not really," she said, and she tugged at Angela's hand, as if she would refuse to go in.

"Oh, you are fit enough," said Angela, "you are my friend."

When they got inside, Angela said something to a man who was standing near in livery, and then they went down a passage, where they met no one, up some low steps, along another passage and then a door was flung open, and Angela and Nesta entered. They entered a pretty bedroom, furnished as Nesta had never seen a bedroom before. Angela went up to a girl who was sitting by the window sewing.

"Clements," she said, "this is my friend. I want you to put her into one of my pretty dresses, so that she may come down to dinner with me. Attend to her and see to everything she wants; she will sleep here to-night. This room leads out of my room, dear," she said, giving Nesta another smiling glance, and then she left her.

Clements dressed Nesta in white, and she would have thought on another occasion that she had never looked so nice. But she was really past thinking of how she looked, for somehow Angela's treatment was awaking something different within her, something which had never, even on that night when her mother was so terribly ill, been truly awakened before. She looked humble and very sad when Angela came back to her.

"You look quite sweet," said Angela, giving her a kiss. "Come along downstairs. By the way, I have sent a telegram to Marcia to tell her that you are all right, and that I am bringing you back to-morrow."

"Home?" said Nesta.

"Well, to your mother. That will make you happy, won't it?"

"Mothery!" said Nesta, and there was a lump in her throat.

"I'll tell you all about it after dinner. I have excellent news for you," said Angela.

At another time that dinner, eaten in the company of people whom Nesta had never even dreamed about before, might have confused her, but she was past being confused now. She had a curious sensation, however, that the rich and delicately cooked food provided for the guests at Castle Walworth was as little to her taste as fried herrings and pease pudding at Mrs Hogg's cottage. There was a heavy weight about her heart; she could scarcely raise her eyes to look at any one. Angela seemed to know all that, for after dinner she took her away, and out in the cool garden in the shadows of the summer night she talked to Nesta as no one had ever talked to her before.

Chapter Thirty One

The Best of them All

"It is all too wonderful," said Nesta.

"Yes, isn't it?" replied Penelope.

"To think," continued Nesta, "that I should like it, that I should even on the whole be quite pleased."

"As to me," said Penelope, "I can scarcely contain myself. It is all on account of her, too. In fact, it is on account of both of them. They are both coming, you know."

"Oh, it is mostly on account of her, as far as I am concerned," said Nesta.

As Nesta spoke Penelope looked at her.

"You certainly are very much changed," she said. "I wouldn't know you for the same girl."

"And I wouldn't know you for the same girl," retorted Nesta. "You seem to be sort of—sort of watching yourself all the time."

Penelope smiled. She slipped her hand through Nesta's arm.

"Let us walk up and down," she said.

The girls disappeared out of a low French window, and paced slowly up the shrubbery at Court Prospect. When they came to the end of the shrubbery they crossed the lawn and stood for a few moments just where they could get a peep into what had been the rose garden. That old-world garden where Angela used to walk when she was a child, and where her mother had walked before her. When they reached this spot, Penelope said very slowly:

"Do you know, Nesta, it was here, just here, she found me. Here on the ground."

"Were you really just here?" said Nesta.

"I was, and I was about as miserable a girl as could be found in the wide world. I told you all about it, didn't I?"

"Oh, yes, and we needn't go into it now, need we?"

"We need never talk of it any more. It is buried away deep; even God has forgotten it, at least, that is what Angela says."

"I was a thousand times worse than you," said Nesta, "and Angela says—by the way she found me, too, lying on the grass—I was sobbing bitterly. I had cause to sob, I was just fifty times as wicked as you. But we needn't talk of that now."

"Of course not," replied Penelope, "for as Angela says, if God has forgotten, nobody else need mind."

"But it is strange," continued Nesta, "how different you are."

"And how different you are, Nesta, so we both understand each other."

They walked a little further, and then they turned. Wonderful things had happened since that day only two short months ago, when Angela St. Just had found Nesta sobbing her heart out on the banks of the pretty little river Tarn, which flowed not far from Castle Walworth.

Amongst many remarkable things Mrs Aldworth had been restored to comparative health. The great specialist who had come down from London on purpose to see her, declared that all the treatment she had hitherto undergone was wrong. He had suggested a course of electricity, which really had a miraculous effect. It strengthened her nerves and seemed to build up her whole system. Mrs Aldworth was so well that it was no longer in the least necessary for her to be confined to her bedroom. She had remained at Hurst Castle for over six weeks, and a fortnight ago had started for the continent with Molly, and Ethel, and Nurse Davenant as her companions. This was Angela's suggestion. Angela thought that Mrs Aldworth and the girls would really enjoy a little tour in Normandy and Brittany, and afterwards they might go further south. To Mrs Aldworth it seemed like a glimpse of heaven, and Molly and Ethel were in raptures at the thought of their new dresses, and their new surroundings, and had gone off with the cheers and good will of every one concerned.

The final arrangement of all was that Nesta and Penelope were to go for a year to that excellent school at Frankfort, which Mrs Silchester presided over. Marcia was to go back again to her beloved occupation, and Angela was to spend the winter with them. Thus, indeed, was everything couleur de rose.

"For my part," said Nesta, as she continued to talk to her companion, "I can't imagine how I could ever take up with that common girl, Flossie Griffiths."

"Angela says that no one is common, that if we look deep enough we shall find something to love and to care for in every human being," said Penelope. "I never used to think so, and if any one had said that sort of thing to me some time ago, I should have set that person down as a prig, but somehow when Angela says it, I don't seem to mind a bit. It seems to come all right. Isn't it quite wonderful?"

"Yes, she is like no one else," said Nesta.

But just as this moment, when they were both talking and wondering what the future would bring forth, and what golden hopes would be realised, and how many good resolutions carried into effect, there was seen crossing the lawn a stout little woman and a girl walking by her side. This person was no other than Mrs Griffiths, of Scarborough fame. Just for the moment Nesta held back. She had not seen Mrs Griffiths, and had not heard a single word from Flossie since the day she had left Scarborough. Mrs Griffiths had not even acknowledged the letter in which Nesta had returned the half-sovereign.

"Oh, there they come, and I don't one bit want to meet them," said Nesta to Penelope.

But Mrs Griffiths quickly waddled forward.

"Now, my dear Nesta, this is just wonderful. I am glad to see you again. Do you remember the shrimps and the wading, and how we bathed on a certain morning that shall be nameless?"

Nesta coloured and glanced at Penelope. Flossie, without taking any notice of Nesta, went straight up to Penelope.

"Well," she said, "and how are you? What is all this fuss about? Why should you, who hoped to be a grand lady, go off to a dull German school? I am sure I should hate it."

"I don't," said Penelope. "I like it very much."

"Nesta," said Mrs Griffiths, "just come along and have a walk with me all alone."

Nesta was forced to comply.

"Is it true," said Mrs Griffiths, in an awe-struck tone, "that you are hand in glove with those aristocratic St. Justs?"

"I am not," said Nesta, who with all her faults was very downright. "Only Angela, one of the family, has been very kind to me, more than kind. She wouldn't have noticed me but for Marcia, dear Marcia. I owe it all to her."

"To your sister Marcia, that priggish girl, the old maid of the family as you used to call her? Miss Mule Selfish?"

Mrs Griffiths laughed.

"I did roar over that name," she said. "I told Griffiths about it, and I thought he wouldn't never stop laughing. He said it was the best and very smartest thing he had ever heard any girl say. It was you who gave it, wasn't it?"

"I did; I am horrible sorry, for she isn't Miss Mule Selfish at all. The name fits me best," said Nesta.

"Oh, my word," said Mrs Griffiths. "How queer you are. You are much changed; I doubt if you are improved. Flossie, come along here this minute."

Flossie ran forward.

"What do you think Nesta calls herself now?"

"What?" said Flossie, who was not specially inclined to be friendly.

"Why, she says she was all wrong about that fine-lady sister of hers, and that she herself is Miss Mule Selfish."

"Very likely," said Flossie. "I always did think Nesta a remarkably selfish girl, even when she was supposed to be my great friend. Mother, have you told her?"

"No," said Mrs Griffiths, "I have been asking her about herself. She is going to the German school, and she seems quite pleased."

"Yes, I am delighted," said Nesta.

"Well then, you may as well tell her now," said Flossie.

"It's this," said Mrs Griffiths, slightly mincing her words and speaking in a rather affected tone, "that Floss and I are going to London, for father—we always call him father, don't we, Floss?—that is Mr Griffiths, you know, has got a splendid opening there, and he is taking a very fine house in Bayswater, and we are to live there, and Flossie will have masters for music and dancing, and she will come out presently, and perhaps make a great match, for I am given to understand that the men admire her very much, with her black eyes and her rosy cheeks."

"Oh, don't," said Flossie, flushing, it is true, but at the same time flashing her eyes with a delighted glance from Nesta to Penelope. "We'll be very rich in the future," she said, in a modest tone, and then she dropped her eyes.

There was a dead pause for a minute or two.

"Father has been having some luck lately," said Mrs Griffiths, "and so perhaps he'll ride over the heads even of the grand Aldworths, and even of you Carters, although you do own a fine place like Court Prospect."

"We are very glad," said Nesta.

"I thought, perhaps," said Flossie, "it would be best to say that seeing the change in my circumstances, I wish to have nothing more to do with you, Nesta Aldworth."

"It seems unkind," said Mrs Griffiths. "I didn't much like coming up here to say it, but Flossie was determined."

"It was father and I who settled it last night," said Flossie. "I spoke to him about it, and he said that such a very deceitful girl could have nothing to do with me in the future; so this is good-bye. I wish you well, of course. I would not wish my worst enemy anything but well, but whatever happens in the future I cannot know you."

"Very well; of course I am sorry. I know I behaved like a perfect horror," said Nesta.

"You say that!" cried Flossie. There was a queer look in her black eyes. She fully expected that Nesta would make a scene and get, in short, into one of her celebrated tantrums; but Nesta's eyes kept on being sorry, and Penelope said:

"Oh, don't let's talk about disagreeables. If we are all happy in our own way, why should we nag and jar at one another? Do come into the house, Mrs Griffiths, and have some tea, and if father is anywhere round I'll ask him to have a chat with you. I am sure he will be delighted to hear that Mr Griffiths had made a lot of money."

"Not so much made, my dear," said Mrs Griffiths, going on in front with Penelope, "but in the making. That's it—it's in the making. We are likely to be richer and richer. Father is so excited you can scarcely hold him in bounds. But there, my dear, there. I am sorry Flossie is so rude, but the child's head is turned by her fine prospects."

When they got near the house Nesta turned and looked at Flossie.

"So you are never going to speak to me again, even though—"

"Well?" said Flossie.

"Even though we were such friends always."

"You never really loved me; I don't believe it a bit," was Flossie's response. "Did you, now?"

"I think I did," said Nesta; "in a horribly selfish way perhaps."

"Well, you were fairly generous, that I will say," continued Flossie, "with regard to your yellow-boy. Anyhow, I'll try to think kindly of you. Take a kiss and we'll say no more about it."

Nesta thought that to kiss Flossie at that moment was one of the hardest things she had to do. But then she was doing a great many hard things just then, and she found as life went on that she had to go on doing hard things, harder and harder each day; a fault to be struggled with each day, a lesson to be learnt, for hers was by no means an easy character. She was not naturally amiable; she was full of self-will, pride, and obstinacy; but nevertheless, that sweet germ of love which Angela had planted in her heart that day down by the river, kept on growing and growing, sometimes, it is true, very nearly nipped by the frosts of that wintry side of her nature, or scorched by the tempests of her violent passions, but nevertheless, the fires of summer, and the frosts of winter could not quite destroy it, for it was watered by something higher than anything Nesta could herself impart to it.

"Nesta is the best of them all," said Marcia, a long time afterwards to Angela, "and she owes it to you."

"No," said Angela, "she owes it to God."

The End

Milton Keynes UK
Ingram Content Group UK Ltd.
UKHW020144190324
439698UK00012B/628

9 781835 912904